The Fourth Generation

Walter Besant

The Fourth Generation

BY

SIR WALTER BESANT

Author of
"All Sorts and Conditions of Men," "The Master Craftsman," "A Fountain Sealed," "The City of Refuge," etc.

The Fourth Generation

The FOURTH GENERATION

BY

SIR WALTER BESANT

Author of
"ALL SORTS AND CONDITIONS OF MEN," "THE MASTER CRAFTSMAN," "A FOUNTAIN SEALED," "THE CITY OF REFUGE," ETC.

FOURTH EDITION

NEW YORK
Frederick A. Stokes Company
Publishers

COPYRIGHT, 1899, 1900,
BY WALTER BESANT.

CONTENTS

Chapter

    I. A Remote Ancestor

    II. What he Wanted

    III. Something to Come

    IV. The Complete Supply

    V. A Learned Profession

    VI. The Return of the Prodigal

    VII. The Child of Sorrows

    VIII. In the Land of Beeches

    IX. Mary Anne

    X. A Dinner at the Club

    XI. The Book of Extracts

    XII. On the Site

    XIII. A Compromise

    XIV. Consultation

    XV. "Barlow Brothers"

XVI. AND ANOTHER CAME

XVII. YET ANOTHER!

XVIII. THE LIGHT THAT BROKE

XIX. THE SIGNS OF CHANGE

XX. HE SPEAKS AT LAST

XXI. THE WILL

PREFACE

IT is perhaps well to explain that this story first appeared as a serial early in 1899: that on revision it was found desirable partly to rewrite certain chapters and to enlarge upon certain points. The structure of the story, the characters, and the situations remain unaltered.

The question with which the story deals is not fully answered. It is one of those questions which can never be answered; from time to time every man must ask himself why the innocent must suffer, and do suffer every day and in every generation, for the follies and the sins of their forefathers. Every man must find his own answer, or must acknowledge sorrowfully that he can find none. I venture to offer in these pages an answer that satisfies myself. It substitutes consequence for punishment, and puts effect that follows cause in place of penalties. And, as I hope is made plain, it seems to me that I have no less an authority for this view than the greatest of the Prophets of Israel. The consequences of ancestral and paternal actions may be a blessing and a help: or they may be a curse and a burden for generations; in either case they are consequences which can only affect the body, or the mind, or the social position of the descendants. They may make ambition impossible: they may make action impossible: they may keep a man down among the rank and file: but they cannot do more. The Prophet defines and limits their power. And the consequences, whatever they are, may be made a ladder for the soul to rise or a weight to drag it down. In the pages which follow they are shown as to some a ladder, but to others a way of descent.

W. B.

UNITED UNIVERSITY CLUB,
June, 1900.

CHAPTER I

A REMOTE ANCESTOR

IT was a morning of early March, when a northeast wind ground together the dry branches on which as yet there were no signs of coming spring; the sky was covered by a grey cloud of one even shade, with no gleams of light or streak of blue, or abatement or mitigation of the sombre hue; the hedges showed as yet no flowers, not even the celandine; the earth had as yet assumed no early vernal softening; there were no tender shoots; dolefully the birds cowered on the branches, or flew up into the ivy on the wall, where they waited for a milder time, with such patience as hunger only half appeased would allow. Those who lived upon berries and buds remembered with anxiety that they had already eaten up all the haws and stripped the currant bushes of all their buds, and must now go further afield; those who hunt the helpless chrysalis, and the slug and the worm and the creeping creatures of the field, reflected that in such weather it was impossible to turn over the hard earth in search of the former, or to expect that the latter would leave their winter quarters on such a day. At such a time, which for all created things is far worse than any terrors offered by King Frost, the human creatures who go abroad wrap themselves in their warmest, and hurry about their business in haste, to finish it and get under shelter again.

The south front of the house looked down upon a broad terrace paved with red bricks; a balustrade of brick ran along the edge of the terrace; a short but nobly designed and dignified flight of stairs led into the garden, which began with a broad lawn. The house itself, of the early eighteenth century, was stately and spacious; it consisted of two stories only; it had narrow and very high windows; above the first-floor windows ran a row of small circular louvres set in the roof, which was of a high pitch and of red tiles; the chimneys were arranged in artistic groups or stacks. The house had somewhat of a foreign appearance; it was one of considerable pretension; it was a house which wanted to be surrounded by ancient trees, by noble gardens and stately lawns, and to be always kept deep in the country, far away from town houses and streets; in the surroundings of a city, apart from gardens, lawns, park and lordly trees, it would have been out of place and incongruous. The warm red brick of which it was built had long since mellowed with age; yellow lichen clung to the walls here and there; over one wing, that of the west, ivy grew, covering the whole of that end of the house.

The gardens were more stately than the house itself. They began with a most noble lawn. On one side grew two cedars of Lebanon, sweeping the bare earth with their drooping branches. On the other side rose three glorious walnut-trees. The space between was a bowling-green, on which no flower-beds had ever been permitted. Beyond the bowling-green, however, were flower-beds in plenty. There were also box-trees cut into the old-fashioned shapes which one only sees in old-fashioned gardens. Beyond these was a narrow plantation of shrubs, mostly evergreen. Then stretched out, in order, the ample kitchen-gardens, the crowded orchard, and the "glass." Here, also, were ranged the beehives in a row, for the owners of the house were bee-masters as well as gardeners.

The whole was stately. One was filled with admiration and respect for so noble a house, so richly set, only by walking along the road outside the park and gazing upon the house from a distance. There were, however, certain bounds imposed upon the admiration and respect of the visitor. These were called for, in fact, by the gardens, and the lawns, and the "glass," as they must have been in the past. As for the garden of the present, it was difficult even to guess when the hand of man, the spade of the gardener, had last touched any part of the place. Everything was overgrown; weeds covered the ground which had once been beds of asparagus and celery; the strawberry plants fought for existence with thistles, and maintained it, by the sacrifice of fruit; couch grass and those thistles, with shepherd's-purse and all the weeds of the field, covered and concealed the flower-beds. The lanes and walks were covered ways, long since rendered impassable by reason of branches that had shot across them; the artificial shapes of the box-trees, formerly so trim and precise, showed cloudy and mysterious through the branches which had grown up outside them; the bowling-green was covered with coarse grass never mown from year to year. In the glass houses the doors stood open: the glass was broken; the vines grew wild, pushing their way through the broken panes. There could be no respect possible for a garden in such a condition. Yet, the pity of it! the pity of it! So fine a place as it had been, as it might again become, if gardeners were once more ordered to restore it to its ancient splendours!

If one turned from the garden and walked towards the house, he would notice, first, that the stairs of brick leading to the terrace were a good deal battered and broken; that many bricks had been displaced, that weeds grew between the bricks, that in the balustrade there were places where the square brick pillars were broken away; that if he mounted the stairs, the brick pavement of the terrace showed holes and damaged places here and there; that if he looked at the house itself he would discern there, as well as in the garden, a certain air of neglect and decay. The window-frames wanted painting, the door wanted painting, there were no curtains or blinds visible anywhere; one or two panes of glass were broken, and not even patched. Stately, even in decay, were house and gardens; but the spectator shivered, as one shivers at the sight of age and decay and death hovering over what should still be rejoicing in the strength of manhood.

On this morning, when the cold of winter ushered in the deceitful spring, a man was walking to and fro on the brick terrace. He was a man very far advanced in life. Cold as he was, he wore no overcoat; he had no wrapper or handkerchief round his neck; he wore no gloves.

When one looked more closely, he was not only advanced in years: he was full of years—overfull, running over. His great age was apparent in the innumerable lines of his face; not in the loss of his hair, for his abundant white locks fell flowing, uncut and untrimmed, upon his shoulders, while a full white beard lay over his ample chest. His age was shown by the heightening of the cheek-bones and the increased prominence of the nose, in the sunken mouth, and the thin lips, and the deep-set eyes. But though his face had been roughly handled by time, his frame seemed to have escaped any touch. Old as he was, he bore himself upright still; he walked with a firm, if not an elastic, step; he carried a stick, but did not use it. He was still six feet four, or even more, in stature; his shoulders were still broad, his back was not curved, nor was his huge, strong body bowed, nor were his strong legs bent or weakened. Nothing could be more anomalous than the difference between the man's face, chipped and lined and covered with curves and diagrams, like an Ordnance Survey map, and his figure, still so strong, so erect, so vigorous.

He walked from one end of the terrace to the other rapidly, and, so to speak, resolutely. Then he turned and walked back. He look neither to one side nor to the other; he was absorbed in some kind of meditation, for his face was set. It was a stern face naturally; the subject of his thoughts made it, perhaps, still harder and more stern. He wore a kind of shooting-jacket, a broad-brimmed felt hat, stout boots fit for the fields, and leggings, as if he were going to take out his gun, and he carried his stick as if it had been a gun. A masterful man — that was apparent at the outset; aggressive — that was also apparent at the moment; defiant — of what? of whom? Evidently a man built originally as a fighting man, endowed with great courage and enormous strength; probably, also, with a quick temper; retaining still the courage, though some of the strength had gone, and the fighting temperament, though his fighting days were done.

There was no sound about the place — no clatter of servants over their work, no footsteps in the house or outside it, no trampling of horses from the stables, or sight of gardeners working quietly among the forlorn flower-beds: all was silent. And the cold wind whistled, and the old man, without the common protection from the wintry wind, walked methodically and rapidly from east to west and from west to east.

So he went on all the morning, hour after hour, untiring over this meaningless exercise. He began it at nine, and at half-past twelve he was still marching in this aimless manner, turning neither to the right nor to the left, and preserving unchanged that fixed expression which might have meant patience — a very old man has to be patient — or it might have been, as I have called it, defiance: a man who has known misfortunes sometimes acquires this expression of defiance, as one who bids Fortune do her very worst, and, when she can do no more, still repeats with courage, 'Come what may.'

In the distance, half a mile or so away, was a clock in a church-tower. If one listened from the garden, one might hear the striking of the hours; without waiting for it and expecting it, one would not hear the clock at all. A melodious clock at a distance falls in with the general whisper of the atmosphere. We call it silence, but, indeed, there is no such thing in Nature. Silence would drive us mad. In the country we hear a gentle whisper, tuneful and soothing, and we say it is the sweet silence of the country; but it is not—it is the blend of all the country sounds.

The morning dragged on slowly. The beat of the old man's footstep on the terrace was as regular as the ticking of a clock. Neither in his carriage, nor in his pace, nor in his face was there the least change. He walked like a machine, and his face was as expressionless as any face of idol or of an image.

It was about eleven o'clock that another step might have been heard. The step of a man on dry branches and among dead leaves. The old man on the terrace paid no attention: he made as if he heard nothing: when the figure of a rustic emerged from the orchard and stood under the walnut-trees, the old man of the terrace made as if he saw nothing.

The rustic was also well advanced in age, though far short of the tale of years which belonged to the other. He was dressed as one who goes afield: he walked as one who has spent his life in the ridges and furrows of the ploughed field: he carried a spade over his shoulder.

Standing under the walnut-trees, he lowered his spade and laid his hands upon the handle as if to support himself. And then he gazed upon the old man of the terrace. He did not, after the wont of some men, pretend to be at work and cast a furtive glance of curiosity. On the contrary, he made no pretence at all: he leaned upon his spade, and he gazed boldly and without any shame. He marked the steady and firm step of the man: his own step was not half so firm or half so steady: he marked the bearing of the man: his own back was bent and his shoulders lowered: he marked the health and strength that still lay in his face: his own cheeks were wrinkled and his eyes were dim. Presently he lifted his spade to his shoulder and he turned away. "If I go first——" he said.

Whether he came or whether he departed, whether he walked in silence over the coarse grass or snapped the twigs and rustled the dead leaves, the old man of the terrace took no notice. He neither saw nor heard anything.

Then the east wind continued dry and cold, and the birds chirped in discomfort, and the branches in the orchard fell to grinding each other, and the old man walked on. And the quarters struck from the church-tower somewhere, not far off.

At the open door of the house, at about half-past twelve, there appeared a young man dressed warmly, as was due to the weather. He was tall—over six feet in height; his face resembled that of the old man strikingly; he was certainly some close relation. He stood at the door looking on while that walk, as dismal, as monotonous, as purposeless as that of prisoners in their yard, went on minute after minute, hour after hour. He stood there, not hour after hour, but for a full half-hour, watching and wondering.

"Always and every day—and for all these years!"—to give words to his thoughts. "Why this tramp day by day every morning; always alone, always silent, seeing and not seeing, dead to outward things, apart from the world, taking no interest in the world? No recluse in a vault could be more lonely. No occupation; nothing to do; nothing to think about. Good heavens! what does he think about? No books, no newspapers to read; no letters to write. Why?"

The young man was the great-grandson of this ancient person: he was not only the great-grandson, but the heir to the house and the estates which belonged to the house: next to this old man he was the head of the family. He therefore, as a mark of respect and a matter of duty, ran down from London occasionally to see that his ancestor was properly cared for and in health. He was also in communication with the solicitors who managed the property.

It was a very curious case: from childhood the young man had been told of the strange and eccentric great-grandfather. He lived alone: he had no other servant than a woman with her daughter: he only saw them when they brought his meals: he received no visitors: he never went out of the house except to walk every morning, whatever the weather, for four hours up and down the terrace: he never spoke even to his housekeeper: if anyone spoke to him, he made no reply: he never read anything—neither book nor paper: his affairs were in the hands of a firm of solicitors in the neighbouring market-town: when they wanted his signature to a cheque, they drew it and sent it in to him, when he signed and returned it; when they consulted him concerning business, he received their statements in writing, and replied with the greatest brevity: there was no sign of mental derangement: so far as the solicitors, the only persons who were able to speak on the subject, understood, the man's faculties were perfectly sound and his intellect as clear as ever. Moreover, there was no sign upon him of any hallucination, any melancholia, any mental trouble: if he maintained silence, his face betrayed no perturbation. Day after day he presented to the morning sun a calm and cloudless face: if he smiled not, neither did he sigh.

Now, the most remarkable thing was that this eccentricity, which might have been explained on the theory of great age and the loss of all his friends and contemporaries, had been practised for nearly seventy years. As a young man, quite a young man, he began this life, and he had continued it ever since. The reason, his great-grandson had always understood, was the shock caused by the sudden death of his wife. Further than this he neither knew nor did he inquire. If one grows up in presence of a certain strange line of conduct, it becomes accepted without inquiry. The old man had become a solitary when this young man's grandfather was a boy: his grandfather, his father, and he himself had always had before them the knowledge, if not the sight, of this eccentricity. There was no curiosity in his mind at all about the possible cause.

Seventy years! It is the whole life of the average man, and this strange creature had spent the whole time alone, in silence, in solitude, and without occupation. It was not the whole span of the man's own life, for he was now completing his ninety-fourth year.

From the distant church-tower came presently the striking of the quarters followed by the stroke of one. At that moment an old woman came out; she passed in front of the visitor in the doorway, and stood watching to catch the eye of the master. She said nothing, but waited there until he noticed her presence. Perhaps he was expecting her. He stopped; the old woman retired; her master entered the house, taking no notice whatever of the young man as he passed him; his eyes looked through him with no gleam of recognition or even of intelligence as to his presence. Yet this young man, the only one of all his descendants, paid him a visit once a month or so to see if he was still in health.

He walked straight into the room which was the single sitting-room and dining-room and living-room. It had been the library—a large room with a north aspect, lofty, and at all times of the year rather dark and cold. A good fire burned in the broad old-fashioned grate. Before the fire was a small table—it had formerly stood in the window for a reading or writing table; now it served as a table set there for the old man's meals. The cloth was, in fact, spread, and the early dinner laid upon it—a plain dinner of steak, potatoes, and a bottle of port, which is a beverage proper to old age; it warms and comforts; it pleases and exhilarates; it imparts a sense of strength, and when the common forms of food can no longer be taken, this generous drink supplies their place. The walls were lined with shelves which were filled with books. Evidently some former member of the family had been a scholar and a bibliophile. The books were all bound in leather; the gilt of the titles had mostly disappeared. If you took a volume from the shelf, you found that it had parted from the binding; if not, it took advantage of the movement to remove itself from the binding; if you examined the shelves long enough, you would have found that there was not one book in the whole library of a date later than 1829. Of all the thousands upon thousands of books published in the seventy years since that time, not one was in this library. For instance, the *Quarterly* and *Edinburgh Reviews*—they stood here bound; they stopped at 1829. The *Annual Register* was here also, bound; it stopped at 1829. And on this great library table there were lying, as if for daily use, scattered volumes and magazines which had been placed there for the reading of the house in 1829. No one had touched the table since some time in that year. A long low leather chair stood beside the fire—the leather was in rags and tatters, worn to shreds; at the table was placed a splendid great wooden chair, which looked like the chair of a hall-porter; the carpet was in rags and tatters, except the part along the front of the shelves; there it was whole, but its colour was faded. In front of the fire was placed a common thick sheepskin.

The young man followed his ancestor into the library. He took a chair, placed it by the fire, and sat down, his long legs curled, watching and waiting. He had been in the same place before. The silence of the old man, the meaningless look in his eyes, terrified him on the first occasion. He was then unaccustomed to the manner of the man. He had gradually grown accustomed to the sight; it no longer terrified him, and he now sat in his place on the other side of the fire, resolved upon making sure that the old man was properly cared for, properly fed, properly clad, properly looked after in all respects, that his health was good and that there was no need of seeking advice. He sat down therefore, by the fire and looked on while the old man took his dinner.

The visitor, I have said, was the great-grandson of the recluse. He was also the heir of his house and the future owner of the place and its possessions. As for what he was by calling you shall hear presently. Being the heir-presumptive, he assumed the duty of making these occasional visits, which were received—as has been stated—in silence, and with not the slightest show of recognition.

Without heeding his presence, then, the old man took his seat at the table, lifted the cover, and began his dinner. It consisted every day of the same dish. Perhaps there are not many men at ninety-four who can devour every day a full-sized steak with potatoes and bread, and can drink with it a whole bottle of port. Yet this is what the recluse did. The descendant for his part made it his business that the port should be of the best and that the steak should be "treated" scientifically, in order to ensure its tenderness and juiciness.

The recluse took his food fast and eagerly. One could perceive that in earlier days he must have enjoyed a great and noble power of putting away beef. He took his steak with fierceness, he devoured an immense quantity of bread, he drank his wine off in goblets as in the old days he had tossed off the great glasses of beer. He did not sip the generous wine, nor did he roll it about in his glass and hold it up to the light; he drank it, as a child drinks water, unconsciously and yet eagerly, regardless of the taste and careless of its qualities.

When the bottle was empty and there was nothing more to eat, he left the wooden chair and cast his great length into the long easy-chair, where he stretched out his legs towards the fire, and, leaning his head upon his hand and his elbow on the arm of the chair, he gazed into the fire, but with eyes which had in them no kind of expression. "Evidently," thought the spectator, "the old man has two senses left; he likes strong meat and drink; he likes the physical comfort that they provide, and he likes the warmth of a fire." Then he rose slowly and stood with his back to the fire, looking down upon his ancestor, and began a remonstrance, which he repeated with variations on every visit.

"Sir," he said, "I come to see you from time to time, as you know. I come to make sure that you are cared for, and that you are well. I come to see if anything can be done for you. On these occasions you never fail to pretend that you do not see me. You make believe that I am not present. You do see me; you know I am here; you know who I am; you know why I am here. Very well. It is, I suppose, your humour to affect silence and solitude. Nothing that I can say will, I fear, induce you to break this silence."

There was no sign of recognition, no reply, nor any change of movement.

"Why you have imposed upon yourself this lifelong misery I do not know, nor shall I inquire. Perhaps I shall never know. It seems to me a great mistake, whatever the cause—a sudden bereavement, I have always understood. If it was in consequence of another person's fault, or another person's misfortune, the waste and wreck of your own life would not remove the cause; and if it was any fault of your own, such a wreck and waste of life would only be an aggravation of the offence. But if it was bereavement, surely it would be the manlier part to bear it and to go on with the duties of life. However, as I do not know all the circumstances, I have no right to speak on this point. It is too late," he went on, "to make up for all the years you have thrown away, but is it too late for a change? Can you not, even now, at this late hour, go back among your fellow-creatures and become human again, if it is only for a year or two? I should say it was harder to continue this life of loneliness and misery than to go back to the life for which you were born."

There was no answer.

"I have been over the house this morning," the young man went on pitilessly. "You have allowed it to fall into a shameful condition. The damp has got into pictures and wall-paper; it will need many thousands to restore the place to a condition proper to a gentleman's house. Don't you think you ought to spend that money and live in it as a gentleman of your position ought to do?"

There was still no answer. But, then, the heir expected none.

The Fourth Generation

The old man lifted his head from his hand and dropped it back on the chair. His eyes closed, his hands dropped, his breathing was soft and regular; he was asleep.

His great-grandson still stood over him. This kind of scene affected him but little, because it occurred on every visit. He arrived at eleven or so; he walked across the park; he saw the old man doing his morning tramp as usual; he spent an hour going over the empty, desolate house; he watched the old man taking his walk; he followed him into the library; he watched him taking his food; he stood over him afterwards and addressed his remonstrances. This was always received, as George the Third used to receive the remonstrances of the City of London, in silence discouraging. And always in the midst of the remonstrance the patriarch fell asleep.

The young man waited awhile, watching his great-grandfather of ninety-four. There is very little resemblance between a man of that age and himself at twenty-six. Yet there may be some. And no one could look upon that old man without becoming conscious that in early manhood he must have been of singular and wonderful comeliness—full of strength and vigour, of fine proportions, of noble stature, and of remarkable face and head. All these things the descendant possessed as well, but in less marked degree, with more refinement, perhaps the refinement of scholarship and culture, but with less strength. He had done what he came to do; he had delivered his message; it was a failure; he expected nothing less. He might as well go; there was nothing more to do, or to be obtained, by staying.

But then a very remarkable event happened. He heard for the first time the voice of his great-grandfather. He was to hear it once more, and only once more. No one, except himself on this occasion, had heard it for nearly seventy years.

The patriarch moved in his sleep, his fingers twitched, his legs jerked, he rolled his head. Then he sat up and clutched the arms of his chair; his face became twisted and distorted, as if under the possession of some evil spirit. He half rose to his feet, still holding to the arms of the chair, and he spoke. His voice was rough and harsh, as if rusted with long disuse. His eyes remained fixed, yet his attitude was that of someone whom he saw—with whom he was conversing. What he said was this:

"That will end it."

Then he sank back. The distortion went out of him. He laid his head upon the chair; calm and peace, as of a child, returned to his face; he was again asleep—if he had been awake.

"A dream," said the looker on. But he remembered the words, which came back to him, and remained with him—why, he could not tell.

He looked about the room. He thought of the strange, solitary, meaningless life, the monotonous life, the useless life, that this patriarch had lived for so many years. Seventy long years! This recluse during the whole of that time—for seventy long years—had never got outside the walls of his garden; he had seen none of his old friends; only his great-grandson might from time to time visit the place to ascertain if he were still living. He had done no kind of work during that long time; he had not even put a spade into the ground; he had never opened a book or seen a newspaper; he knew nothing that had happened. Why, for him the world was still the world before the Reform Act. There were no railways, there were no telegraph-wires; none of the inventions and improvements and new ideas and new customs were known to him, or suspected by him; he asked for nothing, he cared for nothing, he took interest in nothing: he never spoke. Oh, the wretchedness of it! The folly of it! What excuse could there be—what reason—sufficient for this throwing away of a life in which so much might have been done? What defence could a man have for thus deserting from the Army of Humanity?

As long as this young man remembered anything, he had heard of this old man: it was always the same story; there was a kind of family bogie, who wore always the same clothes, and took the same walk every morning and slept every afternoon. Sometimes his mother would tell him, when he was a boy, scraps of history about the Recluse. Long ago, in the reign of George the Fourth, the gloomy solitary was a handsome, spirited, popular young man; fond of hunting, fond of shooting and fishing and all out-door sports, yet not a boor or a barbarian; one who had passed through the University with credit, and had learning and cultivation. He had a fine library which he used, he enjoyed conversations with scholars, he had travelled on the Continent, a thing which then was rare; he was thinking of entering the House. He had a fine, though not a large, estate, and a lovely house and stately gardens. No one in the county had greater reason to be satisfied with his lot, no one had a clearer right to look forward to the future with confidence, than Mr. Algernon Campaigne. The boy remembered all this talk.

He now contemplated the sleeping figure with a curious blend or mixture of emotions. There was pity in the blend, there was contempt in it, there was something of the respect or reverence due to an ancestor. One does not often get the chance of paying respect to so remote an ancestor as a great-grandfather. The ancestor lay back in his chair, his head turned a little on one side; his face, perfectly calm, had something of the transparent waxen look that belongs to the newly dead.

The young man went on thinking of what he had heard of this old man, who was at once the pride and the shame of the family. No one can help being proud of having a recluse, an anchorite, in the family—it is uncommon, like an early Shakespeare; moreover, the recluse was the head of the family, and lived in the place where the family had always lived from time beyond the memory of man.

He remembered his mother, a sad-faced widow, and his grandmother, another sad-faced widow. A certain day came back to him—it was a few weeks after his father's early death, when he was a child of seven—when the two women sat together in sorrow, and wept together, and conversed, in his presence—but the child could not understand—and said things which he recalled at this moment for the first time.

"My dear," said the elder lady, "we are a family of misfortune."

"But why—why—why?" asked the other. "What have we done?"

The elder lady shook her head. "Things are done," she said, "that are never suspected. Nobody knows, nobody finds out, but the arm of the Lord is stretched out and vengeance falls, if not upon the guilty, then upon his children and his grandchildren unto the third and fourth generation. It has fallen heavily upon that old man—for the sins of his father, perhaps—and upon us—and upon the children——"

"The helpless, innocent children? Oh! It is cruel."

"We have Scripture for it."

These words—this conversation—came back suddenly and unexpectedly to the young man. He had never remembered them before.

"Who did what?" he asked. "The guilty person cannot be this venerable patriarch, because this affliction has fallen upon him and still abides with him after seventy years. But they spoke of something else. Why do these old words come back to me? Ancestor, sleep on."

In the hall he saw the old housekeeper, and stopped to ask her after the master.

"He spoke just now," he said.

"Spoke, sir? Spoke? The master spoke?"

"He sat up in his sleep and spoke."

"What in the name o' mercy did he say?"

"He said, quite clearly, 'That will end it.'"

"Say it again."

He said it again.

"Sir," she said, "I don't know what he means. It's most time to end it. Master Leonard, something dreadful will happen. It is the first time for seventy years that he have spoken one single word."

"It was in his sleep."

"The first time for seventy years! Something dreadful, for sure, is going to happen."

CHAPTER II

WHAT HE WANTED

IN the lightest and sunniest rooms of an unpretending flat forming part of the Bendor Mansions, Westminster, sat a young man of six-and-twenty. You have already seen him when he called upon his irresponsive ancestor at the family seat in the shire of Buckingham. He was now in his study and seated at what used to be called his desk. This simple piece of the scholar's furniture has long since given way to a table as big as the dimensions of the room permit—in this case one of eight feet long and five broad. It did not seem to be any too large for the object of its construction, because it was completely covered with books, papers, Blue-books, French and German journals, as well as Transactions of English learned and scientific societies. There was no confusion. The papers were lying in orderly arrangement; the books stood upright along the back of the table facing the writer. They were all books of political history, political economy, or of reference. A revolving bookcase stood ready at hand filled with other books of reference. These, it might have been observed, were principally concerned with statistics of trade—histories of trade, books on subjects connected with trade, Free Trade, Protection, the expansion of trade, and points connected with manufactures, industries, exports, and imports.

Mr. Leonard Campaigne was already in the House. It would be too much to say that he had already arrived at a position of authority, but he was so far advanced that on certain subjects of the more abstruse kind, which he endeavoured to make his own and to speak upon them with the manner of a specialist, he was heard with some deference and reported at some length. More than this is not permitted to six-and-twenty.

These subjects were such as demand a clear head, untiring industry, the grasp of figures, and the power of making them attractive. They also required a prodigious memory. All these valuable qualities this young man possessed. At Cambridge, where he went out in mathematics, he tore himself reluctantly away from examiners who gave him all they could, with tears that it could be no more than "Part

II., Division I., Class I.," and wept that they could not, as all good examiners hope to do before long, carry their examinations on to Part III., divided into three parts and each part into three classes, and then to Part IV., also divided into three divisions and each division into three classes, and so to go on examining their candidates, always decreasing in number, once a year for the rest of their natural lives, ending with a disgraceful pluck at eighty.

"Part II., Division I., Class I." No one can do better than that. I believe that only one man in Leonard's year did as well. Therefore he went down having a very good record and a solid reputation for ability to begin with. As to private fortune, he was independent, with an income derived from his mother of about £800 a year, and with those expectations which, as you have seen, were certainties. He also had a Fellowship worth at least five shillings a year, it having gone up recently in consequence of an unexpected looking-up or recovery in the agricultural interest. He came up to London, therefore, thus adequately equipped, entered at the Bar, got called, without any intention of practising, looked out for a borough, nursed it carefully for a twelvemonth, and got in, without a contest, at a by-election, on the Liberal side. So far he had followed the traditions of his family. He was the third, in sequence of father to son, of University distinction. His grandfather, son of the dumb recluse whom you have already seen, had also done well at Cambridge, and had also entered the House, and had also made a highly successful beginning when he was cut off prematurely at the early age of thirty-two. His father, who in his turn distinguished himself at the University, also in his turn entered the House, and was also in his turn considered a young man of promise, when he, too, was carried off at about the same age. There were moments when Leonard asked himself whether this untoward fate was to be his as well. There were, indeed, special reasons for asking this question, of which he as yet knew nothing. Meantime, he asked no questions of the future, nor did he concern himself about the decrees of fate.

The study was pleasantly furnished with two or three easy chairs and the student's wooden chair. Books lined the walls; two or three cups stood on the mantelshelf, showing that the tenant of the room was no pale student, consumer of the midnight oil; above it there was a drawing of a country house, the same house which you have already seen. One observed also, with pleasure, further proofs that the occupant had his hours of relaxation. Tobacco and that vulgar thing the briar-root were conspicuously present. That a young man who hoped to rise by the most severe of all studies should habitually smoke a pipe should be, to any well-regulated mind, a most promising circumstance. The study opened into the dining-room, which was a dining-room only, and a formal, even a funereal place, with a few books and a few pictures—evidently not a room which was inhabited. The tenant took his breakfast in it, and sometimes his luncheon, and that was all. There were two bedrooms; beyond them, the kitchen and the room for the man and wife who "did" for Mr. Campaigne.

The occupant of the flat presently laid down his pen, and sat up turning his face to the light. Then he rose and paced the chamber.

He was a young man of somewhat remarkable appearance. In stature, as you have seen, he was much above the average, being at least six feet two and of strong build, though not so massive a man as his great-grandfather, the hermit of Campaigne Park. His features were good and strongly marked; his forehead was broad rather than high; his eyes, small rather than large, were keen and bright, the eyebrows were nearly straight. His appearance at this moment was meditative; but, then, he was actually meditating; in conversation and in debate his expression was alert, and even eager. He did not, in fact, belong to that school which admires nothing, desires nothing, and believes in nothing. He believed strongly, for instance, that the general standard of happiness could be raised by wise laws—not necessarily new laws—and by good education—not necessarily that of the School Boards. And he ardently desired to play his part in the improvement of that standard. That is a good solid lump of belief to begin with. For a statesman such a solid lump of belief is invaluable.

Presently he sat down again and renewed the thread of his investigations. After an hour or so he threw aside his pen; he had accomplished what he had proposed to do that morning. If a man is going to succeed, you will generally find that he knows what he means to do and the time that he will take over it, and that he sets to work with directness as well as resolution.

The task was finished, then, and before twelve o'clock Leonard pushed back his chair and sprang to his feet with a sigh of relief. Much as men may love work, it is always a satisfaction to get it done. On the table beside his papers lay a little pile of letters not yet opened. He took up one and opened it. The letter was from the editor of a leading magazine, accepting a proposal to contribute a paper on a certain economic theory. Leonard smiled with satisfaction. The *Nineteenth Century* is the ladder of ambition. It is by means of this magazine, and of one or two like unto it, that the ambitious young man is enabled to put himself forward as a student, if not yet an authority, on any subject—a more rapid way of advance than by means of the House.

Leonard had already written on this subject, and with success, as a student; he was now to write upon it with authority. You will understand from all this that Leonard was a young man whose mind was fully occupied, even absorbed, with work which was at once his greatest delight and the ladder for his ambitions; that he occupied a good position in society, and that his work, his thoughts, his relaxations were those of one who lived and moved habitually on a high level, free from meanness or sordid cares or anxieties of any kind.

On the same staircase and the same floor was a flat exactly corresponding in every particular to his own except that the windows looked out towards the opposite pole. This flat, into which we will not penetrate, was occupied by a young lady, who lived in it, just as Leonard lived in his, with a man and his wife to look after her. People may be neighbours in a "Mansion" and yet not know each other. It is not likely that Leonard would have made the acquaintance of Miss Constance Ambry but for the fortunate circumstance that he belonged to the same club as well as the same collection of flats; that he was introduced to her at the club; that he met her at dinner day after day; that he speedily discovered the fact that they were neighbours; that they became friends; that they often dined together at the club, and that they frequently walked home together.

It will be understood, therefore, that Miss Constance Ambry would have been called, a few years ago, an emancipated young woman. The word has already become belated; in a year or two it will be obsolete. Emancipation has ceased to carry any reproach or to excite any astonishment. Many girls and unmarried women live alone in flats and mansions and similar places; they have their latch-key; they marvel that there could have been formerly a time when the latch-key was withheld from girls; they go where they like; they see what they wish to see; they meet people they wish to meet. The emancipated woman twenty years ago thought it necessary, in order to prove her superiority of intellect, to become at least an atheist. That was part of the situation; other prancings and curvettings there were; now she has settled down, the question of comparative intellect being no longer discussed, and goes on, in many respects, almost as if she were still in the ancient House of Bondage. In this case there were strong reasons, comfortably running into a good many hundreds a year, why Constance Ambry should dare to go her own way and live at her own will. She began her independent career by three years at Girton. During her studentship she distinguished herself especially by writing critical essays, in which it was remarked that the passion of Love, as depicted and dwelt upon by poets, was entirely ignored by the critic; not so much, her friends explained, from maidenly reserve, as from a complete inability to sympathize even with the woman's point of view—which, indeed, women who write poetry and love-songs have always done their utmost to conceal, or mendaciously to represent in the same terms and under the same form as the masculine passion. On leaving Girton she accepted a post as Lecturer on English Literature in a women's college. It was a poorly-paid office, and hitherto it had been difficult to find a good lecturer to keep it. Constance could afford not only to take it, but also to make it the sole object of her work and thoughts. One is pleased to add that her ideas of the liberty of women included their liberty to dress as well as they can afford. She presented to her admiring and envious class the constant spectacle of a woman dressed as she should be—not splendidly, but beautifully. The girls regarded their lecturer, clad, like a summer garden, in varied beauty, with far greater awe than they had entertained for her predecessor, who was dumpy, wore her hair short, and appeared habitually in a man's jacket.

The two were friends close and fast. Leonard was not afraid of compromising her by taking tea in her drawing-room, nor was Constance afraid of compromising herself by venturing alone into the opposite flat if she wanted to talk about anything. It is a dangerous position even for a young man whose ambitions absorb his thoughts;

who has put the question of marriage into the background—to be taken up at some convenient moment not yet arrived. It is dangerous also for a girl even when she is emancipated.

As regards the young man the usual consequences happened. First he perceived that it gave him a peculiar pleasure to sit beside her at dinner and to walk home with her: then he became disappointed if he did not meet her: presently he found himself thinking a great deal about her: he also detected himself in the act of confiding his ambitions to her sympathetic ear—this is one of the worst symptoms possible. He had now arrived at that stage when the image of the girl is always present in a young man's mind: when it sometimes interferes with work: when an explanation becomes absolutely necessary if there is to be any peace or quiet work. The Victorian lover no longer speaks or writes about flames and darts, but he is still possessed and held by the dominant presence in his mind, night and day, of his mistress.

In these matters, there comes a time, the one moment, when words have to be spoken. As with a pear which has half an hour of perfect ripeness, so in love there is a day—an hour—a moment—when the words that mean so much must be spoken. It is a most unfortunate thing if the lover chooses the wrong moment. It is also very unfortunate if the ripeness is on one side only.

Leonard Campaigne made this mistake. Being a self-contained young man, he thought about himself a great deal more than he thought of other people: it is not necessarily a sign of selfishness or of obtuseness—not at all; it is a defect with men of strong natures and ambitious aims to think habitually about themselves and their aims. Therefore, while he himself was quite ripe for a declaration, he did not ask himself whether the ripeness was also arrived at by the other person concerned. Unfortunately, it was not. The other person concerned was still in the critical stage: she could consider her friend from the outside: she felt, as yet, no attraction towards the uncritical condition, the absorption of love.

Leonard did not suspect this arrest, so to speak, of development. He assumed that the maiden's heart had advanced *pari passu* with his. He wrote a letter, therefore, a method of wooing which is less embarrassing than that of speech—I believe that girls prefer the latter.

Certainly, it is difficult to be glowing in a letter; nor, if there should be any doubt, is a letter so persuasive as the voice, aided by the pressure of the hand and the ardour of the eye.

"My Dear Friend,

"I am about to imperil a situation the preservation of which is my greatest happiness. You have allowed me to talk to you freely about my cherished ambitions. You have even done me the honour of consulting me about your own. I would not throw away this position of confidence for any consideration whatever. Let me, however, venture to put before you a simple question. I ask you to consider the possibility of a change in this situation. This change—there is only one which we can consider—would not in any way affect this confidence, but should draw it more closely. How it would affect me I will tell you if you allow me.

"Your friend,
"L. C."

Not a loverlike letter at all, is it? Yet there were possibilities about it. You see, he held out the hope that more would be told. The young lady answered by asking a few days for consideration. She was to send or bring her reply that morning.

Constance knocked at the door. She came in from her rooms without a hat. She took a chair—Leonard's own wooden chair—and sat down, beginning to talk about other things, as if such a matter as a proposal of marriage was of no importance. But that was only her way, which was always feminine.

"I was told last night," she said, "at the club—fancy, at the club!—that I have been compromising myself by dining night after night with you and letting you walk home with me. That is their idea of woman's liberty. She is not to form friendships. Don't abuse our members. Pray remember, Leonard, that I do not in the least mind what they say."

At the first glance at her face, one could understand that this girl was not in the least alarmed as to what women might say of her. It was a proud face. There are many kinds of pride—she might have been proud of her family, had she chosen that form; or of her intellect and attainments; or of her beauty—which was remarkable. She was not proud in any such way; she had that intense self-respect which is pride of the highest kind. "She was a woman, therefore, to be wooed," but the wooer must meet and equal that intense self-respect. This pride made her seem cold. Everybody thought her intensely cold. Leonard was perhaps the only man who knew by a thousand little indications that she was very far from cold. The pose of her head, the lines of the mouth, the intellectual look in her eyes, the clear-cut regularity of her features, proclaimed her pride and seemed to proclaim her coldness.

"I always remember what you say, Constance. And now tell me what you came to say."

She rose from the chair and remained standing. She began by looking at the things over the mantel as if she was greatly interested in tobacco and cigarettes. Then she turned upon him abruptly, joining her hands. "What I came to say was this."

He read the answer in her face, which was frank, hard, and without the least sign of embarrassment, confusion, or weakening. It is not with such a look that a girl gives herself to her lover. However, he pretended not to understand.

"What is it?"

"Well, it is just this. I have thought about it for a whole week, and it won't do. That is my answer. It won't do for either of us. I like you very much. I like our present relations. We dine together at the club. I come in here without fuss. You come to my place without fuss. We talk and walk and go about together. I do not suppose that I shall ever receive this kind of invitation from any man whom I regard so much. And yet——"

"'Yet!' Why this obstructive participle? I bring you"—but he spoke with coldness due to the discouragement in the maiden's face—"the fullest worship of yourself."

She shook her head and put up her hand. "Oh no!—no!" she said. "Worship? I want no worship. What do you mean by worship?"

"I mean the greatest respect—the greatest reverence—the greatest admiration——"

"For what?"

"For Constance Ambry."

"Thank you, my friend. Some of the respect I accept with gratitude, not all of it. Still, I dare say, at this moment, you mean it all. But consider a little. Do you worship my intellect? Confess, now. You know that it is distinctly inferior to your own. I know it, I say. If you came to me pretending to worship an intellect inferior to your own, I should lose my respect for you, or I should lose my faith in your truthfulness. It cannot be my intellect. Is it, then, worship of my genius? But I have no genius. And that you know very well. Is it worship of my attainments? They are far below most of the scholars of your University and the Fellows of your college. You cannot possibly pretend to worship my attainments——"

"Let me worship Constance Ambry herself."

She laughed lightly.

"It would be very foolish of you to do so. For you could not do so without lowering your standards and your character, by pretending what is not the case. For I am no higher than yourself in any of the virtues possible to us both: not a bit higher: I believe that my standards of everything—truth, honour, courage—patience—all—all—everything are like my intellect, distinctly lower than your own. Such is the respect which I entertain for you. Therefore, my friend, do not, pray, think of offering me worship."

"You wrong yourself, Constance. Your nature is far higher than mine."

She laughed again. "If I were to marry you, in a week you would find out your mistake—and then you might fall into the opposite mistake."

"How am I to make you understand?"

"I do understand. There is something that attracts you. Men are so, I suppose. It is face, or voice, or figure, or manner. No one can tell why a man is attracted."

"Constance, is it possible that you are not conscious of your beauty?"

She looked him full in the face, and replied slowly: "I wish I understood things. I see very well that men are more easily moved to love than women. They make the most appalling mistakes: I know of some—mistakes not to be remedied. Do not let us two make a mistake."

"It would be no mistake, believe me."

"I don't know. There is the question of beauty. Women are not fascinated by the beauty of other women. A man is attracted by a face, and straightway attributes to the soul behind that face all the virtues possible. Women can behold a pretty face without believing that it is the stamp of purity and holiness. Besides—a face! Why, in a dozen years what will it be like? And in thirty years—— Oh! Terrible to think of!"

"Never, Constance. You could never be otherwise than wholly beautiful."

She shook her head again, unconvinced. "I do not wish to be worshipped," she repeated. "Other women may like it. To me it would be a humiliation. I don't want worship; I want rivalry. Let me work among those who truly work, and win my own place. As for my own face, and those so-called feminine attractions, I confess that I am not interested in them. Not in the least."

"If you will only let me go on admiring——"

"Oh!" she shook that admirable head impatiently, "as much as you please."

Leonard sighed. Persuasion, he knew well, was of no use with this young lady; she knew her own mind.

"I will ask no more," he said. "Your heart is capable of every emotion—except one. You are deficient in the one passion which, if you had it, would make you divine."

She laughed scornfully. "Make me divine?" she repeated. "Oh, you talk like a man—not a scholar and a philosopher, but a mere man." She left the personal side of the question, and began to treat it generally. "The whole of poetry is disfigured with the sham divinity, the counterfeit divinity, of the woman. I do not want that kind of ascribed divinity. Therefore I do not regret the absence of this emotion which you so much desire; I can very well do without it." She spoke with conviction, and she looked the part she played—cold, loveless, without a touch of Venus. "I was lecturing my class the other day on this very subject. I took Herrick for my text; but, indeed, there are plenty of poets who would do as well. I spoke of this sham divinity. I said that we wanted in poetry, as in human life, a certain sanity, which can only exist in a condition of controlled emotion."

It was perhaps a proof that neither lover nor maiden really felt the power of the passion called Love that they could thus, at what to some persons would be a supreme moment, drop into a cold philosophic treatment of the subject.

"Perhaps love does not recognise sanity."

"Then love had better be locked up. I pointed out in my lecture that these conceits and extravagancies may be very pretty set to the music of rhythm and rhyme and phrase, but that in the conduct of life they can have no place except in the brains of men who have now ceased to exist."

"Ceased to exist?"

"I mean that the ages of ungoverned passion have died out. To dwell perpetually on a mere episode in life, to magnify its importance, to deify the poet's mistress—that, I told my class, is to present a false view of life and to divert poetry from its proper function."

"How did your class receive this view?"

"Well—you know—the average girl, I believe, likes to be worshipped. It is very bad for her, because she knows she isn't worth it and that it cannot last. But she seems to like it. My class looked, on the whole, as if they could not agree with me."

"You would have no love in poetry?"

"Not extravagant love. These extravagancies are not found in the nobler poets. They are not in Milton, nor in Pope, nor in Cowper, nor in Wordsworth, nor in Browning. I have not, as you say, experienced the desire for love. In any case, it is only an episode. Poetry should be concerned with the whole life."

"So should love."

"Leonard," she said, the doubt softening her face, "there may be something deficient in my nature. I sincerely wish that I could understand what you mean by desiring any change." No, she understood nothing of the sacred passion. "But there must be no difference in consequence. I could not bear to think that my answer even to such a trifle should make any difference between us."

"Such a trifle! Constance, you are wonderful."

"But it seems to me, if the poets are right, that men are always ready to make love: if one woman fails, there are plenty of others."

"Would not that make a difference between us?"

"You mean that I should be jealous?"

"I could not possibly use the word 'jealous' in connection with you, Constance."

She considered the point from an outside position. "I should not be jealous because you were making love to some unseen person, but I should not like another woman standing here between us. I don't think I could stay here."

"You give me hope, Constance."

"No. It is only friendship. Because, you see, the whole pleasure of having a friend like yourself—a man friend—is unrestrained and open conversation. I like to feel free with you. And I confess that I could not do this if another woman were with us."

She was silent awhile. She became a little embarrassed. "Leonard," she said, "I have been thinking about you as well as myself. If I thought that this thing was necessary for you—or best for you—I might, perhaps—though I could not give you what you expect—I mean—responsive worship and the rest of it."

"Necessary?" he repeated.

There was no sign of Love's weakness in her face, which had now assumed the professional manner that is historical, philosophical, and analytical.

"Let us sit down and talk about yourself quite dispassionately, as if you were somebody else."

She resumed the chair—Leonard's own chair—beside the table; it was a revolving chair, and she turned it half round so that her elbow rested on the blotting-pad, while she faced her suitor. Leonard for his part experienced the old feeling of standing up before the Head for a little wholesome criticism. He laughed, however, and obeyed, taking the easy-chair at his side of the fireplace. This gave Constance the slight superiority of talking down to instead of up to him. A tall man very often forgets the advantage of his stature.

"I mean, if companionship were necessary for you. It is, I believe, to weaker and to less fortunate men—to poets, I suppose. Love means, I am sure, a craving for support and sympathy. Some men—weaker men than you—require sympathy as much as women. You do not feel that desire—or need."

"A terrible charge. But how do you know?"

"I know because I have thought a great deal about you, and because I have conceived so deep a regard for you that, at first, when I received your letter I almost—almost—made a great mistake."

"Well—but tell me something more. To learn how one is estimated may be very good for one. Self-conceit is an ever-present danger."

"I think, to begin with, that of all young men that I know you are the most self-reliant and the most confident."

"Well, these are virtues, are they not?"

"Of course, you have every right to be self-reliant. You are a good scholar, and you have been regarded at the University as one of the coming men. You are actually already one of the men who are looked upon as arrived. So far you have justified your self-confidence."

"So far my vanity is not wounded. But there is more."

"Yes. You are also the most fortunate of young men. You are miles ahead of your contemporaries, because where they all lack something you lack nothing. One man wants birth—it takes a very strong man to get over a humble origin: another man wants manner: another has an unfortunate face—a harsh voice—a nervous jerkiness: another is deficient in style: another is ground down by poverty. You alone have not one single defect to stand in your way."

"Let me be grateful, then."

"You have that very, very rare combination of qualities which make the successful statesman. You are good-looking: you are even handsome: you look important: you have a good voice and a good manner as well as a good presence: you are a gentleman by birth and training: you have enough to live upon now: and you are the heir to a good estate. Really, Leonard, I do not know what else you could ask of fortune."

"I have never asked anything of fortune."

"And you get everything. You are too fortunate, Leonard. There must be something behind—something to come. Nature makes no man perfectly happy."

"Indeed!" He smiled gravely. "I want nothing of that kind."

"In addition to everything else, you are completely healthy, and I believe you are a stranger to the dentist; your hair is not getting prematurely thin. Really, Leonard, I do not think that there can be in the whole country any other young man so fortunate."

"Yet you refuse to join your future with mine."

"Perhaps, if there were any misfortunes or drawbacks one might not refuse. Family scandals, now—— Many noble houses have whole cupboards filled with skeletons: your cupboards are only filled with blue china. One or two scandals might make you more human."

"Unfortunately, from your point of view, my people have no scandals."

"Poor relations again! Many people are much pestered with poor relations. They get into scrapes, and they have to be pulled out at great cost. I have a cousin, for instance, who turns up occasionally. He is very expensive and most disreputable. But you? Oh, fortunate young man!"

"We have had early deaths; but there are no disreputable cousins."

"That is what I complain of. You are too fortunate. You should throw a ring into the sea—like the too fortunate king, the only person who could be compared with you."

"I dare say gout or something will come along in time."

"It isn't good for you," she went on, half in earnest. "It makes life too pleasant for you, Leonard. You expect the whole of life to be one long triumphal march. Why, you are so fortunate that you are altogether outside humanity. You are out of sympathy with men and women. They have to fight for everything. You have everything tossed into your lap. You have nothing in common with the working world—no humiliations—no disgraces—no shames and no defeats."

"I hardly understand——" he began, disconcerted at this unexpected array of charges and crimes.

"I mean that you are placed above the actual world, in which men tumble about and are knocked down and are picked up—mostly by the women. You have never been knocked down. You say that I do not understand Love. Perhaps not. Certainly you do not. Love means support on both sides. You and I do not want any kind of support. You are clad in mail armour. You do not—you cannot—even wish to know what Love means."

He made no reply. This turning of the table was unexpected. She had been confessing that she felt no need of Love, and now she accused him—the wooer—of a like defect.

"Leonard, if fortune would only provide you with family scandals, some poor relations who would make you feel ashamed, something to make you like other people, vulnerable, you would learn that Love might mean—and then, in that impossible case—I don't know—perhaps——" She left the sentence unfinished and ran out of the room.

Leonard looked after her, his face expressing some pain. "What does she mean? Humiliation? Degraded relations? Ridiculous!"

Then, for the second time after many years, he heard the voices of his mother and his grandmother. They spoke of misfortunes falling upon one and another of their family, beginning with the old man of the country house and the terrace. Oh! oh! It was absurd. He sprang to his feet. It was absurd. Humiliations! Disgrace! Family misfortunes! Absurd! Well, Constance had refused him. Perhaps she would come round. Meanwhile his eyes fell upon the table and his papers. He sat down: he took up the pen. Love, who had been looking on sorrowfully from a lofty perch on a bookshelf, vanished with a sigh of despair. The lover heard neither the sigh nor the fluttering of Love's wings. He bent over his papers. A moment, and he was again absorbed—entirely absorbed in the work before him.

In her own room the girl sat before her table and took up her pen. But she threw it down again. "No," she said, "I could not. He is altogether absorbed in himself. He knows nothing and understands nothing—and the world is so full of miseries; and he is all happiness, and men and women suffer—how they suffer!—for their sins and for other people's sins. And he knows nothing. He understands nothing. Oh, if he could be made human by something—by humiliation, by defeat! If he could be made human, like the rest, why, then—then— —" She threw away her pen, pushed back the chair, put on her hat and jacket, and went out into the streets among the men and women.

CHAPTER III

SOMETHING TO COME

IF you have the rare power of being able to work at any time, and after any event to concentrate your thoughts on work, this is certainly a good way of receiving disappointments and averting chagrin. Two hours passed. Leonard continued at his table absorbed in his train of argument, and for the moment wholly forgetful of what had passed. Presently his pen began to move more slowly; he threw it down: he had advanced his position by another earthwork. He sat up; he numbered his pages; he put them together. And he found himself, after the change of mind necessary for his work, able to consider the late conversation without passion, though with a certain surprise. Some men—the weaker brethren—are indignant, humiliated, by such a rejection. That is because their vanity is built upon the sands. Leonard was not the kind of man to be humiliated by any answer to any proposal, even that which concerns the wedding-ring. He had too many excellent and solid foundations for the good opinion which he entertained of himself. It was impossible for any woman to refuse him, considering the standards by which women consider and estimate men. Constance had indeed acknowledged that in all things fortune had favoured him, yet owing to some feminine caprice or unexpected perversity he had not been able to touch her heart. Such a man as Leonard cannot be humiliated by anything that may be said or done to him: he is humiliated by his own acts, perhaps, and his own blunders and mistakes, of which most men's lives are so full.

He was able to put aside, as an incident which would perhaps be disavowed in the immediate future, the refusal of that thrice fortunate hand of his. Besides, the refusal was conveyed in words so gracious and so kindly.

But there was this strange attack upon him. He found himself repeating in his own mind her words. Nature, Constance said, makes no man perfectly happy. He himself, she went on, presented the appearance of the one exception to the rule. He was well born, wealthy enough, strong and tall, sound of wind and limb, sufficiently well favoured, with proved abilities, already successful, and without any

The Fourth Generation

discoverable drawback. Was there any other man in the whole world like unto him? It would be better for him, this disturbing girl—this oracle—had gone on to prophesy, if something of the common lot—the dash of bitterness—had been thrown in with all these great and glorious gifts of fortune; something would certainly happen: something was coming; there would be disaster: then he would be more human; he would understand the world. As soon as he had shared the sorrows and sufferings, the shames and the humiliations, of the world, he would become more in harmony with men and women. For the note of the common life is suffering.

At this point there came back to him again out of the misty glades of childhood the memory of those two women who sat together, widows both, in the garb of mourning, and wept together.

"My dear," said the elder lady—the words came back to him, and the scene, as plainly as on that day when he watched the old man sleeping in his chair—"my dear, we are a family of misfortune."

"But why—why—why?" asked the other. "What have we done?"

"Things," said the elder lady, "are done which are never suspected. Nobody knows; nobody finds out: the arm of the Lord is stretched out, and vengeance falls, if not upon the guilty, then upon his children and——"

Leonard drove the memory back—the lawn and the garden: the two women sitting in the veranda: the child playing on the grass: the words—all vanished. Leonard returned to the present. "Ghosts!" he said. "Ghosts! Were these superstitious fears ever anything but ghosts?" He refused to think of these things: he put aside the oracle of the wise woman, the admonition that he was too fortunate a youth.

You have seen how he opened the first of a small heap of letters. His eye fell upon the others: he took up the first and opened it: the address was that of a fashionable West-End hotel: the writing was not familiar. Yet it began "My dear nephew."

"My dear nephew?" he asked; "who calls me his dear nephew?" He turned over the letter, and read the name at the end, "Your affectionate uncle, Fred Campaigne."

Fred Campaigne! Then his memory flew back to another day of childhood, and he saw his mother—that gentle creature—flushing with anger as she repeated that name. There were tears in her eyes—not tears of sorrow, but of wrath—and her cheek was aflame. And that was all he remembered. The name of Frederick Campaigne was never more mentioned.

"I wonder," said Leonard. Then he went on reading the letter:

"My dear Nephew,

"I arrived here a day or two ago, after many years' wandering. I lose no time, after the transaction of certain necessary business, in communicating with you. At this point, pray turn to my signature."

"I have done so already," said Leonard. He put the letter down, and tried to remember more. He could not. There arose before his memory once more the figure of his mother angry for the first and only time that he could remember. "Why was she angry?" he asked himself. Then he remembered that his uncle Christopher, the distinguished lawyer, had never mentioned Frederick's name. "Seems as if there was a family scandal, after all," he thought. He turned to the letter again.

"I am the long-lost wanderer. I do not suppose that you can possibly remember me, seeing that when I went away you were no more than four or five years of age. One does not confide family matters to a child of those tender years. When I left my country I was under a cloud—a light cloud, it is true—a sort of nebulous haze, mysteriously glowing in the sunshine. It was no more than the not uncommon mystery of debt, my nephew. I went off. I was shoved off, in fact, by the united cold shoulders of all the relations. Not only were there money debts, but even my modest patrimony was gone. Thus does fond youth foolishly throw good money after bad. I should have kept my patrimony to go abroad with, and spent nothing but my debts. I am now, however, home again. I should have called, but I have important appointments in the City, where, you may be pleased to learn, my name and my voice carry weight. Meantime, I hear that you will be asked to meet me at my brother Christopher's on Wednesday. I shall, therefore, hope to see you then. My City friends claim all my time between this and Wednesday. The magnitude of certain operations renders it necessary to devote myself, for a day or two, entirely to matters of *haute finance*. It was, I believe, customary in former times for the prodigal son to return in rags. We have changed all that. Nowadays the prodigal son returns in broadcloth, with a cheque-book in his pocket and credit at his bank. The family will be glad, I am sure, to hear that I am prosperous exceedingly."

Leonard read this letter with a little uneasiness. He remembered those tears, to begin with. And then there was a certain false ring in the words, an affectation of light-heartedness which did not sound true. There was an ostentation of success which seemed designed to cover the past. "I had forgotten," he said, "that we had a prodigal son in the family. Indeed, I never knew the fact. 'Prosperous exceedingly,' is he? 'Important appointments in the City.' Well, we shall see. I can wait very well until Wednesday."

He read the letter once more. Something jarred in it; the image of the gentle woman for once in her life in wrath real and undisguised did not agree with the nebulous haze spoken of by the writer. Besides, the touch of romance, the Nabob who returns with a pocket full of money having prospered exceedingly, does not begin by making excuses for the manner of leaving home. Not at all: he comes home exultant, certain to be well received on account of his money-bags. "After all," said Leonard, putting down the letter, "it is an old affair, and my poor mother will shed no more tears over that or anything else, and it may be forgotten." He put down the letter and took up the next. "Humph!" he growled. "Algernon again! I suppose he wants to borrow again. And Constance said that I wanted poor relations."

It is true that his cousin Algernon did occasionally borrow money of him: but he was hardly a poor relation, being the only son of Mr. Christopher Campaigne, of Lincoln's Inn, Barrister-at-law, and in the enjoyment of a large and lucrative practice. It is the blessed privilege of the Bar that every large practice is lucrative; now, in the lower branch of the legal profession there are large practices which are not lucrative, just as in the lower branches of the medical profession there are sixpenny practitioners with a very large connection, and in the Church there are vicars with very large parishes.

Algernon, for his part, was studying with a great and ambitious object. He proposed to become the dramatist of the future. He had not yet written any dramas; he haunted the theatres, attended all the first nights, knew a good many actors and a few actresses, belonged to the Playgoers' Club, spoke and posed as one who is on the stage, or at least as one to whom the theatre is his chosen home. Algernon was frequently stone-broke, was generally unable to obtain more than a certain allowance from his father, and was accustomed to make appeals to his cousin, the head of the family.

The letter was, as Leonard expected, an invitation to lend him money:

"DEAR LEONARD,

"I am sorry to worry you, but things have become tight, and the pater refuses any advances. Why, with his fine practice, he should grudge my small expenses I cannot understand. He complains that I am doing no work. This is most unreasonable, as there is no man who works harder at his art than I myself. I go to a theatre nearly every evening; is it my fault that the stalls cost half a guinea? All this means that I want you to lend me a tenner until the paternal pride breaks or bends.

"Yours,
"ALGERNON."

Leonard read and snorted.

"The fellow will never do anything," he said. Nevertheless, he sat down, opened his cheque-book, and drew the cheque. "Take it, confound you!" he said.

And yet Constance had told him that for want of poor relations he was out of harmony with the rest of the world.

There was a third letter—from his aunt:

"DEAR LEONARD,

"Will you look in, if you possibly can, on Wednesday to meet your uncle Fred? He has come home again. Of course, you cannot remember him. He was wild, I believe, in the old days, but he says that is over now. Indeed, it is high time. He seems to be doing well, and is most cheerful. As the acting head of the family, you will, I am sure, give him a welcome, and forget and forgive, if there is anything to forgive. Algernon is, I fear, working too hard. I could not have believed that the art of play-writing required such close attention to the theatres. He is making many acquaintances among actors and actresses, who will be able, he says, to help him tremendously. I tell his father, who sometimes grumbles, that when the boy makes up his mind to begin there will be no living dramatist who has more conscientiously studied his art.

"Affectionately yours,
"Dorothy Campaigne."

Leonard wrote a note accepting this invitation, and then endeavoured, but without success, to dismiss the subject of the returned prodigal from his mind. It was a relief to feel that he was at least prosperous and cheerful. Now, had Leonard been a person of wider experience, he would have remembered that cheerfulness in a prodigal is a most suspicious attribute, because cheerfulness is the dominant note of the prodigal under all circumstances, even the most unpromising. His cheerfulness is his principal, sometimes his only, virtue. He is cheerful because it is always more pleasant to be cheerful than to be miserable; it is more comfortable to laugh than to cry. Only when the prodigal becomes successful—which is very, very seldom—does he lose his cheerfulness and assume a responsible and anxious countenance like the steady and plodding elder brother.

CHAPTER IV

THE COMPLETE SUPPLY

IT was eleven o'clock that same evening. Leonard sat before his fire thinking over the day's work. It was not a day on which he could congratulate himself. He had been refused: he had been told plain truths: he had been called too fortunate: he had been warned that the gods never make any man completely happy: he had been reminded that his life was not likely to be one long triumphal march, nor was he going to be exempt from the anxieties and the cares which beset other people. Nobody likes to be told that he is too fortunate, and that he wants defeated ambition, poor relations, and family scandals to make him level with the rest of mankind. Moreover, he had received, as if in confirmation of the oracle, the addition to his family of a doubtful uncle.

The Mansion was quiet: no pianos were at work: those of the people who were not out were thinking of bed.

Leonard sat over the fire feeling strangely nervous: he had thought of doing a little work: no time like the quiet night for good work. Yet somehow he could not command his brain: it was a rebellious brain: instead of tackling the social question before him, it went off wandering in the direction of Constance and of her refusal and of her words—her uncomfortable, ill-boding words.

Unexpectedly, and without any premonitory sound of steps on the stair, there came a ring at his bell. Now, Leonard was not a nervous man, or a superstitious man, or one who looked at the present or the future with apprehension. But this evening he felt a chill shudder: he knew that something disagreeable was going to happen. He looked at the clock: his man must have gone to bed: he got up and went out to open the door himself.

There stood before him a stranger, a man of tall stature, wrapped in a kind of Inverness cape, with a round felt hat.

"Mr. Leonard Campaigne?" he asked.

"Certainly," he replied snappishly. "Who are you? What do you want here at this time of night?"

"I am sorry to be so late. I lost my way. May I have half an hour's talk with you? I am a cousin of yours, though you do not know me."

"A cousin of mine? What cousin? What is your name?"

"Here is my card. If you will let me come in, I will tell you all about the relationship. A cousin I am, most certainly."

Leonard looked at the card.

"Mr. Samuel Galley-Campaigne." In the corner were the words, "Solicitor, Commercial Road."

"I know nothing about you," said Leonard. "Perhaps, however—will you come in?"

He led the way into the study, and turned on one or two more lights. Then he looked at his visitor.

The man followed him into the study, threw off his cape and hat, and stood before him—a tall, thin figure, with a face which instantly reminded the spectator of a vulture; the nose was long, thin, and curved; his eyes were bright, set too close together. He was dressed in a frock-coat which had known better days, and wore a black tie. He looked hungry, but not with physical pangs.

"Mr. Samuel Galley-Campaigne," he repeated. "My father's name was Galley; my grandmother's maiden name was Campaigne."

"Oh, your grandmother's name was Campaigne. Your own name, then, is Galley?"

"I added the old woman's name to my own; it looks better for business purposes. Also I took her family crest—she's got a coat of arms—it looks well for business purposes."

"You can't take your grandmother's family shield."

"Can't I? Who's to prevent me? It's unusual down our way, and it's good for business."

"Well, as you please—name and coat of arms and everything. Will you explain the cousinship?"

"In two words. That old man over there"—he indicated something in the direction of the north—"the old man who lives by himself, is my grandmother's father. He's ninety something, and she's seventy something."

"Oh! she is my great-aunt, then. Strange that I never heard of her."

"Not at all strange. Only what one would expect. She went down in the world. You went up—or stayed up—of course they didn't tell you about her."

"Well—do you tell me about her. Will you sit down? May I offer you anything—a cigarette?"

The visitor looked about the room; there was no indication of whisky. He sighed and declined the cigarette. But he accepted the chair.

"Thank you," he said. "It is more friendly sitting down. You've got comfortable quarters. No Mrs. C. as yet, is there? The old woman said that you were a bachelor. Now, then. It's this way: She married my grandfather, Isaac Galley. That was fifty years ago—in 1849. No, 1850. Isaac Galley failed. His failure was remarked upon in the papers on account of the sum—the amount—of his liabilities. The *Times* wanted to know how he managed to owe so much."

"Pray go on. I am interested. This part of our family history is new to me."

Leonard continued standing, looking down upon his visitor. He became aware, presently, of a ridiculous likeness to himself, and he found himself hoping that the vulture played a less prominent part in his own expression. All the Campaigne people were taller—much taller—than the average; their features were strongly marked; they were, as a rule, a handsome family. They carried themselves with a certain dignity. This man was tall, his features were strongly marked; but he was not handsome, and he did not carry himself with dignity. His shoulders were bent, and he stooped. He was one of the race, apparently, but gone to seed; looking "common." No one could possibly mistake him for a gentleman by birth or by breeding. "Common" was the word to apply to Mr. Galley-Campaigne. "Common" is a word much used by certain ladies belonging to a certain stage of society about their neighbours' children; it will do to express the appearance of this visitor.

"Pray go on," Leonard repeated mechanically, while making his observations; "you are my cousin, clearly. I must apologise for not knowing of your existence."

"We live at the other end of town. I'm a gentleman, of course, being in the Law—lower branch——"

"Quite so," said Leonard.

"But the old woman—I mean my grandmother—takes jolly good care that I shall know the difference between you and me. You've had Eton and College to back you up. You've got the House of Commons and a swagger club. That's your world. Mine is different. We've no swells where I live, down the Commercial Road. I'm a solicitor in what you would call a small way. There are no big men our way."

"It is a learned profession."

"Yes. I am not a City clerk, like my father."

"Tell me more about yourself. Your grandfather, you say, was bankrupt. Is he living?"

"No. He went off about ten years ago, boastful to the end of his great smash. His son—that's my father—was in the City. He was a clerk all his life to a wine-merchant. He died four or five years ago. He was just able to pay for my articles—a hundred pounds—and the stamp—another eighty—and that pretty well cleared him out, except for a little insurance of a hundred. When he died I was just beginning to get along; and I've been able to live, and to keep my mother and my grandmother—it's a tight fit, though—with what I can screw out of Mary Anne."

"Who is Mary Anne?"

"My sister, Mary Anne. She's a Board School teacher. But she shoves all the expenses on to me."

"Oh! I have a whole family of cousins, then, previously unknown. That is interesting. Are there more?"

He remembered certain words spoken only that morning, and he winced. Here were poor relations, after all. Constance would be pleased.

"No more—only me and Mary Anne. That is to say, no more that you would acknowledge as such. There's all father's cousins and their children: and all mother's cousins and brothers and nephews and nieces: but you can't rightly call them your cousins."

"Hardly, perhaps, much as one would like...."

"Now, Mr. Campaigne. The old woman has been at me a long time to call upon you. I didn't want to call. I don't want to know you, and you don't want to know me. But I came to please her and to let you know that she's alive, and that she would like, above all things, to see you and to talk to you."

"Indeed! If that is all, I shall be very pleased to call."

"You see, she's always been unlucky—born unlucky, so to speak. But she's proud of her own family. They've never done anything for her, whatever they may have to do—have to do, I say." He became threatening.

"Have to do," repeated Leonard softly.

"In the future. It may be necessary to prove who we are, and that before many years—or months—or even days—and it might save trouble if you were to understand who she is, and who I am."

"You wish me to call upon my great-aunt. I will certainly do so."

"That's what she wants. That's why I came here to-night. Look here, sir: for my own part, I would not intrude upon you. I've not come to beg or to borrow. But for the old woman's sake I've ventured to call and ask you to remember that she is your great-aunt. She's seventy-two years of age, and now and then she frets a bit after a sight of her own people. She hasn't seen any of them since your grandfather committed suicide. And that must have been about the year 1860, before you and I were born."

Leonard started.

"My grandfather committed suicide? What do you mean? My grandfather died somewhere about 1860. What do you mean by saying that he killed himself?"

"What! Don't you know? Your grandfather, sir," said the other firmly, "died of cut-throat fever. Oh yes, whatever they called it, he died of cut-throat fever. Very sudden it was. Of that I am quite certain, because my grandmother remembers the business perfectly well."

"Is it possible? Killed himself? Then, why did I never learn such a thing?"

"I suppose they didn't wish to worry you. Your father was but a child, I suppose, at the time. Perhaps they never told him. All the same, it's perfectly true."

Committed suicide! He remembered the widow who never smiled — the pale-faced, heavy-eyed widow. He now understood why she went in mourning all the days of her life. He now learned in this unexpected manner, why she had retired to the quiet little Cornish village.

Committed suicide! Why? It seemed a kind of sacrilege to ask this person. He hesitated; he took up a trifling ornament from the mantelshelf, and played with it. It dropped out of his fingers into the fender, and was broken.

"Pray," he asked, leaving the other question for the moment, "how came your grandmother to be separated from her own people?"

"They went away into the country. And her father went silly. She never knew him when he wasn't silly. He went silly when his brother-in-law was murdered."

"Brother-in-law murdered? Murdered! What is this? Good Lord, man! what do you mean with your murder and your suicide?"

"Why, don't you know? His brother-in-law was murdered on his grounds. And his wife died of the shock the same day. What else was it that drove him off his old chump?"

"I—I—I—know nothing"—the vulgarity of the man passed unnoticed in the face of these revelations—"I assure you, nothing of these tragedies. They are all new to me. I have been told nothing."

The Fourth Generation

"Never told you? Well, of all the—— Why, the old woman over there is never tired of talking about these things. Proud of them she is. And you never to know anything!"

"Nothing. Is there more? And why do you call my great-grandfather mad?"

"He's as much my great-grandfather as yours. Mad? Well, I've seen him over the garden wall half a dozen times, walking up and down his terrace like a Polar bear. I don't know what you call mad. As for me, I'm a man of business, and if I had a client who never opened or answered a letter, never spoke a word to anybody, neglected his children, let his house go to ruin, never went to church, would have no servants about the place—why, I should have that mis'rable creature locked up, that's all."

Leonard put this point aside.

"But you have not told me about his wife's death. It is strange that I should be asking you these particulars of my own family."

"Mine as well, if you please," the East End solicitor objected, with some dignity. "Well, sir, my grandmother is seventy-two years of age. Therefore it is just seventy-two years since her mother died. For her mother died in child-birth, and she died of the shock produced by the news of her own brother's murder. Her brother's name was Langley Holme."

"Langley? My grandfather's name."

"Yes, Langley Holme. I think he was found lying dead on a hillside. So our great-grandfather, I say, lost in one day his wife and his brother-in-law, who was the best friend he had in the world. Why, sir, if you ever go down to see him and find him in that state, does it not occur to you to ask how it came about?"

"I confess—he is so old. I thought it eccentricity of age."

"No!" His cousin shook his head. "Age alone would not make a man go on like that. I take it, sir, that extreme age makes a man care nothing about other people, not even his own children; but it does not cut him off from money matters."

"You are perhaps right. Yet—well, I know nothing. So the old man's mind was overthrown by the great shock of a double loss. Strange that they never told me! And his son, my grandfather, committed suicide. And his sister's husband became a bankrupt."

"Yes; there are misfortunes enough. The old woman is never tired of harping on the family misfortunes. The second son was drowned. He was a sailor, and was drowned. My father was never anything better than a small clerk. I've known myself what it is to want the price of a dinner. If you want to know what misfortune is like, wait till you're hungry."

"Indeed!" Leonard replied thoughtfully. "And all these troubles are new to me. Strange that they should be told me on this very day!"

"Then there's your own father. He died young, too, and the last case that the old woman talks about is your father's brother. I forget his name; they packed him off to Australia after he had forged your father's name."

"What?"

"Forged. That's a pretty word to use, isn't it? Yes, sir, there are misfortunes enough." He got up. "Well, the point is, will you come and see the old woman?"

"Yes. I will call upon her. When shall I find her at home?"

"She lies down on the sofa beside the fire every afternoon from two to four or half-past four, then wakes up refreshed and able to talk. Come about half-past four. It's the back-parlour; the front is my office, and my clerk—I have only one as yet—works in the room over the kitchen—the gal's bedroom it is, as a rule. It is a most respectable house, with my name on a door-plate, so you can't miss it."

"I will call, then."

"There is one thing more, Mr. Campaigne. We have not thrust ourselves forward, or tried to force ourselves on the family, and we shall not, sir, we shall not. We live six miles apart, and we have our own friends, and my friends are not yours. Still, in a business way, there is a question which I should like to ask. It is a business question."

The man's face became suddenly foxy. He leaned forward and dropped his voice to a whisper. Leonard was on his guard instinctively.

"If it has to do with the Campaigne estates, I have nothing whatever to say. Would it not be well to go to the lawyers who manage the estate?"

"No. They would not tell me anything. What I want to know is this. He has, I believe, a large estate?"

"He has, I believe. But he has no power to part with any portion of it."

"The estate produces rents, I suppose?"

"That is no doubt the case."

"Well, for seventy years the old man has spent nothing. There must be accumulations. In case of no will, these accumulations would be divided equally between your grandfather's heirs and my grandmother. Do you know of any will, if I may be so bold as to ask?"

"I know nothing of any will."

"It is most unlikely that there should be any will. A man who has been off his head for nearly seventy years can hardly leave a will. If he did, one could easily set it aside. Mr. Campaigne, it is on the cards that there may be enormous accumulations."

"There may be, as you say, accumulations."

"In that case, it is possible—I say possible—that my sister and I may become rich, very rich—I hardly dare to put the possibility upon myself—but there must be—there must be—accumulations, and the question which I would put to you, sir, is this: Where are those accumulations invested? And can a man find out what they amount to—what they are worth—who draws the dividends—how are they applied—and is there a will? Was it made before or after the old man went off his chump? And if the money is left out of the family, would you, sir, as the head of the family, be ready to take steps to set aside that will? Those are my questions, Mr. Campaigne." He threw himself back again in the chair, and stuck his thumbs in his waistcoat armholes.

"These are very important questions," said Leonard. "As a lawyer, you must be aware that I cannot give you any answer. As to the administration of the property, I believe I have no right to ask the lawyers and agents any questions. We must assume that the owner of the estate is in his right mind. As for disputing a will, we must wait till a will is produced."

"Sir"—the cousin leaned over his knees and whispered hoarsely—"sir, the accumulations must be a million and a half. I worked it all out myself with an arithmetic book. I learned the rule on purpose. For I never got so far in the book as compound interest. It meant hundreds of sums; I did 'em all, one after the other. I thought I should never get to the end. Mary Anne helped. Hundreds of sums at compound interest, and it tots up to a million and a half—a million and a half! Think of that! A million and a half!"

He got up and put on his overcoat slowly.

"Sir," he added, with deep emotion and a trembling voice, "this money must not be suffered to go out of the family. It must not. It would be sinful—sinful. We look to you to protect the rights of the family."

Leonard laughed. "I fear I have no power to help you in this respect. Good-night. I hope to call upon my great-aunt as she wishes."

He shut the door upon his visitor. He heard his feet going down the stairs. He returned to his empty room.

It was no longer empty. The man had peopled it with ghosts, all of whom he had brought with him.

There was the old man—young again—staggering under the weight of a double bereavement—wife and best friend in the same day. There was his own grandfather killing himself. Why? The young sailor going out to be drowned; his own father dying young; the returned colonial—the prosperous gentleman who, before going out, had forged his brother's name. Forged! forged! The word rang in his brain. There was the daughter of the House—deserted by the House, married into such a family as Mr. Galley represented. Were not these ghosts enough to bring into a quiet gentleman's flat?

Yes, he had been brought up in ignorance of these things. He knew nothing of the cause of the old man's seclusion; not the reason of his grandfather's early death; not any of those other misfortunes. He had been kept in ignorance of all. And now these things were roughly exploded upon his unsuspecting head.

He sat down before the fire; he worked at the "Subject" no more that night. And in his brain there rang still the strange warnings of Constance—that he wanted something of misfortune, such as harassed the rest of the world, in order to bring him down to a level with the men and women around him.

"I have got that something," he said. "Poor relations, family scandals, and humiliations and all. But so far I feel no better."

CHAPTER V

A LEARNED PROFESSION

IN one of the streets lying east of Chancery Lane is a block of buildings, comparatively new, let out as offices. They generally consist of three rooms, but sometimes there are four, five, or even six. The geographical position of the block indicates the character of the occupants: does not every stone in Chancery Lane and her daughters belong to the Law? Sometimes, however, there are exceptions. A few trading companies are established here, for instance; and occasionally one finds written across the door such an announcement as "Mr. George Crediton, Agent." The clerks and people who passed up and down the stairs every day sometimes asked each other what kind of agency was undertaken in this office. But the clerks had their own affairs to think about. Such a mystery as a business conducted in a quiet office to which no clients ever come is a matter of speculation for a while, but soon ceases to excite any attention. Some twenty years and more had passed since that name had first appeared on the door and since the clerks began to wonder.

"Mr. George Crediton, Agent." There are many kinds of agents. Land, houses, property of all kinds, may be managed by an agent; there are agents for taking out patents—several of these run offices near the Patent Office; there are literary agents—but Chancery Lane is not Parnassus; there are agents for the creation and the dissolution of partnership; there are theatrical agents—but what has law land to do with sock and buskin? And what kind of Agent was Mr. George Crediton?

Mr. George Crediton, Agent, sat in his inner office. The room was furnished solidly with a view to work. The large and ponderous table, covered with papers so dear to the solicitor, was not to be seen here; in its place was an ordinary study table. This was turned at an angle to the wall and window. There was a warm and handsome carpet, a sheepskin under the table, a wooden chair for the Agent, and two others for his visitors. A typewriter stood on the table. The walls were covered with books—not law books, but a miscellaneous collection. The Agent was apparently a man who revelled in light reading; for, in fact, all the modern humorists were there—those from America as well as those of our own production. There was also a collection of the English poets, and some, but not many, of France and Germany. On a table before him stood half a dozen bound folios with the titles on the back—"Reference A—E," and so on. In one corner, stood an open safe, to which apparently belonged another folio, entitled "Ledger."

The Agent, engaged upon his work, evidently endeavoured to present an appearance of the gravest responsibility. His face was decorated by a pair of small whiskers cut straight over and set back; the chin and lips were smooth-shaven. The model set before himself was the conventional face of the barrister. Unfortunately, the attempt was not successful, for the face was not in the least like that conventional type. It had no severity, it had no keenness; it was not set or grave or dignified. It might have been the face of a light comedian. In figure the man was over six feet high and curiously thin, with a slightly aquiline nose and mobile, sensitive lips.

He began his morning's work by opening his letters; there were only two or three. He referred to his ledger and consulted certain entries; he made a few pencil notes. Then he took down from one shelf Sam Slick, Artemus Ward, and Mark Twain, and from another a collection of Burnand's works and one or two of Frederick Anstey's. He turned over the pages, and began to make brief extracts and more notes. Perhaps, then, a bystander might have thought he was about to write a paper on the comparative characteristics of English and American humour.

Outside, his boy—he had a clerk of fourteen at five shillings a week—sat before the fire reading the heroic jests and achievements of the illustrious Jack Harkaway. He was a nice boy, full of imagination, resolved on becoming another Jack Harkaway when the time should arrive, and for the moment truly grateful to fortune for providing him with a situation which demanded no work except to post letters and to sit before the fire reading in a warm and comfortable outer room to which no callers or visitors ever came except his employer and the postman; and if you asked that boy what was the character of the agency, he would not be able to tell you.

When Mr. George Crediton had finished making his extracts, he pinned the papers together methodically, and laid them on one side. Then he opened the last letter.

"He's answered it," he chuckled. "Fred's handwriting. I knew it—I knew it. Called himself Barlow, but I knew it directly. Oh, he'll come—he'll come." He sat down and laughed silently, shaking the room with his chuckling. "He'll come. Won't he be astonished?"

Presently he heard a step and a voice:

"I want to see Mr. George Crediton."

"That's Fred," said the Agent, chuckling again. "Now for it."

"There's nobody with him," the boy replied, not venturing to commit himself, and unaccustomed to the arrival of strangers.

The caller was a tall man of about forty-five, well set up, and strongly built. He was dressed with the appearance of prosperity, therefore he carried a large gold chain. His face bore the marks which we are accustomed to associate with certain indulgences, especially in strong drink. It is needless to dwell upon these evidences of frailty; besides, one may easily be mistaken. It was a kind of face which might be met with in a snug bar-parlour with a pipe and a glass of something hot—a handsome face, but not intellectual or refined. Yet it ought to have been both. In spite of broadcloth and white linen the appearance of this gentleman hardly extorted the immediate respect of the beholder.

"Tell Mr. Crediton that Mr. Joseph Barlow is outside."

"Barlow?" said the boy. "Why don't you go in, then?" and turned over now to his book of adventures.

Mr. Barlow obeyed, and passed into the inner office. There he stopped short, and cried:

"Christopher, by all that's holy!"

The Agent looked up, sprang to his feet, and held out his hand.

"Fred! Back again, and become a Barlow!"

Fred took the outstretched hand, but doubtfully.

"Come to that, Chris, you're a Crediton."

"In the way of business, Crediton."

"Quite so. In the way of business, Barlow."

Then they looked at each other and burst into laughter.

"I knew your handwriting, Fred. When I got your letter I knew it was yours, so I sent you a type-written reply. Typewriting never betrays, and can't be found out if you want to be secret."

"Oh, it's mighty funny, Chris. But I don't understand it. What the devil does it all mean?"

"The very question in my mind, Fred. What does it mean? New rig-out, gold chain, ring—what does it mean? Why have you never written?"

"The circumstances of my departure—you remember, perhaps."

The Agent's face darkened.

"Yes, yes," he replied hastily; "I remember. The situation was awkward—very."

"You were much worse than I was, but I got all the blame."

"Perhaps—perhaps. But it was a long time ago, and—and—well, we have both got on. You are now Barlow—Joseph Barlow."

"And you are now Crediton—George Crediton."

"Sit down, Fred; let us have a good talk. And how long have you been back?"

Fred took a chair, and sat down on the opposite side of the table.

"Only a fortnight or so."

"And why didn't you look me up before?"

"As I told you, there was some doubt —— However, here I am. Barlow is the name of my Firm, a large and influential Firm."

"In Sydney? or Melbourne?"

"No, up-country—over there." He pointed over his left shoulder. "That's why I use the name of Barlow. I am here on the business of the

Firm—it brought me to London. It takes me every day into the City—most important transactions. Owing to the magnitude of the operation, my tongue is sealed."

"Oh!" There was a little doubt implied by the interjection. "You a business man? You? Why, you never understood the simplest sum in addition."

"As regards debts, probably not. As regards assets and property——But in those days I had none. Prosperity, Chris—prosperity brings out all a man's better qualities. You yourself look respectable."

"I've been respectable for exactly four-and-twenty years. I am married. I have a son of three-and-twenty, and a daughter of one-and-twenty. I live in Pembridge Crescent, Bayswater."

"And you were by way of being a barrister."

"I was. But, Fred, to be honest, did you ever catch me reading a law book?"

"I never did. And now you're an Agent."

"Say, rather, that I practice in the higher walks of Literature. What can be higher than oratory?"

"Quite so. You supply the world—which certainly makes a terrible mess of its speeches—with discourses and after-dinner oratory."

"Oratory of all kinds, from the pulpit to the inverted tub: from the Mansion House to the Bar Parlour: from the House of Commons to the political gathering."

"What does your wife say?"

"My wife? Bless you, my dear boy, she doesn't know anything. She doesn't suspect. At home I'm the prosperous and successful lawyer: they wonder why I don't take silk."

"What? Don't they know?"

"Nobody knows. Not the landlord of these rooms. Not the boy outside. Not any of my clients. Not my wife, nor my son, nor my daughter."

"Oh! And you are making a good thing out of it?"

"So good that I would not exchange it for a County Court Judgeship."

"It's wonderful," said Fred. "And I always thought you rather a half-baked lump of dough."

"Not more wonderful than your own success. What a blessing it is, Fred, that you have come home without wanting to borrow any money"—he watched his brother's face: he saw a cloud as of doubt or anxiety pass over it, and he smiled. "Not that I could lend you any if you did want it—with my expensive establishment. Still, it is a blessing and a happiness, Fred, to be able to think of you as the Head—I believe you said the Head—of the great and prosperous Firm of Barlow & Co." Fred's face distinctly lengthened. "I suppose I must not ask a business man about his income?"

"Hardly—hardly. Though, if any man—— But—I have a partner who would not like these private affairs divulged."

"Well, Fred, I'm glad to see you back again—I am indeed."

They shook hands once more, and then, for some unknown reason, they were seized with laughter, long and not to be controlled.

"Distinguished lawyer," murmured Fred, when the laugh had subsided with an intermittent gurgle.

"Influential man of business," said Christopher. "Oh! Ho, Lord!" cried he, wiping his eyes, "it brings back the old times when we used to laugh. What a lot we had to laugh at! The creditors and the duns—you remember?"

"I do. And the girls—and the suppers! They were good old times, Chris. You carried on shameful."

"We did—we did. It's pleasant to remember, though."

"Chris, I'm thirsty."

"You always are."

His brother remembered this agreeable trait after five-and-twenty years. He got up, opened a cupboard, and took out a bottle and glasses and some soda-water. Then they sat opposite each other with the early tumbler and the morning cigar, beaming with fraternal affection.

"Like old times, old man," said the barrister.

"It is. We'll have many more old times," said Fred, "now that I'm home again."

In the words of the poet, "Alas! they had been friends in youth," as well as brothers. And it might have been better had they not been friends in youth. And they had heard the midnight chimes together. And they had together wasted each his slender patrimony. But now they talked friendly over the sympathetic drink that survives the possibility of port and champagne, and even claret.

"Don't they really suspect—any of them?" asked Brother Fred.

"None of them. They call me a distinguished lawyer and the Pride of the Family—next to Leonard, who's in the House."

"Isn't there a danger of being found out?"

"Not a bit. The business is conducted by letter. I might as well have no office at all, except for the look of it. No, there's no fear. Nobody ever comes here. How did you find me out?"

"Hotel clerk. He saw my name as a speaker at the dinner to-morrow, and suggested that I should write to you."

"Good. He gets a commission. I say, you must come and see us, you know. Remember, no allusions to the Complete Speech-maker—eh?"

"Not a word. Though, I say, it beats me how you came to think of it."

"Genius, my boy—pure genius. When you get your speech you will be proud of me. What's a practice at the Bar compared with a practice at the after-dinner table? And now, Fred, why Barlow?"

"Well, you remember what happened?" His brother nodded, and dropped his eyes. "Absurd fuss they made."

"Nobody has heard anything about you for five-and-twenty years."

"I took another name—a fighting name. Barlow, I called myself— Joseph Barlow. Joe—there's fight in the very name. No sympathy, no weakening about Joe."

"Yes. For my own part, I took the name of Crediton. Respectability rather than aggressiveness in that name. Confidence was what I wanted."

"Tell me about the family. Remember that it was in 1874 that I went away—twenty-five years ago."

His brother gave him briefly an account of the births and deaths. His mother was dead; his elder brother was dead, leaving an only son.

"As for Algernon's death," said the speech-merchant, "it was a great blow. He was really going to distinguish himself. And he died—died at thirty-two. His son is in the House. They say he promises well. He's a scholar, I believe; they say he can speak; and he's more than a bit of a prig."

"And about the old man—the ancient one—is he living?"

"Yes. He is nearly ninety-five."

"Ninety-five. He can't last much longer. I came home partly to look after things. Because, although the estate goes to Algernon's son—deuced bad luck for me that Algernon did have a son—there's the accumulations. I remembered them one evening out there, and the thought went through me like a knife that he was probably dead, and the accumulations divided, and my share gone. So I bundled home as fast as I could."

"No—so far you are all right. For he's hearty and strong, and the accumulations are still rolling up, I suppose. What will become of them no one knows."

"I see. Well, I must make the acquaintance of Algernon's son."

"And about this great Firm of yours?"

"Well, it's a—as I said—a great Firm."

"Quite so. It must be, with Fred Campaigne at the head of it."

"Never mind the Firm, but tell me about this astonishing profession of yours."

The Professor smiled.

"Fortunately," he said, "I am alone. Were there any competition I might be ruined. But I don't know: my reputation by this time stands on too firm a basis to be shaken."

"Your reputation? But people cannot talk about you."

"They cannot. But they may whisper—whisper to each other. Why, just consider the convenience. Instead of having to rack their brains for compliments and pretty things and not to find them, instead of hunting for anecdotes and quotations, they just send to me. They get in return a speech just as long as they want—from five minutes to an hour—full of good things! In this way they are able to acquire it at a cheap, that is, a reasonable rate, for next to nothing, considering the reputation of wit and epigram and sparkles. Then think of the company at the dinner. Instead of having to listen to a fumbler and a stammerer and a clumsy boggler, they have before them a speaker easy in his mind, because he has learned it all by heart, bright and epigrammatic. He keeps them all alive, and when he sits down there is a sigh to think that his speech was so short."

"You must give me just such a speech."

"I will—I will. Fred, you shall start with a name that will make you welcome at every City Company's dinner. It will help you hugely over your enormous transactions for the Firm. Rely on me. Because, you see, when a man has once delivered himself of a good speech, he is asked to speak again: he must keep it up; so he sends to me again. Look here"—he laid his hands upon a little pile of letters—"here are yesterday's and to-day's letters." He took them up and played with them as with a pack of cards. "This man wants a reply for the Army. This is a return for Literature. This is a reply for the House of Commons. The Ladies, the American Republic, Science, the Colonies—see?"

"And the pay?"

"The pay, Fred, corresponds to the privilege conferred. I make orators. They are grateful. As for yourself, now——"

"Mine is a reply for Australia. The dinner is on Friday at the Hotel Cecil—Dinner of Colonial Enterprise."

"Really!" The Agent smiled and rubbed his hands. "This is indeed gratifying. Because, Fred—of course you are as secret as death—I may tell you that this request of yours completes the toast-list for the evening. The speeches will be all—all my own—all provided by the Agent. But the plums, my brother, the real plums, shall be stuffed in yours. I will make it the speech of the evening. Mr. Barlow—Barlow—Barlow of New South Wales."

Fred rose. "Well," he said, "I leave you to my speech. Come and dine with me to-night at the Hôtel Métropole—half-past seven. We might have a look round afterwards."

They had that dinner together. It was quite the dinner of a rich man. It was also the dinner of one who loved to look upon the winecup.

After dinner Fred looked at his watch. "Half-past nine. I say, Chris, about this time we used to sally forth. You remember?"

"I believe I do remember. I am now so respectable that I cannot allow myself to remember."

"There was the Holborn Casino and the Argyll for a little dance: the Judge and Jury, Evans's, and the Coalhole for supper and a sing-song: Caldwell's to take a shop-girl for a quiet dance: Cremorne——"

"My dear Fred, these are old stories. All these things have gone. The Holborn and the Argyll are restaurants, Cremorne is built over, Evans's is dead and gone: the Judge and Jury business wouldn't be tolerated now."

"What do the boys do now?"

"How should I know? They amuse themselves somehow. But it's no concern of mine, or of yours. You are no longer a boy, Fred."

"Hang it! What am I to do with myself in the evenings? I suppose I can go and look on if I can't cut in any more?"

"No; you mustn't even look on. Leave the boys to themselves. Join a club and sit by yourself in the smoking-room all the evening. That's the amusement for you."

"I suppose I can go to the theatre—if that's all?"

"Oh yes! You must put on your evening clothes and go to the stalls. We used to go to the pit, you know. There are music-halls and variety shows of sorts—you might go there if you like. But, you know, you've got a character to maintain. Think of your position."

"Hang my position, man! Get up and take me somewhere. Let us laugh and look on at something."

"My dear Fred, consider. I am a respectable barrister with a grown-up son. Could I be seen in such a place? The head of the firm of Barlow and Co., allow me to point out, would not improve his chances in the City if he were seen in certain places."

"Nobody knows me."

"Remember, my dear brother, that if you mean to get money out of the City you must be the serious and responsible capitalist in the evening as well as in the morning."

"Then we'll go and have tobacco in the smoking-room. One is apt to forget, Chris, the responsibilities of success."

"Quite so." Christopher smiled. "Quite so. Well put. The responsibilities of success. I will introduce the phrase in your speech. The responsibilities of success."

CHAPTER VI

THE RETURN OF THE PRODIGAL

Mrs. Christopher Campaigne was at home. The rooms were filled with people—chiefly young people, friends of her son and daughter. Most of them were endowed with those literary and artistic leanings which made them severe critics, even if they had not yet produced immortal works of their own. The chief attraction of the evening, however, was the newly-returned Australian, said to be a millionaire, who took up a large space in the room, being tall and broad; he also took up a large space in the conversation: he talked loud and laughed loud. He presented successfully the appearance he desired, namely, that of a highly prosperous gentleman, accustomed to the deference due to millions.

Leonard came late.

"I am glad to see you here," said his hostess. "Frederick, you can hardly remember your other nephew, son of Algernon."

Frederick held out a manly grasp. "When I left England," he said, "you were a child of four or five; I cannot pretend to remember you, Leonard."

"Nor can I remember you." He tried to dismiss from his mind a certain ugly word. "But you are welcome home once more. This time, I hope, to stay."

"I think not. Affairs—affairs are sometimes peremptory, particularly large affairs. The City may insist upon my staying a few weeks, or the City may allow me to go back. I am wholly in the hands of the City."

If you come to think of it, a man must be rich indeed to be in the hands of the City.

The people gazed upon the speaker with increased interest, and even awe. They were not in the hands of the City.

"I confess," he went on, "that I should like to remain. Society, when one returns to it after many years, is pleasing. Some people say that it is hollow. Perhaps. The frocks vary"—he looked round critically—

"they are not the same as they were five-and-twenty years ago; but the effect remains the same. And the effect is everything. We must not look behind the scenes. The rough old colonist"—yet no one in the room was better groomed—"looks on from the outside and finds it all delightful."

"Can things unreal ever be delightful?" murmured a lady in the circle with a sigh.

"At all events," Leonard continued, "you will not leave us for a time."

"There, again, I am uncertain. I have a partner in Australia. I have connections to look up in the City. But for a few weeks I believe I may reckon on a holiday and a look round, for Colonials have to show the City that all the enterprise is not theirs, nor all the wealth—nor all the wealth. And what," he asked with condescension, "what are you doing, Leonard?"

"I am in the House."

"As your father was—and your grandfather. It is a great career."

"It may be a great career."

"True—true. There must be many failures—many failures. Where and when are you most likely to be found?"

Leonard told him.

"Give me a note of it before we go to-night. I dare say I can get round some time."

The ugly word once more unpleasantly returned to Leonard's mind.

Mr. Frederick Campaigne proceeded with his interrupted discourse, which proved the necessity of the existence of the poor in order to make the condition of the rich possible and enviable. He took the millionaire's point of view, and dwelt not only on the holiness of wealth, but also on the duties of the poor towards their superiors.

Leonard slipped away. He felt uncomfortable. He could not forget what had been told him about this loud and prosperous and self-satisfied person. Besides, he seemed to be overdoing it—acting a part. Why?

The Fourth Generation

In the inner drawing-room he found his two cousins, Algernon and Philippa. The former, a young man of three-or four-and-twenty, was possessed of a tall figure, but rather too small a head. He smiled a good deal, and talked with an easy confidence common to his circle of friends. It was a handsome face, but it did not suggest possibilities of work.

Leonard asked him how he was getting on.

"Always the same," he replied, with a laugh. "The study of the dramatic art presents endless difficulties. That is why we are loaded up with plays."

"Then it remains for you to show the world what a play should be."

"That is my mission. I shall continue my studies for a year or so more; and then—you shall see. My method is to study the art on the stage itself, not in books. I go to men and women on the stage. I sit in various parts of the stalls and watch and learn. Presently I shall sit down to write."

"Well, I look forward to the result."

"Look here, Leonard"—he dropped his voice. "I hear that you go to see the old man sometimes. He is nearly ninety-five. He can't last much longer. Of course the estate is yours. But how about the accumulations."

"I know nothing about the accumulations."

"With the pater's large practice and our share of the accumulations, don't you think it is too bad of him to keep up this fuss about my work? Why should I trouble my head about money? There will be—there must be—plenty of money. My work," he said proudly, "shall be, at least, the work of one who is not driven by the ignoble stimulus of necessity. It will be entirely free from the ignoble stimulus of necessity. It will be free from the commercial taint—the curse of art—the blighting incubus of art—the degrading thought of money."

Leonard left him. In the doorway stood his cousin Philippa.

"You have just been talking to Algernon," she said. "You see, he is always stretching out his hands in the direction of dramatic art."

"So I observe," he replied dryly. "Some day, perhaps, he will grasp it. At present, as you say, he is only stretching out arms in that direction. And you?"

"I have but one dream—always one dream," she replied, oppressed with endeavour.

"I hope it will come true, then. By the way, Philippa, I have just found a whole family of new cousins."

"New cousins? Who are they?"

"And a great aunt. I have seen one of the cousins; and I am going to-morrow to see the great-aunt and perhaps the other cousin."

"Who are they? If they are your cousins, they must be cousins on papa's side. I thought that we three were the only cousins on his side."

"Your uncle Fred may have children. Have you asked him if he is married?"

"No; he has promised to tell all his adventures. He is a bachelor. Is it not interesting to get another uncle, and a bachelor, and rolling in money? Algernon has already— —" She stopped, remembering a warning. "But who are these cousins?"

"Prepare for a shock to the family pride."

"Why, we have no poor relations, have we? I thought— —"

"Listen, my cousin. Your grandfather's sister Lucy married one Isaac Galley about the year 1847. It was not a good marriage for her. The husband became a bankrupt, and as by this time her father had fallen into his present condition or profession of a silent hermit, there was no help from him. Then they fell into poverty. Her son became a small clerk in the City, her grandson is a solicitor in the Commercial Road—not, I imagine, in the nobler or higher walks of that profession—and her grand-daughter is a teacher in a Board School."

"Indeed!" The girl listened coldly; her eyes wandered round the room filled with well-dressed people. "A teacher in a Board School! And our cousin! A Board School teacher! How interesting! Shall we tell all these people about our new cousins?"

"No doubt they have all got their own second cousins. It is, I believe, the duty of the second cousin to occupy a lower rank."

"I dare say. At the same time, we have always thought our family a good deal above the general run. And it's rather a blow, Leonard, don't you think?"

"It is, Philippa. But, after all, it remains a good old family. One second cousin cannot destroy our record. You may still be proud of it."

He left the girl, and went in search of his uncle, whom he found, as he expected, in his study apart from the throng.

"Always over your papers," he said. "May I interrupt for a moment?"

The barrister shuffled his papers hurriedly into a drawer.

"Always busy," he said. "We lawyers work harder than any other folk, I believe, especially those with a confidential practice like my own, which makes no noise and is never heard of."

"But not the less valuable, eh?"

The barrister smiled.

"We make both ends meet," he said meekly—"both ends meet. Yes, yes, both ends meet."

"I went to see the old man the other day," Leonard went on, taking a chair. "I thought you would like to know. He remains perfectly well, and there is no change in any respect. What I want to ask you is this. It may be necessary before long to get the question decided. Is he in a condition to make a will?"

The lawyer took time to give an opinion. Backed by his long legal experience and extensive practice, it was an opinion carrying weight.

"My opinion," he said gravely, and as one weighing the case judicially—in imagination he had assumed the wig and gown—"my opinion," he repeated, "would be, at first and on the statement of the case, that he is unfit and has been unfit for the last seventy years, to make a will. He is undoubtedly on some points so eccentric as to appear of unsound mind. He does nothing; he allows house and gardens and furniture and pictures to fall into decay; he never speaks;

he has no occupation. This points, I say, to a mind unhinged by the shock of seventy years ago."

"A shock of which I only heard the other day."

"Yes—I know. My sister-in-law—your mother and your grandfather—thought to screen you from what they thought family misfortune by never telling you the truth—that is to say, the whole truth. I have followed the same rule with my children."

"Family misfortune! I hardly know even now what to understand by it."

"Well, they are superstitious. Your father died young, your grandfather died young; like you, they were young men of promise. Your great-grandfather at the age of six-and-twenty or thereabouts was afflicted, as you know."

"And they think——"

"They think that it is the visiting of the unknown sins of the fathers upon the children. They think that the old man's father must have done something terrible."

"Oh, but this is absurd."

"Very likely—very likely. Meantime, as to the power of making a will, we must remember that during all these years the old man has never done anything foolish. I have seen the solicitors. They tell me that from father to son, having acted for him all these years, they have found him perfectly clear-headed about money matters. I could not ask them what he has done with all his money, nor what he intends to do with it. But there is the fact—the evidence of the solicitors as to the clearness of his intellect. My opinion, therefore, is that he will do something astonishing, unexpected, and disgusting with his money, and that it will be very difficult, if not impossible, to set aside his will."

"Oh, that is your opinion, is it? The reason why I ask is that I have just discovered a family of hitherto unknown cousins. Do you know the name of Galley?"

"No. It is not a name, I should say, of the highest nobility."

"Possibly not. It is the name of our cousins, however. One of them is a solicitor of a somewhat low class, I should say; the man has no pretensions whatever to be called a gentleman. He practises and lives in the Commercial Road, which is, I suppose, quite out of the ordinary quarter where you would find a solicitor of standing."

"Quite, quite; as a place of residence—deplorable from that point of view."

"He has a sister, it appears, who is a Board School teacher."

"A Board School teacher? It is at least respectable. But who are these precious cousins of ours?"

"They are the grandchildren of an aunt of yours—Lucy by name."

"Lucy! Yes. I have heard of her; I thought she was dead long ago."

"She married a man named Galley. They seem to have gone down in the world."

"More family misfortune." The lawyer shuddered. "I am not superstitious," he said, "but really—more misfortunes."

"Oh, misfortunes! Nonsense! There are always in every family some who go down—some who go up—some who stay there. You yourself have been borne steadily upwards to name and fortune."

"I have," said the lawyer, with half a groan. "Oh yes—yes—I have."

"And my uncle Fred, you see, comes home—all his wild oats sowed—with a great fortune."

"Truly." The lawyer's face lengthened. "A great fortune. He told you so, didn't he? Yes; we have both been most fortunate and happy, both Fred and I. Go on, Leonard. About these cousins——"

"These are the grandchildren of Lucy Campaigne. I am to see the old lady in a day or two."

"Do they want anything? Help? Recognition?"

"Nothing, so far as I know. Not even recognition."

"That is well. I don't mind how many poor relations we've got, provided they don't ask for money, or for recognition. If you give them money, they will infallibly decline to work, and live upon you.

If you call upon them and give them recognition, they will infallibly disgrace you."

"The solicitor asked for nothing. This cousin of ours has been building hopes upon what he calls accumulations. He evidently thinks that the old man is not in a condition to make a will, and that all that is left of personal property will be divided in two equal shares, one moiety among your father's heirs on our side, while the other will go to the old lady his grandmother on the other side."

"That is, I am afraid, quite true. But there may have been a Will before he fell into—eccentricity. It is a great pity, Leonard, that these people have turned up—a great misfortune—because we may have to share with them. Still, there must be enormous accumulations. My mother did not tell us anything about possible cousins; yet they do exist, and they are very serious and important possibilities. These people will probably interfere with us to a very serious extent. And now Fred has turned up, and he will want his share, too. Another misfortune."

"How came my grandfather to die so young?" Leonard passed on to another point.

"He fell into a fever. I was only two years old at the time."

Leonard said nothing about the suicide. Clearly, not himself only, but his uncles also, had been kept in the dark about the true cause of that unexpected demise.

He departed, closing the door softly, so as not to shake up and confuse the delicate tissues of a brain always occupied in arriving at an opinion.

As soon as he was gone the barrister drew out his papers once more, and resumed the speech for which he had prepared half a dozen most excellent stories. In such a case the British public does not ask for all the stories to be new.

Leonard rejoined the company upstairs.

His uncle Fred walked part of the way home with him.

"I hadn't expected," he said, "to find the old man still living. Of course, it cannot go on much longer. Have you thought about what may happen—when the end comes?"

"Not much, I confess."

"One must. I take it that he does not spend the fiftieth part of his income. I have heard as a boy that the estate was worth £7,000 a year."

"Very likely, unless there has been depression."

"Say he spends £150 a year. That leaves £5,850 a year. Take £800 for expenses and repairs—that leaves £5,000 a year. He has been going on like this for seventy years. Total accumulations, £420,000. At compound interest for all these years, it must reach two millions or so. Who is to have it?"

"His descendants, I suppose."

"You, my brother Christopher, and myself. Two millions to divide between us. A very pretty fortune—very pretty indeed. Good-night, my boy—good-night."

He walked away cheerfully and with elastic step.

"Accumulations—accumulations!" said Leonard, looking after him. "They are all for accumulations. Shall I, too, begin to calculate how much has been accumulated? And how if the accumulations turn out to be lost—wasted—gone—to somebody else?"

CHAPTER VII

THE CHILD OF SORROWS

ON a cold day, with a grey sky and an east wind, Leonard for the first time walked down the Commercial Road to call upon the newly-found cousins. It is a broad thoroughfare, but breadth does not always bring cheerfulness with it; even under a warm summer sun some thoroughfares cannot be cheerful. Nothing can relieve the unvarying depression of the Commercial Road. It is felt even by the children, who refuse to play in it, preferring the narrow streets running out of it; the depression is felt even by the drivers and the conductors of the tram-cars, persons who are generally superior to these influences. Here and there is a chapel, here and there is a model lodging-house or a factory, or a square or a great shop. One square was formerly picturesque when the Fair of the Goats was held upon it; now it has become respectable; the goats are gone, and the sight provokes melancholy. North and south of the road branch off endless rows of streets, crossed by streets laid out in a uniform check pattern. All these streets are similar and similarly situated, like Euclid's triangles. One wonders how a resident finds his own house; nevertheless, the houses, though they are all turned out according to the same pattern, are neat and clean and well kept. The people in them are prosperous, according to their views on prosperity; the streets are cheerful, though the road to which they belong is melancholy. "Alas!" it says, "how can such a road as myself be cheerful? I lead to the Docks, and Limehouse, and Poplar, and Canning Town, and the Isle of Dogs."

Mr. Galley's house was on the north side, conveniently near to a certain police-court, in which he practised daily, sometimes coming home with as much as three or four half-crowns in his pocket, sometimes with less—for competition among the professional solicitors in the police-courts is keen, and even fierce. Five shillings is a common fee for the defence of a prisoner, and rumour whispers that even this humble sum has to be shared secretly with a certain functionary who must be nameless.

A brass plate was on the door: "Mr. Samuel Galley-Campaigne, Solicitor." It was a narrow three-storied house, quite respectable, and as depressing as the road in which it stood.

Leonard knocked doubtfully. After a few moments' delay the door was opened by a boy who had a pen stuck behind his ear.

"Oh, you want Mrs. Galley!" he said. "There you are—back-parlour!" and ran up the stairs again, leaving the visitor on the doormat.

He obeyed instructions, however, and opened the door indicated. He found himself in a small back room—pity that the good old word "parlour" has gone out!—where there were sitting three ladies representing three stages of human life—namely, twenty, fifty, and seventy.

The table was laid for tea; the kettle was on the old-fashioned hob—pity that the hospitable hob has gone!—and the kettle was singing; the buttered toast and the muffins were before the fire, within the high old-fashioned fender; the tea-things and the cake and the bread-and-butter were on the table, and the ladies were in their Sunday "things," waiting for him. It was with some relief that Leonard observed the absence of Mr. Samuel.

The eldest of the three ladies welcomed him.

"My grand-nephew Leonard," she said, giving him her hand, "I am very glad—very glad indeed to make your acquaintance. This"—she introduced the lady of middle life—"is my daughter-in-law, the widow—alas!—of my only son. And this"—indicating the girl—"is my grand-daughter."

The speaker was a gentlewoman. The fact was proclaimed in her speech, in her voice, in her bearing, in her fine features. She was tall, like the rest of her family; her abundant white hair was confined by a black lace cap, the last of the family possessions; her cheek was still soft, touched with a gentle colour and a tender bloom; her eyes were still full of light and warmth; her hands were delicate; her figure was still shapely; there were no bending of the shoulders, no dropping of the head. She reminded Leonard of the Recluse; but her expression was different: his was hard and defiant; hers was gentle and sad.

The second lady, who wore a widow's cap and a great quantity of black crape, evidently belonged to another class. Some people talk of a lower middle class. The distinction, I know, is invidious. Why do we say the lower middle class? We do not say the lower upper class. However, this lady belonged to the great and numerous class which has to get through life on slender means, and has to consider, before all things, the purchasing power of sixpence. This terrible necessity, in its worst form, takes all the joy and happiness out of life. When every day brings its own anxieties about this sixpence, there is left no room for the graces, for culture, for art, for poetry, for anything that is lovely and delightful. It makes life the continual endurance of fear, as dreadful as continued pain of body. Even when the terror of the morrow has vanished, or is partly removed by an increase of prosperity, the scars and the memory remain, and the habits of mind and of body.

Mrs. Galley the younger belonged to that class in which the terror of the morrow has been partly removed. But she remembered. In what followed she sat in silence. But she occupied, as of right, the proud position of pouring out the tea. She was short of stature, and might have been at one time pretty.

The third, the girl, who was Mary Anne, the Board School teacher, in some respects resembled her mother, being short and somewhat insignificant of aspect. But when she spoke she disclosed capacity. It is not to girls without capacity and resolution that places in Board Schools are offered.

"Let me look at you, Leonard." The old lady still held his hand. "Ah! what a joy it is to see once more one of my own people! You are very tall, Leonard, like the rest of us: you have the Campaigne face: and you are proud. Oh yes!—you are full of pride—like my father and my brothers. It is fifty years—fifty years and more—since I have seen any of my own people. We have suffered—we have suffered." She sighed heavily. She released his hand. "Sit down, my dear," she said gently, "sit down, and for once take a meal with us. Mary Anne, give your cousin some cake—it is my own making—unless he will begin with bread-and-butter."

The tea was conducted with some ceremony; indeed, it was an occasion: hospitalities were not often proffered in this establishment.

Leonard was good enough to take some cake and two cups of tea. The old lady talked while the other two ministered.

"I know your name, Leonard," she said. "I remember your birth, seven-and-twenty—yes, it was in 1873, about the same time as Samuel was born. Your mother and your grandmother lived together in Cornwall. I corresponded with my sister-in-law until she died; since then I have heard nothing about you. My grandson tells me that you are in the House. Father to son—father to son. We have always sent members to the House. Our family belongs to the House. There were Campaignes in the Long Parliament." So she went on while the cups went round, the other ladies preserving silence.

At last the banquet was considered finished. Mary Anne herself carried out the tea-things, Mrs. Galley the younger followed, and Leonard was left alone with the old lady, as had been arranged. She wanted to talk with him about the family.

"Look," she said, pointing to a framed photograph on the wall, "that is the portrait of my husband at thirty. Not quite at his best—but—still handsome, don't you think? As a young man he was considered very handsome indeed. His good looks, unfortunately, like his good fortune and his good temper—poor man!—went off early. But he had heavy trials, partly redeemed by the magnitude of his failure."

Leonard reflected that comeliness may go with very different forms of expression. In this case the expression was of a very inferior City kind. There also appeared to be a stamp or brand upon it already at thirty, as of strong drinks.

"That is my son at the side. He was half a Campaigne to look at, but not a regular Campaigne. No; he had too much of the Galley in him. None of the real family pride, poor boy!"

The face of the young man, apparently about twenty years of age, was handsome, but weak and irresolute, and without character.

"He had no pride in himself and no ambition, my poor boy! I could never understand why. No push and no ambition. That is why he remained only a clerk in the City all his life. If he had had any pride he would have risen."

"I must tell you," said Leonard, "that I have been kept, no doubt wisely, in ignorance of my own family history. It was only yesterday that I heard from your son that there have been troubles and misfortunes in our records."

"Troubles and misfortunes? And you have never heard of them! Why, my children, who haven't nearly so much right as you to know, have learned the history of my people better than that of their own mother or their grandfather's people. To be sure, with the small folk, like those who live round here, trouble is not the same thing as with us. Mostly they live up to the neck in troubles, and they look for nothing but misfortune, and they don't mind it very much so long as they get their dinners. And you haven't even heard of the family misfortunes? I am astonished. Why, there never has been any family like ours for trouble. And you might have been cut off in your prime, or struck off with a stroke, or been run over with a waggon, and never even known that you were specially born to misfortune as the sparks fly upwards."

"Am I born to misfortune? More than other people?"

It was in a kind of dream that Leonard spoke. His brain reeled; the room went round and round: he caught the arms of a chair. And for a moment he heard nothing except the voice of Constance, who warned him that Nature makes no one wholly happy: that he had been too fortunate: that something would fall upon him to redress the balance: that family scandals, poor relations, disgraces and shames, were the lot of all mankind, and if he would be human, if he would understand humanity, he must learn, like the rest of the world, by experience and by suffering. Was she, then, a Prophetess? For, behold! a few days only had passed, and these things had fallen upon him. But as yet he did not know the full extent of what had happened and what was going to happen.

He recovered. The fit had lasted but a moment; but thought and memory are swifter than time.

The old lady was talking on. "To think that you've lived all these years and no one ever told you! What did they mean by keeping you in the dark? And I've always thought of you as sitting melancholy, waiting for the Stroke whenever it should fall."

"I have been ignorant of any Stroke, possible or actual. Let me tell you that I have no fear of any Stroke. This is superstition."

"No—no!" The old lady shook her head, and laid her hand on his. "Dear boy, you are still under the curse. The Stroke will fall. Perhaps it will be laid in mercy. On me it fell with wrath. That is our distinction. That's what it is to be a Campaigne. The misfortunes, however, don't go on for ever. They will leave off after your generation. It will be when I am dead and gone; but I should like, I confess, to see happiness coming back once more to the family."

"Your grandson spoke of a murder and of a suicide among other things."

"Other things, indeed! Why, there was my husband's bankruptcy. There was your uncle Fred, my nephew, and what he did, and why he was bundled out of the country. I thought your mother would have fallen ill with the shame of it. And there was my poor father, too; and there was the trial. Did they not tell you about the trial?"

"What trial?"

"The great trial for the murder. It's a most curious case. I believe the man who was tried really did it, because no one else was seen about the place. But he got off. My father was very good about it. He gave the man Counsel, who got him off. I've got all the evidence in the case—cut out of newspapers and pasted in a book. I will lend it to you, if you like."

"Thank you. It might be interesting," he said carelessly.

"It is interesting. But don't you call these things enough misfortunes for a single family?"

"Quite enough, but not enough to make us born to misfortune."

"Oh, Leonard! If you had seen what I have seen, and suffered what I have suffered! I've been the most unfortunate of all. My brothers gone; poor dear Langley by his own hand; Christopher, dear lad, drowned; my father a wreck. Like him, I live on. I live on, and wait for more trouble." She shook her head, and the tears came into her eyes.

"I was a poor neglected thing with no mother, and as good as no father, to look after me. Galley came along; he was handsome, and I thought, being a silly girl, that he was a gentleman; so I married him. I ran away with him and married him. Then I found out. He thought I had a large fortune, and I had nothing; and father would not answer my letters. Well, he failed, and he used me cruelly—most cruelly, he did. And poverty came on—grinding, horrible poverty. You don't know, my dear nephew, what that means. I pray that you never may. There is no misfortune so bad as poverty, except it is dishonour. He died at last"—the widow heaved a sigh of relief, which told a tale of woe in itself—"and his son was a clerk, and kept us all. Now he's dead, and my grandson keeps me. For fifty years I have been slave and housemaid and cook and drudge and nurse to my husband and my son and my grandson. And, oh! I longed to speak once more with one of my own people."

Leonard took her hand and pressed it. There was nothing to be said.

"Tell me more," she said, "about yourself."

He told her, briefly, his position and his ambitions.

"You have done well," she said, "so far—but take care. There is the Family Luck. It may pass you over, but I don't know. I doubt. I fear. There are so many kinds of misfortune. I keep thinking of them all." She folded her hands, resigned. "Let trouble come to me," she said, "not to you or the younger ones. To me. That is what I pray daily. I am too old to mind much. Trouble to me means pain and suffering. Rather that than more trouble to you young people. Leonard, I remember now that your grandmother spoke in one of her letters of keeping the children from the knowledge of all this trouble. Yes, I remember."

She went on talking; she told the whole of the family history. She narrated every misfortune at length.

To Leonard, listening in that little back room with the gathering twilight and the red fire to the soft, sad voice of the mournful lady, there came again the vision of two women, both in widows' weeds, in the cottage among the flowers—tree fuchsias, climbing roses, myrtles, and Passion-flowers. All through his childhood they sat together, seldom speaking, pale-faced, sorrowful. He understood now. It was not their husbands for whom they wept; it was for the fate which they imagined to be hanging over the heads of the children. Once he heard his mother say—now the words came back to him—"Thank God! I have but one."

"Leonard," the old woman was going on, "for fifty years I have been considering and thinking. It means some great crime. The misfortunes began with my father; his life has been wrecked and ruined in punishment for someone else's crime. His was the first generation; mine was the second. All our lives have been wrecked in punishment for that crime. His was the first generation, I say"—she repeated the words as if to drive them home—"mine was the second; all our lives have been wrecked in punishment for that crime. Then came the third—your father died early, and his brother ran away because he was a forger. Oh! to think of a Campaigne doing such a thing! That was the third generation. You are the fourth—and the curse will be removed. Unto the third and fourth—but not the fifth."

"Yes," said Leonard. "I believe—I now remember—they thought—at home—something of this kind. But, my dear lady, consider. If misfortune falls upon us in consequence of some great crime committed long ago, and impossible to be repaired or undone, what is there for us but to sit down quietly and to go on with our work?"

She shook her head.

"It is very well to talk. Wait till the blows begin. If we could find out the crime—but we never can. If we could atone—but we cannot. We are so powerless—oh, my God! so powerless, and yet so innocent!"

She rose. Her face was buried in her handkerchief. I think it consoled her to cry over the recollection of her sorrows almost as much as to tell them to her grand-nephew.

"I pray daily—day and night—that the hand of wrath may be stayed. Sitting here, I think all day long. I have forgotten how to read, I think——"

Leonard glanced at the walls. There were a few books.

"Until Mary Anne began to study, there were no books. We were so poor that we had to sell everything, books and all. This room is the only one in the house that is furnished decently. My grand-daughter is my only comfort; she is a good girl, Leonard. She takes after the Galleys to look at, but she's a Campaigne at heart, and she's proud, though you wouldn't think it, because she's such a short bunch of a figure, not like us. She's my only comfort. We talk sometimes of going away and living together—she and I—it would be happier for us. My grandson is not—is not—altogether what one would wish. To be sure, he has a dreadful struggle. It's poverty, poverty, poverty. Oh, Leonard!"—she caught his hand—"pray against poverty. It is poverty which brings out all the bad qualities."

Leonard interrupted a monologue which seemed likely to go on without end. Besides, he had now grasped the situation.

"I will come again," he said, "if I may."

"Oh, if you may! If you only knew what a joy, what a happiness, it is only to look into your face! It is my brother's face—my father's face—oh, come again—come again."

"I will come again, then, and soon. Meantime, remember that I am your nephew—or grand-nephew, which is the same thing. If in any way I can bring some increase to your comforts——"

"No, no, my dear boy. Not that way," she cried hastily. "I have been poor, but never—in that way. My father, who ought to help me, has done nothing, and if he will not, nobody shall. I would, if I could, have my rights; no woman of our family, except me, but was an heiress. And, besides—*he*"—she pointed to the front of the house, where was the office of her grandson—"he will take it all himself."

"Well, then, but if——"

"If I must, I will. Don't give him money. He is better without it. He will speculate in houses and lose it all. Don't, Leonard."

"I will not—unless for your sake."

"No—no—not for my sake. But come again, dear boy, and we will talk over the family history. I dare say there are quantities of misfortunes that I have left out—oh, what a happy day it has been to me!"

He pressed her hand again. "Have faith, dear lady. We cannot be crushed in revenge for any crime by any other person. Do not think of past sorrows. Do not tremble at imaginary dangers. The future is in the hands of Justice, not of Revenge."

They were brave words, but in his heart there lurked, say, the possibilities of apprehension.

In the hall Samuel himself intercepted him, running out of his office. "I had my tea in here," he said, "because I wanted her to have a talk with you alone; and I'm sick of her family, to tell the truth, except for that chance of the accumulations. Did she mention them?" he whispered. "I thought she wouldn't. I can't get her to feel properly about the matter. Women have got no imagination—none. Well, a man like that can't make a will. He can't. That's a comfort. Good-evening, Mr. Campaigne. We rely entirely upon you to maintain the interests of the family, if necessary, against madmen's wills. Those accumulations—ah! And he's ninety-five—or is it ninety-six? I call it selfish to live so long unless a man's a pauper. He ought to be thinking of his great-grandchildren."

CHAPTER VIII

IN THE LAND OF BEECHES

LEONARD met Constance a few days later at the club, and they dined at the same table. As for the decision and the rejection, they were ignored by tacit consent. The situation remained apparently unaltered. In reality, everything was changed.

"You look thoughtful," she said presently, after twice making an observation which failed to catch his attention. "And you are absent-minded."

"I beg your pardon, yes. That is, I do feel thoughtful. You would, perhaps, if you found your family suddenly enlarged in all directions."

"Have you received unknown cousins from America?"

"I have received a great-aunt, a lesser aunt, and two second cousins. They are not from America. They are, on the contrary, from the far East End of this town—even from Ratcliffe or Shadwell, or perhaps Stepney."

"Oh!" Constance heard with astonishment, and naturally waited for more, if more was to follow. Perhaps, however, her friend might not wish to talk of connections with Shadwell.

"The great aunt is charming," he continued; "the lesser aunt is not so charming; the second cousins are—are—well, the man is a solicitor who seems to practice chiefly in a police-court, defending those who are drunk and disorderly, with all who are pickpockets, hooligans, and common frauds."

"A variegated life, I should say, and full of surprises and unexpectedness."

"He is something like my family—tall, with sharp features—more perhaps of the vulture than the eagle in him. But one may be mistaken. His sister is like her mother, short and round and plump, and—not to disguise the truth—common-looking. But I should say that she was capable. She is a Board School teacher. You were saying the other day,

Constance, that it was a pity that I had never been hampered by poor relations."

"I consider that you are really a spoiled child of fortune. I reminded you that you have your position already made; you have your distinguished University career; you are getting on in the House; you have no family scandals or misfortunes, or poor relations, or anything."

"Well, this loss is now supplied by the accession of poor relations and—other things. Your mention of things omitted reminded Fortune, I suppose. So she hastened to turn on a supply of everything. I am now quite like the rest of the world."

"Do the poor relations want money?"

"Yes, but not from me. The solicitor thinks that there must be great sums of money accumulated by the Patriarch of whom I have spoken to you. Cupidity of a sort, but not the desire to borrow, sent him to me. Partly he wanted to put in his claim informally, and partly he prepared the way to make me dispute any will that the old man may have made. He is poor, and therefore he is grasping, I suppose."

"I believe we all have poor relations," said Constance. "Mine, however, do not trouble me much."

"There has been a Family enlargement in another direction. A certain uncle of mine, who formerly enacted with much credit the old tragedy of the Prodigal Son, has come back from Australia."

"Has he been living on the same diet as the Prodigal?"

"Shucks and bean-pods! He hardly looks as if that had been his diet. He is well dressed, big, and important. He repeats constantly, and is most anxious for everybody to know, that he is prosperous. I doubt, somehow——"

Leonard paused; the expression of doubt is not always wise.

"The return of a middle-aged Prodigal is interesting and unusual. I fear I must not congratulate you altogether on this unexpected enlargement."

"Yet you said I ought to have poor relations. However, there is more behind. What was it you said about disgraces? Well, they've come too."

"Oh!" Constance changed colour. "Disgraces? But, Leonard, I am very sorry, and I really never supposed— —"

"Of course not; it is the merest coincidence. At the same time, like all coincidences, it is astonishing just after your remarks, which did really make me very uncomfortable. But I've stepped into quite a remarkable family history, full of surprising events, and all of them disasters."

"But you had already a remarkable family history."

"So I thought—a long history and a creditable history, ending with the ancient recluse of whom I have told you. We are rather proud of this old, old man—this singular being who has been a recluse for seventy years. I have always known about him. One of the very earliest things I was told was the miraculous existence of this eccentric ancestor. They told me so much, I suppose, because I am, as a matter of fact, heir to the estate whenever that happens to fall in. But I was never told—I suppose because it is a horrible story—why the old man became a recluse. That I only learned yesterday from this ancient aunt, who is the only daughter of the still more ancient recluse."

"Why was it? That is, don't let me ask about your private affairs."

"Not at all. There is nothing that might not be proclaimed from the house-top; there never is. There are no private affairs if we would only think so. Well, it seems that one day, seventy years ago, the brother-in-law of this gentleman, then a hearty young fellow of five-or six-and-twenty, was staying at the Hall. He went out after breakfast, and was presently found murdered in a wood, and in consequence of hearing this dreadful thing suddenly, his sister, my ancestor's wife, died on the same day. The ancient aunt was born on the day that the mother died. The blow, which was certainly very terrible, affected my ancestor with a grief so great that he became at once, what he is now, a melancholy recluse, taking no longer the least interest in anything. It is to me very strange that a young man, strong physically and mentally, should not have shaken off this obsession."

"It does seem very strange. I myself had an ancestor murdered somewhere—father of one of my grandmothers. But your case is different."

"The aged aunt told me the story. She had a theory about some great crime having been committed. She suggests that the parent of the recluse must have been a great unknown, unsuspected criminal—a kind of Gilles de Retz. There have been misfortunes scattered about—she related a whole string of calamities—all, she thinks, in consequence of some crime committed by this worthy, as mild a Christian, I believe, as ever followed the hounds or drank a bottle of port."

"She is thinking, of course, of the visitation upon the third and fourth generation. To which of them do you belong?"

"I am of the fourth according to that theory. It is tempting; it lends a new distinction to the family. This lady is immensely proud of her family, and finds consolation for her own misfortunes in the thought that they are in part atonement for some past wickedness. Strange, is it not?"

"Of course, if there is no crime there can be no consequences. Have the misfortunes been very marked?"

"Yes, very marked and unmistakable misfortunes. They cannot be got over or denied or explained away. Misfortunes, Dooms—what you please."

"What does your recluse say about them?"

"He says nothing; he never speaks. Constance, will you ride over with me and see the man and the place? It is only five-and-twenty miles or so. The roads are dry; the spring is upon us. Come to-morrow. There is a pretty village, an old church, an eighteenth-century house falling into ruins, great gardens all run to bramble and thistle, and a park, besides the recluse himself."

"The recluse might not like my visit."

"He will not notice it. Besides, he sleeps all the afternoon. And when he is awake he sees nobody. His eyes go straight through one like a Röntgen ray. I believe he sees the bones and nothing else."

The least frequented of the great highroads running out of London is assuredly that which passes through Uxbridge, and so right into the heart of the shire of Buckingham—the home or clearing or settlement of the Beeches. Few bicycles attempt this road; the ordinary cyclist knows or cares nothing for the attractions. Yet there is much to see. In one place you can visit the cottage where Milton finished "Paradise Lost." It is still kept just as when the poet lived in it. There are churches every two or three miles, churches memorable, and even historical, for the most part, and beautiful. Almost every church in this county has some famous man associated with it. On the right is the burial-place of the Russells, with their ancient manor-house, a joy and solace for the eyes: also, on the right, is another ancient manor-house. On the left is the quiet and peaceful burial-place of Penn and Elwood, those two illustrious members of the Society of Friends. Or, also on the left, you may turn aside to see the church and the road and the house of England's patriot John Hampden. The road goes up and the road goes down over long low hills and through long low valleys. On this side and on that are woods and coppices and parks, with trees scattered about and country houses. No shire in England is more studded with country houses than this of Bucks. At a distance of every six or eight miles there stands a town. All the towns in Bucks are small; all are picturesque. All have open market-places and town-halls and ancient inns and old houses. I know of one where there is an inn of the fourteenth century. I have had it sketched by a skilful limner, and I call it the Boar's Head, Eastcheap, and I should like to see anybody question the authenticity of the name. If any were so daring, I would add the portrait of Jack Falstaff himself, sitting in the great chair by the fire.

On a fine clear day in early spring, two cyclists rode through this country. They were Leonard and his friend Constance. They went by train as far as Uxbridge, and then they took the road.

At first it was enough to breathe the pure air of the spring; to fly along the quiet road, while the rooks cawed in the trees, and over the fields the larks sang. Then they drew nearer and began to talk.

"Is this what you brought me out to see?" asked Constance. "I am well content if this is all. What a lovely place it is! And what a lovely air! It is fragrant; the sun brings out the fragrance from the very fields as well as the woods."

"This is the quietest and the most beautiful of all the roads near London. But I am going to show you more. Not all to-day. We must come again. I will show you Milton's cottage and Penn's burial-ground, John Hampden's church and tomb, and the old manor-house of Chenies and Latimer. To-day I am only going to show you our old family house."

"We will come when the catkins have given place to the leaves and the hedge-rose is in blossom."

"And when the Park is worth looking at. Everything, however, at our place is in a condition of decay. You shall see the house, and the church, and the village. Then, if you like, we will go on to the nearest town and get some kind of dinner, and go home by train."

"That pleases me well."

They went on in silence for a while.

Leonard took up the parable again about his family.

"We have been in the same place," he said, "for an immense time. We have never produced a great man or a distinguished man. If you consider it, there are not really enough distinguished men to go round the families. We have twice recently made a bid for a distinguished man. My own father and my grandfather were both promising politicians, but they were both cut off in early manhood."

"Both? What a strange thing!"

"Yes. Part of what the ancient aunt calls the family luck. We have had, in fact, an amazing quantity of bad luck. Listen. It is like the history of a House driven and scourged by the hand of Fate."

She listened while he went through the terrible list.

"Why," she said, "your list of disaster does really suggest the terrible words 'unto the third and fourth generation.' I don't wonder at your aunt looking about for a criminal. What could your forefathers have done to bring about such a succession of misfortunes?"

"Let us get down and rest a little." They sat down on a stile, and turned the talk into a more serious vein.

"What have my forefathers done? Nothing. Of that I am quite certain. They have always been most respectable squires, good fox-hunters, with a touch of scholarship. They have done nothing. Our misfortunes are all pure bad luck, and nothing else. Those words, however, do force themselves on one. I am not superstitious, yet since that venerable dame—— However, this morning I argued with myself. I said, 'It would be such a terrible injustice that innocent children should suffer from their fathers' misdeeds, that it cannot be so.' "

"I don't know," said Constance. "I am not so sure."

"You, too, among the superstitious? I also, however, was brought up with that theory——"

"I suppose you went to church?"

"Yes, we went to church. And now I remember that my mother, for the reason which I have only just learned, believed that we were ourselves expiating the sins of our forefathers. It is very easy for me to go back to the language and ideas of my childhood, so much so that this morning I made a little search after a certain passage which I had well-nigh forgotten."

"What was that?"

"It is directed against that very theory. It expresses exactly the opposite opinion. The passage is in the Prophet Ezekiel. Do you remember it?"

"No. I have never read that Prophet, and I have never considered the subject."

"It is a very fine passage. Ezekiel is one of the finest writers possible. He ought to be read more and studied more."

"Tell me the sense of the passage."

"I can give you the very words. Listen." He stood up and took off his hat, and declaimed the words with much force:

" 'What mean ye that ye use this proverb concerning the land of Israel, saying, The fathers have eaten sour grapes, and the children's teeth are set on edge? As I live, saith the Lord God, ye shall not use this proverb any more. Behold, all souls are Mine: as the soul of the father, so also the soul of the son is Mine. The soul that sinneth, it shall die. But if a man be just, he shall surely live."

"These are very noble words, Constance;" indeed, Leonard spoke them with much solemnity. "The verbal interpretation of the Prophets no longer occupies our minds. Still, they are very noble words. I have never believed myself to be superstitious or to believe in heredity of misfortune; still, after learning for the first time the long string of disasters that have fallen upon my people, I became possessed with a kind of terror, as if the Hand of Fate was pressing upon us all."

"They are very noble words," Constance repeated. "It seems as if the speaker was thinking of a distinction between consequences—certain consequences—of every man's life as regards his children and — —"

"What consequences—from father to son?"

"Why, you have only to look around you. We live in conditions made for us by our forefathers. My people behaved well and prospered: they saved money and bought lands: they lived, in the old phrase, God-fearing lives. Therefore I am sound in mind and body, and I am tolerably wealthy."

"Oh! that, of course. But I was not thinking of consequences like these."

"You must think of them. A man loses his fortune and position. Down go children and grandchildren. The edifice of generations may have to be built up again from the very foundations. Is it nothing to inherit a name which has been smirched? If a man commits a bad action, are not his children disgraced with him?"

"Of course; but only by that act. They are not persecuted by the hand of Fate."

"Who can trace the consequences of a single act? Who can follow it up in all the lines of consequence?"

"Yes; but the third and fourth generation...."

"Who can say when those consequences will cease?"

" 'As I live, saith the Lord.' It is a solemn assurance—a form of words, perhaps—only a form of words—yet, if so, the audacity of it! 'As I live'—the Lord Himself takes the oath—'if a man be just, he shall surely live.' "

"A man may be kept down by poverty and shut out from the world by his father's shame. Yet he may still be just. It is the distinction that the Prophet would draw. What misfortune has fallen upon your House which affects the soul of a man? Death? Poverty? The wrong-doing of certain members?"

Leonard shook his head. "Yes, I understand what you mean. I confess that I had been shaken by the revelations of that old lady. They seemed to explain so much."

"Perhaps they explained the whole—yet not as she meant them to explain."

"Now I understand so many things that were dark—my mother's sadness and the melancholy eyes which rested upon me from childhood. She was looking for the hand of Fate: she expected disaster: she kept me in ignorance: yet she was haunted by the thought that for the third and fourth generation the sins—the unknown sins—of the fathers would be visited upon the children. When I learned these things"—he repeated himself, because his mind was so full of the thought—"I felt the same expectation, the same terror, the same sense of helplessness, as if wherever I turned, whatever I attempted, the Hand which struck down my father, my grandfather, and that old man would fall upon me."

"It was natural."

"So that these words came to me like a direct message from the old Hebrew Prophet. Our ancestors went for consolation and instruction to those pages. They held that every doubt and every difficulty were met and solved by these writers. Perhaps we shall go back to the ancient faith. And yet——" He looked round; it was a new world that he saw, with new ideas. "Not in my time," he said. "We are a scientific age. When the reign of Science is ended, we may begin again the reign of Faith." He spoke as one in doubt and uncertainty.

"Receive the words, Leonard, as a direct message."

"At least, I interpreted the words into an order to look at events from another point of view. And I have taken all the misfortunes in turn. They have nothing whatever to do with heredity. Your illustration about a man losing his money, and so bringing poverty upon his children, does not apply. My great-grandfather has his head turned by a great trouble. His son commits suicide. Why? Nobody knows. The young sailor is drowned. Why? Because he is a sailor. The daughter marries beneath her station. Why? Because she was motherless and fatherless and neglected. My own father died young. Why? Because fever carried him off."

"Leonard"—Constance laid her hand upon his arm—"do not argue the case any more. Leave it. A thing like this may easily become morbid. It may occupy your thoughts too much."

"Let me forget it, by all means. At present, I confess, the question is always with me."

"It explains something in your manner yesterday and to-day. You are always serious, but now you are absent-minded. You have begun to think too much about these troubles."

He smiled. "I am serious, I suppose, from the way in which I was brought up. We lived in Cornwall, right in the country, close to the seashore, with no houses near us, until I went to school. It was a very quiet household: my grandmother and my mother were both in widows' weeds. There was very little talking, and no laughing or mirth of any kind, within the house, and always, as I now understand, the memory of that misfortune and the dread of new misfortunes were upon these unhappy ladies. They did not tell me anything, but I felt the sadness of the house. I suppose it made me a quiet boy—without much inclination to the light heart that possessed most of my fellows."

"I am glad you have told me," she replied. "These things explain a good deal in you. For now I understand you better."

They mounted their cycles, and resumed the journey in silence for some miles.

"Look!" he cried. "There is our old place."

He pointed across a park. At the end of it stood a house of red brick, with red tiles and stacks of red chimneys—a house of two stories only.

In front was a carriage-drive, but no garden or enclosure at all. The house rose straight out of the park itself.

"You see only the back of the house," said Leonard. "The gardens are all in the front: but everything is grown over; nothing has been done to the place for seventy years. I wonder it has stood so long." They turned off the road into the drive. "The old man, when the double shock fell upon him, dropped into a state of apathy from which he has never rallied. We must go round by the servant's entrance. The front doors are never opened."

The great hall with the marble floor made echoes rolling and rumbling about the house above as they walked across it. There were arms on the walls and armour, but all rusted and decaying in the damp air. There were two or three pictures on the walls, but the colour had peeled off and the pictures had become ghosts and groups of ghosts in black frames.

"The recluse lives in the library," said Leonard. "Let us look first at the other rooms." He opened a door. This was the dining-room. Nothing had been touched. There stood the great dining-hall. Against the walls were arranged a row of leather chairs. There was the sideboard; the mahogany was not affected by the long waiting, except that it had lost its lustre. The leather on the chairs was decaying and falling off. The carpet was moth-eaten and in threads. The paper on the wall, the old-fashioned red velvet paper, was hanging down in folds. The old-fashioned high brass fender was black with neglected age. On the walls the pictures were in better preservation than those in the hall, but they were hopelessly injured by the damp. The curtains were falling away from the rings. "Think of the festive dinners that have been given in this room," said Leonard. "Think of the talk and the laughter and the happiness! And suddenly, unexpectedly, the whole comes to an end, and there has been silence and emptiness for seventy years."

He closed the door and opened another. This was in times gone by the drawing-room. It was a noble room—long, high, well proportioned. A harp stood in one corner, its strings either broken or loose. A piano with the music still upon it stood open; it had been open for seventy years. The keys were covered with dust and the wires with rust. The music which had last been played was still in its place. Old-fashioned sofas and couches stood about. The mantel-shelf was ornamented with strange things in china. There were occasional tables in the old fashion of yellow and white and gold. The paper was peeling off like that of the dining-room. The sunshine streamed into the room through windows which had not been cleaned for seventy years. The moths were dancing merrily as if they rejoiced in solitude. On one table, beside the fireplace, were lying, as they had been left, the work-basket with some fancy work in it; the open letter-case, a half-finished letter, an inkstand, with three or four quill pens: on a chair beside the table lay an open volume; it had been open for seventy years.

Constance came in stepping noiselessly, as in a place where silence was sacred. She spoke in whispers; the silence fell upon her soul; it filled her with strange terrors and apprehensions. She looked around her.

"You come here often, Leonard?"

"No. I have opened the door once, and only once. Then I was seized with a strange sense of—I know not what; it made me ashamed. But it seemed as if the room was full of ghosts."

"I think it is. The whole house is full of ghosts. I felt their breath upon my cheek as soon as we came into the place. They will not mind us, Leonard, nor would they hurt you if they could. Let us walk round the room." She looked at the music. "It is Gluck's 'Orpheo'; the song, 'Orpheo and Euridice.' She must have been singing it the day before—the day before——" Her eyes turned to the work-table. "Here she was sitting at work the day before—the day before—— Look at the dainty work—a child's frock." She took up the open book; it was Paschal's "Pensées." "She was reading this the day before—the day before——" Her eyes filled with tears. "The music—no common music; the book—a book only for a soul uplifted above the common level; the dainty, beautiful work—Leonard, it seems to reveal the woman and the household. Nothing base or common was in that woman's heart— or in the management of her house; they are slight indications, but they are sure. It seems as if I knew her already, though I never heard of her until to-day. Oh, what a loss for that man!—what a Tragedy! what a terrible Tragedy it was!" Her eyes fell upon the letter; she took it up. "See!" she said. "The letter was begun, but never finished. Is it not sacrilege to let it fall into other hands? Take it, Leonard."

"We may read it after all these years," Leonard said, shaking the dust of seventy years from it. "There can be nothing in it that she would wish not to be written there." He read it slowly. It was written in pointed and sloping Italian hand—a pretty hand belonging to the time when women were more separated from men in all their ways. Now we all write alike. " 'My dearest....' I cannot make out the name. The rest is easy. 'Algernon and Langley have gone off to the study to talk business. It is this affair of the Mill which is still unsettled. I am a little anxious about Algernon: he has been strangely distrait for this last two or three days; perhaps he is anxious about me: there need be no anxiety. I am quite well and strong. This morning he got up very early, and I heard him walking about in his study below. This is not his way at all. However, should a wife repine because her Lord is anxious about her? Algernon is very determined about that Mill; but I fear that Langley will not give way. You know how firm he can be behind that pleasant smile of his.' That is all, Constance. She wrote no more."

"It was written, then, the day before—the day before—— Keep the letter, Leonard. You have no other letter of hers—perhaps nothing at all belonging to the poor lady. I wonder who Langley was? I had a forefather, too, whose Christian name was Langley. It is not a common name."

"The Christian name of my unfortunate grandfather who committed suicide was also Langley. It is a coincidence. No doubt he was named after the person mentioned in this letter. Not by any means a common name, as you say. As for this letter, I will keep it. There is nothing in my possession that I can connect with this unfortunate ancestress."

"Where are her jewels and things?"

"Perhaps where she left them, perhaps sent to the bank. I have never heard of anything belonging to her."

Constance walked about the room looking at everything; the dust lay thick, but it was not the black dust of the town—a light brown dust that could be blown away or swept away easily. She swept the strings of the harp, which responded with the discords of seventy years' neglect. She touched the keys of the piano, and started at the harsh and grating response. She looked at the chairs and the tables with their curly legs, and the queer things in china that stood upon the mantel shelf.

"Why," she said, "the place should be kept just as it is, a museum of George the Fourth fashion in furniture. Here is a guitar. Did that lady play the guitar as well as the harp and the piano? The pictures are all water-colours. The glass has partly preserved them, but some damp has got in; they are all injured. I should like to get them all copied for studies of the time and its taste. They are good pictures, too. This one looks like a water-colour copy of a Constable. Was he living then? And this is a portrait." She started. "Good heavens! what is this?"

"This? It is evidently a portrait," said Leonard. "Why, Constance — —"

For she was looking into it with every sign of interest and curiosity.

"How in the world did this picture come here?" Leonard looked at it.

"I cannot tell you," he said; "it is only my second visit to this room. It is a young man. A pleasing and amiable face; the short hair curled by the barber's art, I suppose. The face is familiar; I don't know why — —"

"Leonard, it is the face of my own great-grandfather. How did it come here? I have a copy, or the original, in my own possession. How did it come here? Was he a friend of your people?"

"I know nothing at all about it. By the rolled collar and the curly hair and the little whiskers I should say that the original must have been a contemporary of my ancestor the Recluse. Stop! there is a name on the frame. Can you read it?" He brushed away the dust. " 'Langley Holme, 1825,' Langley Holme! What is it, Constance?"

"Oh, Leonard, Langley Holme — Langley Holme — he was my great-grandfather. And he was murdered; I remember to have heard of it — he was murdered. Then, it was here, and he was that old man's brother-in-law, and — and — your Tragedy is mine as well."

"Why, Constance, are you not jumping to a conclusion? How do you know that the murder in Campaigne Park was that of Langley Holme?"

The Fourth Generation

"I don't know it; I am only certain of it. Besides, that letter. Algernon and Langley were in the study. The letter tells us. Oh, I have no doubt—no doubt at all. This is his portrait; he was here the day before—the day before the terrible Tragedy. It must have been none other—it could have been none other. Leonard, this is very strange. You confide your story to me, you bring me out to see the spot where it happened and the house of the Recluse, and I find that your story is mine. Oh, to light upon it here and with you! It is strange, it is wonderful! Your story is mine as well," she repeated, looking into his face; "we have a common tragedy."

"We are not certain yet; there may be another explanation."

"There can be no other. We will hunt up the contemporary papers; we shall find an account of the murder somewhere. A gentleman is not murdered even so far back as 1826 without a report in the papers. But I am quite—quite certain. This is my great-grandfather, Langley Holme, and his death was the first of all your many troubles."

"This was the first of the hereditary misfortunes."

"The more important and the most far-reaching. Perhaps we could trace them all to this one calamity."

Leonard was looking into the portrait.

"I said it was a familiar face, Constance; it is your own. The resemblance is startling. You have his eyes, the same shape of face, the same mouth. It is at least your ancestor. And as for the rest, since it is certain that he met with an early and a violent end, I would rather believe that it was here and in this Park, because it makes my Tragedy, as you say, your own. We have a common history; it needs no further proof. There could not have been two murders of two gentlemen, both friends of this House, in the same year. You are right: this is the man whose death caused all the trouble."

They looked at the portrait in silence for awhile. The thought of the sudden end of this gallant youth, rejoicing in the strength and hope of early manhood, awed them.

"We may picture the scene," said Constance—"the news brought suddenly by some country lad breathless and panting; the old man then young, with all his future before him; a smiling future, a happy life; his wife hearing it; the house made terrible by her shriek; the sudden shock; the heavy blow; bereavement of all the man loved best; the death of his wife for whom he was so anxious; the awful death of the man he loved. Oh, Leonard, can you bear to think of it?"

"Yes; but other young men have received blows as terrible, and have yet survived, and at least gone about their work as before. Is it in nature for a man to grieve for seventy years?"

"I do not think that it was grief, or that it was ever grief, that he felt or still feels. His brain received a violent blow, from which it has never recovered."

"But he can transact business in his own way—by brief written instructions."

"We are not physicians, to explain the working of a disordered brain. We can, however, understand that such a shock may have produced all the effect of a blow from a hammer or a club. His brain is not destroyed: but it is benumbed. I believe that he felt no sorrow, but only a dead weight of oppression—the sense of suffering without pain—the consciousness of gloom which never lifts. Is not the story capable of such effects?"

"Perhaps. There is, however, one thing which we have forgotten, Constance. It is that we are cousins. This discovery makes us cousins."

She took his proffered hand under the eyes of her ancestor, who looked kindly upon them from his dusty and faded frame. "We are cousins—not first or second cousins—but still—cousins—which is something. You have found another relation. I hope, sir, that you will not be ashamed of her, or connect her with your family misfortunes. This tragedy belongs to both of us. Come, Leonard, let us leave this room. It is haunted. I hear again the shrieks of the woman, and I see the white face of the man—the young man in his bereavement. Come."

She drew him from the room, and closed the door softly.

Leonard led the way up the broad oaken staircase, which no neglect could injure, and no flight of time. On the first floor there were doors leading to various rooms. They opened one: it was a room filled with things belonging to children: there were toys and dolls: there were dresses and boots and hats: there was a children's carriage, the predecessor of the perambulator and the cart: there were nursery-cots: there were slates and pencils and colour-boxes. It looked like a place which had not been deserted: children had lived in it and had grown out of it: all the old playthings were left in when the children left it.

"After the blow," said Leonard, "life went on somehow in the House. The Recluse lived by himself in his bedroom and the library: the dining-room and the drawing-room were locked up: his wife's room—the room where she died—was locked up: the boys went away: the girl ran away with her young man, Mr. Galley; then the whole place was deserted." He shut the door and unlocked another. "It was her room," he whispered.

Constance looked into the room. It was occupied by a great four-poster bed with steps on either side in order that the occupant might ascend to the feather-bed with the dignity due to her position. One cannot imagine a gentlewoman of 1820, or thereabouts, reduced to the indignity of climbing into a high bed. Therefore the steps were placed in position. We have lost this point of difference which once distinguished the "Quality" from the lower sort: the former walked up these steps with dignity into bed: the latter flopped or climbed: everybody now seeks the nightly repose by the latter methods. The room contained a great amount of mahogany: the doors were open, and showed dresses hanging up as they had waited for seventy years to be taken down and worn: fashions had come and gone: they remained waiting. There was a chest of drawers with cunningly-wrought boxes upon it: silver patch-boxes: snuff-boxes in silver and in silver gilt: a small collection of old-world curiosities, which had belonged to the last occupant's forefather. There was a dressing-table, where all the toilet tools and instruments were lying as they had been left. Constance went into the room on tiptoe, glancing at the great bed, which stood like a funeral hearse of the fourteenth century, with its plumes and heavy carvings, as if she half expected to find a tenant. Beside the looking-glass stood open, just as it had been left, the lady's jewel-box. Constance took out the contents, and looked at them with admiring eyes. There were rings and charms, necklaces of pearl, diamond brooches, bracelets, sprays, watches—everything that a rich gentlewoman would like to have. She put them all back, but she did not close the box; she left everything as she found it, and crept away. "These things belonged to Langley's sister," she whispered; "and she was one of my people—mine."

They shut the door and descended the stairs. Again they stood together in the great empty hall, where their footsteps echoed up the broad staircase and in the roof above, and their words were repeated by mocking voices, even when they whispered, from wall to answering wall, and from the ceilings of the upper place.

"Tell me all you know about your ancestor," said Leonard.

"Indeed, it is very little. He is my ancestor on my mother's side, and again on her mother's side. He left one child, a daughter, who was my grandmother: and her daughter married my father. There is but a legend—I know no more—except that the young man—the lively young man whose portrait I have—whose portrait is in that room—was found done to death in a wood. That is all I have heard. I do not know who the murderer was, nor what happened, nor anything. It all seemed so long ago—a thing that belonged to the past. But, then, if we could understand, the past belongs to us. There was another woman who suffered as well as the poor lady of this house. Oh, Leonard, what a tragedy! And only the other day we were talking glibly about family scandals!"

"Yes; a good deal of the sunshine has disappeared. My life, you see, was not, as you thought, to be one long succession of fortune's gifts."

"It was seventy years ago, however. The thing must not make us unhappy. We, at least, if not that old man, can look upon an event of so long ago with equanimity."

"Yes, yes. But I must ferret out the whole story. I feel as if I know so little. I am most strangely interested and moved. How was the man killed? Why? Who did it? Where can I look for the details?"

"When you have found what you want, Leonard, you can tell me. For my own part, I may leave the investigation to you. Besides, it was so long ago. Why should we revive the griefs of seventy years ago?"

"I really do not know, except that I am, as I said, strangely attracted by this story. Come, now, I want you to see the man himself who married your ancestor's sister. Her portrait is somewhere among those in the drawing-room, but it is too far gone to be recognised. Pity—pity! We have lost all our family portraits. Come, we will step lightly, not to wake him."

He led her across the hall again, and opened very softly the library door. Asleep in an armchair by the fire was the most splendid old man Constance had ever seen. He was of gigantic stature; his long legs were outstretched, his massive head lay back upon the chair—a noble head with fine and abundant white hair and broad shoulders and deep chest. He was sleeping like a child, breathing as softly and as peacefully. In that restful countenance there was no suggestion of madness or a disordered brain.

Constance stepped lightly into the room and bent over him. His lips parted.

He murmured something in his sleep. He woke with a start. He sat up and opened his eyes, and gazed upon her face with a look of terror and amazement.

She stepped aside. The old man closed his eyes again, and his head fell back. Leonard touched her arm, and they left the room. At the door Constance turned to look at him. He was asleep again.

"He murmured something in his sleep. He was disturbed. He looked terrified."

"It was your presence, Constance, that in some way suggested the memory of his dead friend. Perhaps your face reminded him of his dead friend. Think, however, what a shock it must have been to disturb the balance of such a strong man as that. Why, he was in the full strength of his early manhood. And he never recovered—all these seventy years. He has never spoken all these years, except once in my hearing—it was in his sleep. What did he say? 'That will end it.' Strange words."

The tears were standing in the girl's eyes.

"The pity of it, Leonard—the pity of it!"

"Come into the gardens. They were formerly, in the last century—when a certain ancestor was a scientific gardener—show gardens."

The Fourth Generation

They were now entirely ruined by seventy years of neglect. The lawns were covered with coarse rank grass; the walks were hidden; brambles grew over the flower-beds; the neglect was simply mournful. They passed through into the kitchen-garden, over the strawberry-beds and the asparagus-beds, and everywhere spread the brambles with the thistle and the shepherd's-purse and all the common weeds; in the orchard most of the trees were dead, and under the dead boughs there flourished a rank undergrowth.

"I have never before," said Constance, "realized what would happen if we suffered a garden to go wild."

"This would happen—as you see. I believe no one has so much as walked in the garden except ourselves for seventy years. In the eyes of the village, I know, the whole place is supposed to be haunted day and night. Even the chance of apples would not tempt the village children into the garden. Come, Constance, let us go into the village and see the church."

It was a pretty village, consisting of one long street, with an inn, a small shop, and post-office, a blacksmith's, and one or two other trades. In the middle of the street a narrow lane led to the churchyard and the church. The latter, much too big for the village, was an early English cruciform structure, with later additions and improvements.

The church was open, for it was Saturday afternoon. The chancel was full of monuments of dead and gone Campaignes. Among them was a tablet, "To the Memory of Langley Holme, born at Great Missenden, June, 1798, found murdered in a wood in this parish, May 18, 1826. Married February 1, 1824, to Eleanor, daughter of the late Marmaduke Flight, of Little Beauchamp, in this county; left one child, Constance, born January 1, 1825."

"Yes," said Constance, "one can realise it: the death of wife and friend at once, and in this dreadful manner."

In the churchyard an old man was occupied with some work among the graves. He looked up and straightened himself slowly, as one with stiffened joints.

"Mornin', sir," he said. "Mornin', miss. I hope I see you well. Beg your pardon, sir, but you be a Campaigne for sure. All the Campaignes are alike—tall men they are, and good to look upon. But you're not so tall, nor yet so strong built, as the Squire. Been to see the old gentleman, sir? Ay, he do last on, he do. It's wonderful. Close on ninety-five he is. Everybody in the village knows his birthday. Why, he's a show. On Sundays, in summer, after church, they go to the garden wall and look over it, to see him marching up and down the terrace. He never sees them, nor wouldn't if they were to walk beside him."

"You all know him, then?"

"I mind him seventy years ago. I was a little chap then. You wouldn't think I was ever a little chap, would you? Seventy years ago I was eight—I'm seventy-eight now. You wouldn't think I was seventy-eight, would you?" A very garrulous old man, this.

"I gave evidence, I did, at the inquest after the murder. They couldn't do nohow without me, though I was but eight years old."

"You? Why, what had you to do with the murder?"

"I was scaring birds on the hillside above the wood. I see the Squire—he was a fine big figure of a man—and the other gentleman crossing the road and coming over the stile into the field. Then they went as far as the wood together. The Squire he turned back, but the other gentleman he went on. They found him afterwards in the wood with his head smashed. Then I see John Dunning go in—same man as they charged with the murder. And he came running out—scared-like with what he'd seen. Oh! I see it all, and I told them so, kissing the Bible on it."

"I have heard that a man was tried for the crime."

"He was tried, but he got off. Everybody knows he never done it. But they never found out who done it."

"That is all you know about it?"

"That is all, sir. Many a hundred times I've told that story. Thank you, sir. Mornin', miss. You'll have a handsome partner, miss, and he'll have a proper missus."

"So," said Leonard, as they walked away, "the murder is still remembered, and will be, I suppose, so long as anyone lives who can talk about it. It is strange, is it not, that all these discoveries should fall together; that I should learn the truth about my own people, and only a day or two afterwards that you should learn the truth about your own ancestors? We are cousins, Constance, and a common tragedy unites us."

They mounted their wheels and rode away in silence. But the joy had gone out of the day. The evening fell. The wind in the trees became a dirge; their hearts were full of violence and blood and death; in their ears rang the cries of a bereaved woman, and the groans of a man gone mad with trouble.

CHAPTER IX

MARY ANNE

IT was the Sunday afternoon after these visits to the ancestor and to the group in the Commercial Road. Leonard was slowly returning home after a solitary lunch. He walked with drooping head, touching the lamp-posts as he passed with his umbrella. This, as everybody knows, is a certain sign of preoccupation and dejection.

He was becoming, in fact, conscious of a strange obsession of his soul. The Family History sat upon him like a nightmare: it left him not either by day or by night. He was beginning to realise that he could not shake it off, and that it was come to stay.

When a man is born to a Family History, and has to grow up with it, in full consciousness of it, he generally gets the better of it, and either disregards it or treats it with philosophy, or laughs at it, or even boasts of it. The illustrious Mr. Bounderby was one of the many who boast of it. But, then, he had grown up with it, and it had become part of him, and he was able to present his own version of it.

Very different is the case when a man has a Family History suddenly and quite unexpectedly sprung upon him. What could have been more desirable than the position of this young man for a whole quarter of a century? Sufficiently wealthy, connected for generations with gentlefolk, successful, with nothing whatever to hamper him in his career, with the certainty of succeeding to a large property—could mortal man desire more?

And then, suddenly, a Family History of the darkest and most gloomy kind—murder, sudden death, suicide, early death, the shattering of a strong mind, bankruptcy, poverty, cousins whom no kindliness could call presentable—all this fell upon him at one blow. Can one be surprised that he touched the lamp-posts as he went along?

Is it wonderful that he could not get rid of the dreadful story? It occupied his whole brain; it turned everything else out—the great economical article for the *Nineteenth Century*, all his books, all his occupations. If he read in the printed page, his eyes ran across the lines and up and down the lines, but nothing reached his brain. The Family History was a wall which excluded everything else; or it was a jealous tenant who drove every intruder out as with a broom. If he tried to write, his pen presently dropped from his fingers, for the things that lay on his brain were not allowed by that new tenant to escape. And all night long, and all day long, pictures rose up and floated before his eyes; terrible pictures—pictures of things that belonged to the History; pictures that followed each other like animated photographs, irrepressible, not to be concealed, or denied, or refused admission.

This obsession was only just beginning: it intended to become deeper and stronger: it was going to hold him with grip and claw, never to let him go by night or day until—— But the end he could not understand.

You know how, at the first symptoms of a long illness, there falls upon the soul a premonitory sadness: the nurses and the doctors utter words of cheerfulness and hope: there is a loophole, there always is a loophole, until the climax and the turning-point. The patient hears, and tries to receive solace. But he knows better. He knows without being told that he stands on the threshold of the torture chamber: the door opens, he steps in, because he must: he will lie there and suffer— O Lord! how long?

With such boding and gloom of soul—boding without words, gloom inarticulate—Leonard walked slowly homewards.

It was about three in the afternoon that he mounted his stairs. In his mood, brooding over the new-found tragedies, it seemed quite natural, and a thing to be expected, that his cousin Mary Anne should be sitting on the stairs opposite his closed door. She rose timidly.

"The man said he could not tell when you would come home, so I waited," she explained.

"He ought to have asked you to wait inside. Did you tell him who you were?"

"No. It doesn't matter. I'm sorry to disturb your Sabbath calm."

"My—— Oh yes! Pray come in."

She obeyed, and sat down by the fire, glancing round the room curiously. In her lap lay a brown-paper parcel.

"I thought you would come home to dinner after chapel," she began, "so I got here about one."

She observed that his face showed some trouble, and she hesitated to go on.

"Have you come to tell me of more family misfortunes?" he asked abruptly.

"Oh," she said, "I wish I hadn't come. I told her you didn't want it and you wouldn't like it. Besides, what's the use? It all happened so long ago. But granny would have it. I've brought you a book. She says you must read it. If you'd rather not have it, I will take it back again. Granny ought to know that you don't want to be worried about these old things."

He pulled himself together, and assumed a mask of cheerfulness.

"Nonsense!" he said. "Why should I not read about these old things which are to me so new? They belong to me as much as to you."

He observed the girl more narrowly while he spoke. Her words and her hesitation showed perception and feeling at least. As for her appearance, she was short and sturdy; her features were cast in one of the more common moulds. She wore a black cloth jacket and a skirt of dark green serge, a modest hat with black plumes nodding over her head in the hearse-like fashion of the day before yesterday, and her gloves were doubtful.

The first impression was of complete insignificance; the second impression was of a girl who might interest one. Her eyes were good—they were the eyes of her grandmother; her hands were small and delicate—they were the hands of her grandmother; her voice was clear and soft, with a distinct utterance quite unlike the thick and husky people among whom she lived. In all these points she resembled her grandmother. Leonard observed these things—it was a distraction to think of the cousin apart from the Family History—and became interested in the girl.

"My cousin," he said unexpectedly, "you are very much like your grandmother."

"Like granny?" She coloured with pleasure. As she was not a girl who kept company with anyone, she had never before received a compliment. "Why, she is beautiful still, and I — — Oh!"

She laughed.

"You have her voice and her eyes. She seems to be a very sweet and gentle lady."

"She is the sweetest old lady in the world and the gentlest, and, oh! she's had an awful time."

"I am sorry to think so."

"She cried with pleasure and pride when you went away. For fifty years not a single member of her family has been to see her. I never saw her take on so, and you so kind and friendly. Sam said you had as much pride as a duke."

"Your brother should not judge by first appearances."

"And you were not proud a bit. Well, granny said: 'Nobody ever told him of the family misfortunes, and it's shameful. I've told him some, but not all, and now I'll send him my Scrap-book with the trial in it— the trial, you know, of John Dunning for the wilful murder of Langley Holme.' And I've brought it; here it is." She handed him the parcel in her lap. "That's why I came."

"Thank you," said Leonard, laying it carelessly on the table: "I will read it or look at it some time. But I own I am not greatly interested in the trial; it took place too long ago."

"Once she had another copy, but she gave it to your grandfather a few days before he killed himself."

Leonard remembered these words afterwards. For the moment they had no meaning for him.

"Granny says we've got hereditary misfortunes."

"So she told me. Hereditary? Why?" His brow contracted. "I don't know why. Hereditary misfortunes are supposed to imply ancestral crimes."

"She puts it like this. If it hadn't been hereditary misfortune she wouldn't have married grandfather; he wouldn't have been bankrupt; father wouldn't have been only a small clerk; Sam would have been something in a large way; and I should be a lady instead of a Board School teacher."

"You can be both, my cousin. Now look at the other side. Your grandfather was ruined, I take it, by his own incompetence; his poverty was his own doing. Your father never rose in the world, I suppose, because he had no power of fight. Your brother has got into a respectable profession; what right has he to complain?"

"That's what I say sometimes. Granny won't have it. She's all for hereditary ill-luck, as if we are to suffer for what was done a hundred years ago. I don't believe it, for my part. Do you?"

He thought of his talk with Constance in the country road.

"It is a dreadful question; do not let it trouble us. Let us go on with our work and not think about it."

"It's all very well to say 'Don't think about it,' when she talks about nothing else, especially when she looks at Sam and thinks of you. There was something else I wanted to say." She dropped her head, and began nervously to twitch with her fingertips. "I'm almost ashamed to say it. Sam would never forgive me, but I think of granny first and of all she has endured, and I must warn you." She looked round; there was nobody else present. "It's about Sam, my brother. I must warn you—I must, because he may make mischief between you and granny."

"He will find that difficult. Well, go on."

"He goes to your village in the country. He sits and talks with the people. He pretends that he goes to see how the old man is getting on. But it is really to find out all he can about the property."

"What has he to do with the property?"

"He wants to find out what is to become of all the money."

"Does he think that the rustics can tell him?"

"I don't know. You see, his head is filled with the hope of getting some of the money. He wants to get it divided among the heirs. It's what he calls the 'accumulations.'"

"Accumulations!" Leonard repeated impatiently. "They are all in a tale. I know nothing about these accumulations, or what will be done with them."

"Sam is full of suspicions. He thinks there is a conspiracy to keep him out."

"Oh, does he? Well, tell him that my great-grandfather's solicitor receives the rents and deals with them as he is instructed. I, for one, am not consulted."

"I said you knew nothing about it. Granny was so angry. You see, Sam can think of nothing else. He's been unlucky lately, and he comforts himself with calculating what the money comes to. He's made me do sums—oh! scores of sums—in compound interest for him: Sam never got so far himself. If you've never worked it out——"

"I never have. Like Sam, I have not got so far."

"Well, it really comes to a most wonderful sum. Sometimes I think that the rule must be wrong. It mounts up to about a million and a half."

"Does it?" Leonard replied carelessly. "Let your brother understand, if you can, that he builds his hopes on a very doubtful succession."

"Half of it he expects to get. Granny and you, he says, are the only heirs. What is hers, he says, is his. So he has made her sign a paper giving him all her share."

"Oh! And where do you come in?"

"There will be nothing for me, because it will all be granny's: and she has signed that paper, so that it is to be all his."

"I am sorry that she has signed anything, though I do not suppose such a document would stand."

"Sam says she owes the family for fifty years' maintenance: that is, £20,000, without counting out-of-pocket expenses, incidentals, and rent. How he makes it out I don't know, because poor old granny doesn't cost more than £30 a year, and I find that. Can't he claim that money?"

"Of course not. She owes him nothing. Your brother is not, I fear, quite a—a straight-walking Christian, is he?"

She sighed.

"He's a Church member; but, then, he says it's good for business. Mother sides with Sam. They are both at her every day. Oh, Mr. Campaigne, is it all Sam's fancy? Will there be no money at all? When he finds it out, he'll go off his head for sure."

"I don't know. Don't listen to him. Don't think about the money."

"I must sometimes. It's lovely to think about being rich, after you've been so poor. Why, sometimes we've had to go for days—we women—with a kippered herring or a bloater and a piece of bread for dinner. And as for clothes and gloves and nice things——"

"But now you have an income, and you have your work. Those days are gone. Don't dream of sudden wealth."

She got up.

"I won't think about it. It's wicked to dream about being rich."

"What would you do with money if you had it?"

"First of all, it would be so nice not to think about the rent and not to worry, when illness came into the house, how the Doctor was to be paid. And next, Sam would be always in a good temper."

"No," said Leonard decidedly; "Sam would not always be in a good temper."

"Then I should take granny away, and leave mother and Sam."

"You would have to give up your work, you know—the school and the children and everything."

"Couldn't I go on with the school?"

"Certainly not."

"I shouldn't like that. Oh, I couldn't give up the school and the children!"

"Well—but what would you buy?"

"Books—I should buy books."

"You can get them at the Free Library for nothing. Do you want fine clothes?"

"Every woman likes to look nice," she said. "But not fine clothes—I couldn't wear fine clothes."

"Then you'd be no better off than you are now. Do you want a carriage?"

"No; I've got my bike."

"Do you want money to give away?"

"No. It only makes poor people worse to give them money."

"Very well. Now, my cousin, you have given yourself a lesson. You have work that you like: you have a reasonably good salary: you have access to books—as many as you want: you can dress yourself as you please and as you wish: would you improve your food?"

"Oh, the food's good enough! We women don't care much what we eat. As for Sam, he's always wanting more buttered toast with his tea."

"Rapacious creature! Now, Mary Anne, please to reflect on these things, and don't talk about family misfortunes so long as you yourself are concerned. And just think what a miserable girl you would be if you were to become suddenly rich."

She laughed merrily.

"Miserable!" she said. "I never thought of that. You mean that I shouldn't know what to do with the money?"

"No, not that. You wouldn't know what to do with yourself. You have been brought up to certain standards. If you were rich, you would have to change them. The only way to be rich," said this philosopher who was going to inherit a goodly estate, "is to be born rich, and so not to feel the burden of wealth."

"I suppose so. I wish you would say it all over again for Sam to hear. Not that he would listen."

"And how would you like just to have everything you want by merely calling for it? There is no desire for anything with a rich girl: no trying to get it: no waiting for it: no getting it at last, and enjoying it all the more. Won't you think of this?"

"I will. Yes, I will."

"Put the horrid thought of the money out of your head altogether, and go on with your work. And be happy in it."

She nodded gravely.

"I am happy in it. Only, sometimes — —"

"And remember, please, if there is anything—anything at all that it would please your grandmother to have, let me know. Will you let me know? And will you have the pleasure of giving it to her?"

"Yes, I will—I will. And will you come again soon?"

"I will call again very soon."

"I will tell granny. It will please her—oh! more than I can say. And you'll read the book, won't you, just to please her?"

"I will read the book to please her."

"She longs to see you again. And so do I. Oh, Mr. Campaigne—cousin, then—it's just lovely to hear you talk!"

CHAPTER X

A DINNER AT THE CLUB

LEONARD stood looking straight before him when the girl had gone. Well, the omissions so much regretted by Constance seemed to be fully supplied. He was now exactly like other people, with poor relations and plenty of scandals and people to be ashamed of. Only a week ago he had none of these things. Now he was supplied with all. Nothing was wanting. He was richly, if unexpectedly, endowed with these gifts which had been at first withheld. As yet he hardly rose to the situation: he felt no gratitude: he would have resigned these new possessions willingly: the tragedies, the new cousins, the ennobling theory of hereditary sorrow.

He remembered the brown-paper parcel which he had promised to read; he tore off the covering. Within there was a foolscap volume of the kind called "scrap-book." He opened it, and turned over the pages. It was more than half filled with newspaper cuttings and writing between and before and after the cuttings. As he turned the pages there fell upon him a sense of loathing unutterable. He threw the book from him, and fell back upon an easy-chair, half unconscious.

When he recovered, he picked up the book. The same feeling, but not so strong, fell upon him again. He laid it down gently as a thing which might do him harm. He felt cold; he shivered: for the first time in his life, he was afraid of something. He felt that deadly terror which superstitious men experience in empty houses and lonely places in the dark—a terror inexplicable, that comes unasked and without cause.

This young man was not in the least degree superstitious. He had no terror at all concerning things supernatural; he would have spent a night alone in a church vault, among coffins and bones and grinning skulls, without a tremor. Therefore this strange dread, as of coming evil, astonished him. It seemed to him connected with the book. He took it up and laid it down over and over again. Always that shiver of dread, that sinking of the heart, returned.

He thought that he would leave the book and go out; he would overcome this weakness on his return. And he remembered that the returned Australian—the man of wealth, the successful man of the family—was to dine with him at the club. He left the book on the table; he took his hat, and he sallied forth to get through the hours before dinner away from the sight of this enchanted volume charged with spells of fear and trembling.

Uncle Fred arrived in great spirits, a fine figure of Colonial prosperity, talking louder than was considered in that club to be good form. He called for a brandy and bitters, and then for another, which astonished the occupants of the morning-room. Then he declared himself ready for dinner.

He was; he displayed not only an uncommon power of putting away food, but also an enviable power of taking his wine as a running stream never stopping. He swallowed the champagne, served after the modern fashion with no other wine, as if it was a brook falling continuously into a cave, without pause or limit.

When the dinner was over, a small forest of bottles had been successively opened and depleted. Never had the club-waiters gazed upon a performance so brilliant in a house where most men considered a mere little pint of claret to be a fair whack, a proper allowance. After dinner this admirable guest absorbed a bottle of claret. Then, on adjourning to the smoking-room, he took coffee and three glasses of curaçoa in rapid succession. Then he lit a cigar, and called for a soda and whisky. At regular intervals of a quarter of an hour he called for another soda and whisky. Let us not count them. They were like the kisses of lovers, never to be counted or reckoned, either for praise or blame. It was half-past nine when this phenomenal consumption of wine and whisky began, and it lasted until half-past eleven.

Leonard was conscious that the other men in the room were fain to look on in speechless wonder; the increased seriousness in the waiters' faces showed their appreciation and envy. The club-waiter loveth most the happy few who drink with freedom. His most serious admiration and respect go forth to one who becomes a mere cask of wine, and yet shows no signs of consequences. Now, this performer, from start to finish, turned not a hair; there was no thickness in his speech; there was no sign of any effect of strong drink upon this big man.

That he talked more loudly than was at this club generally liked is true. But, then, he always talked loud enough to be heard in every part of the largest room. The things of which he spoke; the stories he told; the language in which he clothed these stories, astonished the other members who were present—astonished and delighted them beyond measure, because such a loud and confident guest had never before been known in the place, and because it had been the fortune of Campaigne, Leonard Campaigne—the blameless, the austere, the cold—who had brought this elderly Bounder, this empty hogshead or barrel to be filled with strong drink, this trumpet-voiced utterer of discreditable stories. Next day there were anecdotes told in the club by those who had been present, and scoffers laughed, and those who had not been present envied those who had.

"Leonard," said this delightful guest, late in the evening, and in a louder voice than ever, "I suppose someone has told you about the row—you know—when I had to leave the country. There had been plenty of rows before; but I mean the big row. You were only three or four years old at the time. I suppose you can't remember."

The other men lifted their heads. They were like Mrs. Cluppins. Listening they scorned, but the words were forced upon them.

"No one told me—that is to say, I heard something the other day. No details—something alleged as the cause."

"Would you like to know the real truth?"

"No! Good heavens, no! Let bygone scandals rest," he replied, in a murmur as low as extreme indignation would allow. "Let the thing die—die and be forgotten."

"My dear nephew"—he laid a great hand on Leonard's knee—"I dare say they told you the truth. Only, you see"—he said this horrid thing loud enough to gratify the curiosity of all present—"the real truth is that the fellow who put the name at the bottom of you know what, and did the rest of it, was not me, but the other fellow—Chris. That's all. Chris the respectable it was—not me."

"I tell you I want to know nothing about it."

"I don't care. You must. After all these years, do you think now that I am home again, with my pile made, that I'm going to labour under such an imputation any longer? No, sir. I've come to hold up my head like you. Chris may hang his if he likes. I won't. (Boy, another whisky and soda.) In those days Chris and I hunted in couples. Very good sport we had, too. Then we got through the money, and there was tightness. Chris did it. Run him in if you like. For, you see — —"

"Enough said—enough said." Leonard looked round the room. There were only three or four men present: they sat singly, each with a magazine in his hand: they preserved the attitude of those who read critically, but there was a *je-ne-sais-quoi* about them which suggested that they had heard the words of this delightful guest. Indeed, he spoke loud enough for all to hear. It is not every day that one can hear in a respectable club revelations about putting somebody's name on the front and on the back of a document vaguely described as "you know what."

"Enough said," Leonard repeated impatiently.

"My dear fellow, you interrupt. I am going to set the whole thing right, if you'll let me."

"I don't want to hear it."

"It isn't what you want to hear; it's what you've got to hear," said uncle Fred impressively and earnestly. He had taken, even for him, a little more than was good for him: it made him obstinate: it also made his speech uncertain as to loudness and control: he carried off these defects with increased earnestness. "Character, Leonard, character is involved; and self-respect; also forgiveness. I am not come home to bear malice, as will be shown by my testamentary dispositions when Abraham calls me to his bosom — —"

"Oh! But really — —"

"Really—you shall hear! (Boy, why the devil do you keep me waiting for another whisky and soda?) Look here, Leonard. There was a money-lender in it — —"

"Never mind the money-lender — —"

"I must mind him. Man! he was in it. I quite forget at this moment where old Cent. per Cent. got in. But he was there—oh yes! he was there. He always was there in those days either for Chris or for me.

Devil of a fellow, Chris! Now, then. The money-lending Worm—or Crocodile—wanted to be paid. He was always wanting to be paid. Either it was Chris or it was me. Let me think——"

"Does it matter?"

"Truth, sir, and character always matter. What the money-lender said I forget at this moment. I dare say Chris knows; it was more his affair than mine. It amounted to this——" He drained his glass again, and forgot what he had intended to say. "When the fellow was gone, 'Chris,' I said, 'here's a pretty hole you're in.' I am certain that he was in the hole, and not me, because what was done, you know, was intended to pull him out of the hole. So it must have been Chris, and not me. It is necessary," he added with dignity, "to make this revolution—revelation. It is due to self-respect. My brother Chris, then, you understand, was in the hole. (Boy, I'll take another whisky and soda.) I want you to understand exactly what happened." Leonard groaned. "Of course, when it came to sticking a name on a paper, and that paper a cheque——"

"For the Lord's sake, man, stop!" Leonard whispered.

"I knew and told him that the world, which is a harsh world and never makes allowance, would call the thing by a bad name. Which happened. But who could foresee that they would tack that name on to me?"

Leonard sprang to his feet. The thing was becoming serious. "It is eleven o'clock," he said. "I must go."

"Go? Why, I've only just begun to settle down for a quiet talk. I thought we should go on till two or three. And I've nearly done; I've only got to show that the cheque——"

"No—I must go at once. I have an appointment. I have work to do. I have letters to write."

Uncle Fred slowly rose. "It's a degenerate world," he said. "We never thought the day properly begun before midnight. But if these are your habits—well, Leonard, you've done me well. The champagne was excellent. Boy—no, I'll wait till I get back to the hotel. Then two or three glasses, and so to bed. Moderation—temperance—early hours. These are now my motto and my rule."

"This way down the stairs," said Leonard, for his uncle was starting off in the opposite direction.

"One warning. Don't talk to Chris about that story, for you'll hear a garbled version—garbled, sir—garbled." He lurched a little as he walked down the stairs, but otherwise there were no indications of the profound and Gargantuan thirst that he had been assuaging all the evening.

Leonard went home in the deepest depression and shame. Why did he take such a man to such a club? He should have given him dinner in the rowdiest tavern, filled with the noisiest topers.

"He cannot be really what he pretends," Leonard thought. "A man of wealth is a man of responsibility and position. This man talks without any dignity or reticence whatever. He seems to associate still with larrikins and cattle-drovers; he sits in bars and saloons; he ought to keep better company, if only on account of his prosperity."

The Family History asserted itself again.

"You have entertained," it said, "another Unfortunate. Here is a man nearly fifty years of age. He has revealed himself and exposed himself: he is by his own confession, although he is rich and successful, the companion and the friend of riffraff; his sentiments are theirs. He has no morals; he drinks without stint or measure; he has disgraced you in the Club. No doubt the Committee will interfere."

It is, the moralist declares, an age of great laxity. A man may make a living in more ways than were formerly thought creditable; men are admitted to clubs who formerly would not have dared to put their names down. In Leonard's mind there still remained, strong and clear, the opinion that there are some things which a gentleman should not do: things which he must not do: companions with whom he must not sit. Yet it appeared from the revelations of this man that, whatever he had done, he had habitually consorted with tramps, hawkers, peddlers, and shepherds.

CHAPTER XI

THE BOOK OF EXTRACTS

LEONARD turned up his light in the study. His eye fell upon the Book of Extracts. He looked at his watch. Nearly twelve. He took up the book resolutely. Another wave of loathing rolled over his mind. He beat it back; he forced himself to open the book, and to begin from the beginning.

The contents consisted, as he had already seen, of cuttings from a newspaper, with a connecting narrative in writing. On the title-page was written in a fine Italian hand the following brief explanation:

"This book was given to me by Mrs. Nicols, our housekeeper for thirty years. She cut out from the newspapers all that was printed about the crime and what followed. There are accounts of the Murder, the Inquest, and the Trial. She also added notes of her own on what she herself remembered and had seen. She made two cuttings of each extract, and two copies of her own notes; these she pasted in two scrap-books. She gave me one; the other I found in her room after her death. I sent the latter copy to my brother three days before he committed suicide."

This statement was signed "Lucy Galley, née Campaigne." The extracts and cuttings followed. Some of the less necessary details are here suppressed.

The first extract was from the weekly paper of the nearest county town:

"We are grieved to report the occurrence of a crime which brings the deepest disgrace upon our neighbourhood, hitherto remarkably free from acts of violence. The victim is a young gentleman, amiable and respected by everyone—Mr. Langley Holme, of Westerdene House, near the town of Amersham.

"The unfortunate gentleman had been staying for some days at the house of his brother-in-law, Mr. Algernon Campaigne, J.P., of Campaigne Park. On Tuesday, May 18, as will be seen from our Report of the Inquest, the two gentlemen started together for a walk after breakfast. It was about ten o'clock: they walked across the Park, they crossed the highroad beyond, they climbed over a stile into a large field, and they walked together along the pathway through the field, as far as a small wood which lies at the bottom of the field. Then Mr. Campaigne remembered some forgotten business or appointment and left his friend, returning by himself. When Mr. Holme was discovered—it is not yet quite certain how long after Mr. Campaigne left him, but it was certainly two hours—he was lying on the ground quite dead, his head literally battered in by a thick club—the branch of a tree either pulled off for the purpose, or lying on the ground ready to the hand of the murderer. They carried the body back to the house where he had been staying.

"It is sad to relate that the unfortunate man's sister, Mr. Campaigne's wife, was so shocked by the news, which seems to have been announced or shouted roughly, and without any precaution about breaking it gently, that she was seized with the pains of labour, and in an hour was dead. Thus the unfortunate gentleman, Mr. Algernon Campaigne, himself quite young, has been deprived in one moment, so to speak, of wife and brother-in-law. Mr. Langley Holme was also a married man, and leaves one young child, a daughter, to weep with her mother over their irreparable loss. The Inquest was held on Wednesday morning."

Then followed a passage in writing:

"I was in my own room, the housekeeper's room, which is the last room of the south wing on the ground-floor overlooking the garden; there is an entrance to the house at that end for servants and things brought to the house. At ten o'clock in the morning, just after the clock in the stables struck, I saw the master with Mr. Langley Holme walking across the Terrace, down the gardens, and so to the right into the park. They were talking together friendly and full of life, being, both of them, young gentlemen of uncommon vivacity and spirit; with a temper, too, both of them, as becomes the master of such a place as his, which cannot be ruled by a meek and lowly one, but calls for a high spirit and a temper becoming and masterful.

"Three-quarters of an hour afterwards I heard steps in the garden, and looked up from my work. It was the master coming home alone. He was walking fast, and he was swinging his arms, as I'd often seen him do. Now I think of it, his face was pale. One would think that he had a presentiment. He entered the house by the garden door and went into his study.

"Now, this morning, my lady, when we called her, was not at all well, and the question was whether we should send for the doctor at once. But she refused to consent, saying that it would pass away. And so she took breakfast in bed; but I was far from easy about her. I wish now, with all my heart, that I had sent a note to the doctor, who lived three miles away, if it was only for him to have driven over. Besides, as things turned out, he might have been with her when the news came.

"However, about twelve o'clock, or a little after, I heard steps in the garden, and I saw a sight which froze my very blood. For four men were carrying a shutter, walking slowly; and on the shutter was a blanket, and beneath the blanket was a form. Oh! there is no mistaking such a form as that—it was a human form. My heart fell, I say, like lead, and I ran out crying:

" 'Oh! in God's name, what has happened?'

"Said one of them, John Dunning by name:

" 'It's Mr. Holme. I found him dead. Someone's murdered him.'

"I screeched. I ran back to the house; I ran into the kitchen; I told them, never thinking, in the horror of it, of my poor lady.

"Then all over the house, suddenly, the air was filled with the shrieks of women.

"Alas! my lady had got up; she was dressed: she was on the landing; she heard the cries.

" 'What has happened?' she asked.

" 'Mr. Holme is murdered.'

"I do not know who told her. None of the maids confessed the thing, but when she heard the news she fell back, all of a sudden, like a woman knocked down.

"We took her up and carried her to bed. When the doctor came in an hour my lady was dead—the most beautiful, the kindest, the sweetest, most generous-hearted lady that ever lived. She was dead, and all we could do was to look after the new-born babe. And as for her husband, that poor gentleman sat in his study with haggard looks and face all drawn with his grief, so that it was a pity and a terror to look upon him. Wife and brother-in-law—wife and friend—both cut off in a single morning! Did one ever hear the like? As for the unfortunate victim, Mr. Holme that had been, they laid him in the dining-room to wait the inquest."

At this point Leonard laid down the book and looked round. The place was quite quiet. Even from the street there came no noise of footsteps or of wheels. Once more he was overpowered by this strange loathing—a kind of sickness. He closed his eyes and lay back. Before him, as in a vivid dream, he saw that procession with the body of the murdered man; and he saw the murdered lady fall shrieking to the ground; and he saw the old recluse of the Park, then young, sitting alone, with haggard face, while one body lay in the dining-room and the other on the marriage-bed.

The feeling of sickness passed away. Leonard opened his eyes and forced himself, but with a beating heart and a dreadful feeling of apprehension, to go on with the reading:

"I remember that the house was very quiet, so quiet that we could hear in my room—the housekeeper's room—the cries and shouts of the two little boys in the nursery, which was the room next to where the mother lay dead. The boys were Master Langley, the eldest, who was three, and Master Christopher, then a year and a half.

"Little did those innocents understand of the trouble that was coming upon them from the terrible tragedy of that day. They would grow up without a mother—the most terrible calamity that can befall a child: and they were to grow up, as well, without a father, for the master has never recovered the shock, and now, I fear, never will.

"On the Wednesday morning, the next day, the Coroner came with his jury and held the inquest. They viewed the body in the dining-room. I was present and heard it all. The report of the paper is tolerably accurate, so far as I remember."

The newspaper began again at this point:

"On Wednesday last, the 19th inst., an inquest was held at Campaigne Park on the body of Langley Holme, Esquire, Justice of the Peace, of Westerdene House, near Amersham, aged twenty-eight years. The unfortunate gentleman, as narrated in our last number, was found dead under circumstances that pointed directly to murder, in a wood not far from Campaigne Park, where he was staying as the guest of his friend and brother-in-law, Mr. Algernon Campaigne.

"The cause of death was certified by Dr. Alden. He deposed that it was caused by a single blow from a heavy club or branch which had probably been picked up close by. The club was lying on the table—a jagged branch thick at one end, which was red with blood. The nature of the wound showed that it was one blow only, and that by a most determined and resolute hand, which had caused death, and that death must have been instantaneous.

"Mr. Algernon Campaigne, J.P., of Campaigne Park, deposed that the deceased, named Langley Holme, his brother-in-law—his wife's brother, and his most intimate friend—was staying with them, and that on Tuesday morning the two started together after breakfast for a walk. They walked through the park, crossed the road, got over the stile on the other side, and followed the pathway under the hill. They were entering the wood in which the body was found when he himself recollected a letter which had to be written and posted that morning. He therefore stopped and explained that he must return immediately. Unfortunately, his brother-in-law chose to continue his walk alone. Mr. Campaigne turned and walked home as quickly as he could. He saw the deceased no more until he was brought back dead.

"The Coroner asked him if he had observed anyone in the wood: he said he had not looked about him carefully, but that he had seen nobody.

"A little boy, who gave the name of Tommy Dadd, and said that he knew the meaning of an oath, deposed that he was on the hillside scaring birds all day; that he saw the two gentlemen get over the stile, walk along the footpath together, talking fast and loud; that they came to the wood, and that one of them, Mr. Campaigne, turned back; that he looked up and down the path as if he was expecting somebody, and then walked away very fast.

" 'Stop!' said the Coroner. 'Let us understand these facts quite plainly. You saw Mr. Campaigne and the deceased get over the stile and walk as far as the wood?'

" 'Yes.'

" 'And you saw Mr. Campaigne turn back and walk away?'

" 'Yes.'

" 'Go on, then.'

" 'A long time after that I see John Dunning walking from the farm across the field to the pathway; he was carrying a basket of something over his shoulder; he wore his smock-frock. He went into the wood, too. Presently he came out and ran back to the farm-yard, and three other men came and carried something away.'

" 'Did nobody else go into the wood?'

" 'No; nobody.'

"John Dunning said that he was a labourer; that on the day in question he was on his way to some work, and had to pass through the wood; that half-way through he came upon what he thought was a man asleep. When he looked closer, he found that it was a gentleman, and he was dead, and he lay in a pool of blood. There was no scuffle of feet or sign of a struggle. That he tried to lift him, getting his hands and frock covered with blood-stains; that he found a bit of rough and jagged wood lying beside the body, which was covered with blood at one end; that on making this discovery he ran out of the wood, and made his way as fast as he could to the nearest farm, where he gave the alarm, and got four men to come with him, carrying a shutter and a blanket.

"The Coroner cross-examined this witness severely. Where did he work? Was he a native of the village? Had he ever been in trouble? What was it he was carrying on his shoulder? Would he swear it was not the club that had been found near the body?

"To all these questions the man gave a straightforward answer.

"The Coroner then asked him if he had searched the pockets of the deceased.

"At this point the deceased's valet stood up, and said that his master had not been robbed; that his watch and rings and purse were all found upon him in his pockets.

" 'I presume that the murderer had no time,' said the Coroner. 'He must have been disturbed. I never yet heard of a murder that was not a robbery, unless, indeed, there was revenge in it.'

"Mr. Campaigne interposed. 'I would suggest, Mr. Coroner,' he said, 'with submission——'

" 'Sir,' said the Coroner, 'your suggestions are instructions.'

" 'I venture, then, to suggest that perhaps there may have been some person or persons unknown in the wood. The boy's evidence was straightforward, but he could not see through the wood.'

" 'That is true. Call up the parish constable.'

"This officer stood up to give evidence. He was asked if there were any dangerous or suspicious persons in or near the village; if he had seen any tramps, sturdy vagabonds, gipsies, or, in fact, any persons who might reasonably be suspected of this outrage.

"There was no one. The village, he said, was quite quiet and well behaved.

"He was asked if there were poachers about. He said there were poachers, whom he knew very well, and so did his Honour's gamekeeper; but in the month of May there was little or nothing to poach, and no excuse for going into the wood. Besides, why should they go into the wood at ten in the morning? He was quite confident that the village poachers had nothing to do with the business.

" 'My suggestion, sir,' said Mr. Campaigne, 'seems unproductive. Nevertheless, there was the chance that the mystery might be explained if we could in this way light upon a clue.'

" 'There is another way of explanation,' said the Coroner grimly.

"He put other questions to the constable. Had he seen any gipsies or tramps about the village or on the road? The constable declared that he had seen none: that the village, lying as it did off the main road, from which it was not even visible, did not attract gipsies or tramps or vagabonds of any description.

"Had the constable observed any case of drunkenness? He had not: there were men who sometimes took more beer than was good for them, but they carried their liquor peaceably and did not become quarrelsome in their cups.

" 'We come next,' said the Coroner, 'to the question whether the deceased gentleman had any private enmities to fear?'

"To this Mr. Campaigne made reply: 'My brother-in-law, sir, was a man who may have made enemies as a magistrate, especially among poachers; but if so, these enemies would be all in his own part of the county, fifteen miles away. In this place he could have had neither friends nor enemies.'

" 'Then, gentlemen of the jury,' said the Coroner, 'we can find no motive for the crime. I said just now that there was another explanation possible. We can put aside the theory of poachers being disturbed at their work: and the theory of private enmity: and the theory of tramp or gipsy attacking him for the sake of robbery. We come back therefore to the broad facts. At ten in the morning the deceased entered the wood—alone. At twelve the man Dunning ran out, his smock-frock covered with blood. He said that he had found the dead body of this gentleman lying on the grass, and he had tried to lift it, getting his smock-frock stained with blood in doing so. Now, gentlemen, what was the good of trying to lift a dead body? On the other hand, suppose that a man, finding this gentleman unarmed, perhaps asleep, conceived the sudden thought of killing him for the sake of taking his money: suppose him to have been disturbed, or to have thought himself disturbed—it might be by the bird-scaring boy—what would he do? Naturally he would give the alarm, and pretend that the crime was committed by another man. You, gentlemen of the jury, will form your own conclusion. You will return such a verdict as seems to you reasonable, leaving further investigation to the Law. Far be it from me to suggest your verdict or to influence your judgment. You have now to consider how and by whom this murder—as clear a case of murder as has ever been known—was committed.'

"The jury considered their verdict for half an hour. They then returned a verdict of wilful murder against John Dunning.

"The man was standing alone by this time: everybody shunned him. When the verdict was given, he cried out, 'No! No! I never done it! I never done it!' passionately, or with some show of passion.

"The constable arrested him on the spot. After the first ejaculation the man became quite passive, and made no kind of resistance. The Coroner turned to Mr. Campaigne.

" 'You are a magistrate, sir. You can formally commit the man for trial.'

" 'I commit this man?' the bereaved gentleman seemed to have difficulty in understanding the matter. However, he came to himself, and performed his duties mechanically.

"The man, John Dunning, now lies in gaol, awaiting his trial. We would not say anything to forejudge the case, but it certainly looks black, so far, against the accused."

To this the housekeeper added: "The Coroner's Court was full, and a sorrowful sight it was to see the master, tall and handsome and upright, but ashy pale. On the same day, in the afternoon, they buried both the brother and the sister in the parish church. They lie side by side in the chancel."

Then followed the report of the trial of John Dunning. Part of it is a repetition of the evidence heard at the inquest. He was defended by counsel, and a very able counsel, too—a young man who had taken the greatest pains to get up the case. Leonard knew the name. Later on he had become a judge. The cross-examination was keen and searching. Every little point was made the most of.

The Report gave at full length all the evidence and the speeches. In this place it is sufficient to give the most important questions and answers.

The counsel had a map of the wood. He made a great deal out of this map. He called attention to distances; for instance, it would take five minutes only to get from the wood to the farm. On these points he cross-examined Mr. Campaigne closely.

" 'I believe it is a small wood—little more than a coppice?'

" 'It is very little more than a coppice.'

" 'How long, now, would it take you to walk through the wood from end to end?'

" 'Not five minutes.'

" 'Are there any seats in the wood—any places where a man might sit down?'

" 'None.'

" 'Did your friend express any intention of lingering in the wood, or was there any reason why he should linger in the wood?'

" 'No, certainly not. He entered the wood at a quick pace, and, so far as I know, he intended to keep it up. He was walking partly for exercise and partly to look at the condition of the fields.'

" 'There were no seats in the wood.' The counsel returned to the point. 'Were there any fallen trees to sit down upon?'

" 'Not to my knowledge.'

" 'Was it a morning for lying down on the grass?'

" 'No; there had been rain; the path was muddy and the grass was wet.'

" 'Did you suppose that the deceased would loiter about in the wet wood, in the mud and in the long grass in the wood, for two long hours?'

" 'I do not. I think it most improbable—even impossible.'

" 'Your suggestion is that there was someone lurking in the wood?'

" 'Everything points to that, in my opinion.'

" 'Otherwise, on the theory of the prosecution, your brother-in-law must have stood in the wood, doing nothing for nearly two hours; because nobody disputes the fact that the prisoner entered the wood a little before twelve.'

" 'That is so, I think.'

" 'I am sorry to press you, Mr. Campaigne, on a subject so painful, but I have a life to save. Do you suppose that your friend was one who would be likely to yield up his life without a struggle?'

" 'Certainly not. He was a strong and resolute man.'

" 'Again, look at the prisoner,' who was not more than five feet five. 'Do you suppose that your friend would stand still to be killed by a little man like that?'

" 'It is absurd to suppose anything of the kind.'

" 'He might have been taken unawares, but then the blow would have been at the back of the head. Now, it was in the front. Do you suppose it possible that this labouring man should on entering the wood suddenly resolve upon taking a strange gentleman's life without a motive, not even with the hope of plunder?—should rush upon him, find him off his guard, and succeed in taking his life without receiving a blow or a scratch?'

" 'I certainly do not. I consider the thing absolutely impossible.'

" 'Do you suppose that, if all these improbabilities or impossibilities had taken place, the man would have run back covered with blood to tell what he had found, and to pretend that some other man had done it?'

" 'I certainly do not.'

"The boy, who had already given his evidence, was recalled.

" 'How long was it after Mr. Holme went into the wood before John Dunning went in?'

" 'It was a long time.'

" 'We know the facts already,' said the Judge; 'the two gentlemen went out at ten; they would reach the wood, according to this map, about fifteen minutes past ten; the dead body was brought home a little after noon. Therefore, as the prisoner was only a few minutes in the wood, it must have been about twenty minutes to twelve that he went in.'

" 'And remained, my lord, no more than a few minutes.'

" 'So it would seem from the evidence. Much mischief, however, may be done in a few minutes.'

"The counsel recalled the doctor.

" 'When you saw the body it was, I think you said, a little before one o'clock.'

" 'That is so.'

" 'The body was then quite stiff and dead, you say?'

" 'Quite. It had been dead some time—perhaps two hours.'

" 'It had been dead two hours. You are quite sure?'

" 'I will not swear to the exact time. I will say a long while.'

" 'If the boy's evidence as to the time occupied by the prisoner in the wood is correct, death would have been caused a few minutes before the men brought the shutter. The body would have been quite warm.'

" 'It would.'

" 'Now—you saw the wound. Indicate for the jury exactly where it was.'

"The doctor laid his hand on the top of his head.

" 'Not the front, but the top. Very good. Mr. Holme was six feet high. Look at the prisoner. Is it possible that so short a man could have inflicted such a blow on the top of the head?'

" 'Not unless he found his victim seated.'

" 'Quite so. And we have heard from Mr. Campaigne that it was impossible to sit down in the wet wood. Thank you.' "

One need not go on. This was the most important part of the evidence. At first it looked very bad against the prisoner: no one else in the wood; the blood on the smock; the weapon with which the deed was accomplished; the apparent impossibility of anyone else being the criminal. Then came this clever lawyer upon the scene, and in a little while the whole of the case fell to pieces.

First, the doctor's evidence that death had been caused two hours before the prisoner entered the wood; the evidence of the boy that the prisoner had gone in only a few minutes before he came out running. That was positive evidence in his favour. There was, next, the evidence of Mr. Campaigne. His brother-in-law was the last man in the world who would be murdered without making a fight. He was a powerful man, much stronger than the fellow charged with murdering him. He was not taken unawares, but received the fatal blow in full front. Again, there was no robbery. If a poor man commits the crime of murder, he does it either for revenge, or for jealousy, or for robbery. There could be none of those motives at work in the murder of this unfortunate gentleman.

Lastly, there was the best possible testimony in favour of the prisoner's personal character. This is not of much use where the evidence is strong, but when it is weak it may be of the greatest possible help. His employer stated that the prisoner was a good workman who knew his business; that he was sober and industrious and honest; the least likely man on his farm to commit this atrocious act.

The Judge summed up favourably. The jury retired to consider their verdict. They came back after an hour. Verdict: "Not guilty."

"Quite right," said Leonard, laying down the book. "The man John Dunning certainly was innocent of this charge."

Then followed more writing by the housekeeper:

"When the verdict was declared the prisoner stepped down, and was greeted with friendly congratulations by his master, the farmer, and others. The Judge, before leaving the Court, sent for Mr. Campaigne.

" 'Sir,' he said, shaking hands with him, 'we have to deplore our own loss as well as yours in the melancholy events of that day. For my own part, although I consider the verdict of the jury amply justified by the evidence, I should like your opinion on the matter.'

" 'If it is worth your attention, you shall hear it. I had already made up my mind on the point. The evidence at the inquest was quite incomplete. After talking the matter over with the doctor, I was convinced that the murder was most certainly committed long before the man Dunning went into the wood at all. The state of the body showed, if medical evidence is worth anything, that death had taken place two hours before: that is, before eleven—in fact, shortly after I left him. He must have been walking straight to his death when I left him and saw him striding along through the wood.'

" 'And have you been able to form any theory at all?'

" 'None. Had there been robbery, I should have suspected gipsies. Our own people about here are quiet and harmless. Such a thing as wilful and deliberate murder would be impossible for them.'

" 'So the case only becomes the more mysterious.'

" 'I felt so strongly as to the man's innocence that I not only provided him with counsel, but I also provided counsel with my own full statement of the case. The murderer of my brother-in-law, the slayer of my wife'—here Mr. Campaigne turned very pale—'will be discovered; some time or other he must be discovered. I have understood that murder lies on the conscience until life becomes intolerable. Then the man confesses, and welcomes the shameful death to end it. Let us wait till the murderer finds his burden too heavy to be borne.'

" 'Yet,' said the Judge, 'one would like to find him out by means of the Law.'

" 'Well,' said Mr. Campaigne, 'for my own part, I resolved that I would do all in my power so that an innocent man should not suffer for the guilty if I could prevent it.'

" 'Sir,' said the Judge, 'your conduct is what the world expects of a noble gentleman. There remains one conclusion. It is that there was someone concealed in the wood. The boy said that no one went out. He was thinking of the two ends; but he could not perhaps see through the wood, or beyond the wood. It is not yet, perhaps, too late to search for footsteps. However, no doubt all that can be done will be done.'

"So the trial was finished. I have not heard that any further examination of the spot was made. As all the village, and people from neighbouring villages and the nearest market-towns, crowded over every Sunday for weeks after, gazing at the spot where the body was found, it was of very little use to look for footsteps.

"The man John Dunning went back to work. But the village folk—his old friends—turned against him. They would no longer associate with him; the taint of murder was upon him, though he was as innocent a man as ever stepped. The Vicar spoke to the people, but it was in vain; anyone who had been tried for murder must be a murderer, and he was shunned like a leper or a madman.

"Then the Vicar spoke about it to the Squire, who gave John money so that he might emigrate; and with all his family he went to Botany Bay, where the people are not all convicts, I am told. There, at least, it ought not to be thrown in a man's teeth that he had been tried and acquitted for murder. I have never heard what became of John Dunning and his family afterwards.

"The Squire offered a reward of £500 for the apprehension and conviction of some person unknown who had murdered Mr. Langley Holme. The printed bill remained on the church door for years—long after the rain had washed out the letters, until the whole bill was finally washed out and destroyed. But the reward was never claimed, nor was there any attempt to fix the guilt upon another; and as time went on, a belief grew up in the minds of the world that, notwithstanding the acquittal, no other was possible as the criminal than John Dunning himself. So that it was a fortunate thing for him that he went away when he did, before the popular belief was turned quite so dead against him.

"The wood became haunted; no one dared pass through it alone, even by day; because the murdered man walked by day as well as by night. I cannot say, for myself, that I ever actually saw the ghost—not, that is to say, to recognise the poor gentleman, though there are plenty of credible witnesses who swear to having seen it—in the twilight, in the moonlight, and in the sunshine. But one day, when I was walking home from the village—it was in the morning about eleven o'clock—I saw a strange thing which made my heart stand still.

"It was a spring day, with a fresh breeze and sunshine, but with flying clouds. They made light and shadow over the fields. In the wood, which, as was stated at the trial, was more of a coppice than a wood, composed of slender trees such as birches, which were on one side, and firs and larches on the other, with a good deal of undergrowth among the birches, I saw, as clear as ever I saw anything in my life, a figure—oh! quite plain—a figure under the birches and among the bushes and undergrowth. I knew there could be no one there, but I saw a figure, plain as the figure of man or woman. It had its back to me, and I made out head and shoulders and arms; the rest of the body was hidden. While I looked the shadow passed away and the sun came out. Then the figure disappeared. I waited for it to return. It did not.

"I crept slowly through the wood, looking about fearfully to right and left. There was nothing; the birds were singing and calling to each other, but there was no ghost. Yet I had seen it. When I asked myself how it was dressed I could not remember; nay, I had not observed. Then there were some to whom the ghost had appeared clad as when he met the murderer; nay, some to whom it has spoken; so that my own evidence is not of so much importance as that of some others.

"After the funeral we could not fail to observe a great change in the habits of my master.

"Before the trouble Mr. Campaigne was a man fond of society; he would invite friends to dinner two or three times a week. He was fond of the bottle, but no drunkard; once a week he went to the market town, and there dined at the gentlemen's ordinary. He was a Justice of the Peace, and active; he farmed himself some of his own land, and took an interest in the stock and in the crops; he went to church every Sunday morning, and had prayers every morning for the household; he was fond of playing with his children; he talked politics and read the paper every week. He went hunting once or twice a week in the season; he went shooting nearly every day in the autumn; he attended the races; he was a gardener, and looked after his hothouses and conservatories; in a word, he was a country gentleman who pleased himself with the pursuits of the country. He was a good farmer, a good landlord, a good magistrate, a good father, and a good Christian.

"Yet, mark what followed. When the murder happened, the body was placed in the dining-room. The master went into the library; there he had his meals served. He never entered the dining-room afterwards; he sat in the library when he was not walking on the terrace alone.

"Suddenly, not little by little, he abandoned everything. He left off going to church; he left off going to market; he left off shooting, hunting, gardening, farming, reading; he gave up company; he refused to see anyone; he opened no letters; he held no family prayers; he paid no attention to his children; if he found them playing, he passed by the innocents as if they had been strangers; as for the youngest, she who cost her mother her life, I doubt if he ever saw her, or knew who she was if he did see her.

"And so it has continued all these years. Sometimes the lawyer comes over when money is wanted; then the money is obtained. But he never speaks; he listens, and signs a cheque. As his housekeeper, I used to present an open bill from time to time; the money was put upon the bill with no question. The grooms have been long dismissed; the horses turned out to grass are long dead; the dogs are dead; the garden has run to seed and weed; the rooms, in which there has been no fire, or light, or air, or anything, are mouldering in decay.

"As for the poor unfortunate children, they grew up somehow; the master would allow no interference on the part of his own family; the lawyer, Mr. Ducie, was the only person who could persuade him to anything. The boys were sent to a preparatory school, and then to a public school. The second went into the Navy—never was there a more gallant or handsome boy—but he was drowned; the elder went to Oxford and into Parliament, but he killed himself; the girl married a merchant who turned out bad.

"Everything turned out bad. It was a most unfortunate family; father and children alike—all were unfortunate."

* * * * * * *

Here ended the housekeeper's book of extracts and comments. There was appended a letter. It was headed, "Mary's letter, September, 2d, 1855:"

"Dear Lucy,

"I have not been able to answer your letter before—believe me. There are times when the heart must be alone with the heart. I have been alone with my sorrowful heart—oh, my sorrowful heart!—for a month since it happened.

"I can now tell you something—not all—that has fallen upon us, upon my innocent babes and myself. You heard that Langley took his own life with his own hand four weeks ago. You ask now why he did it. He was doing well—no one was more promising, no one had brighter prospects; friends assured me that in proper time I might confidently expect to see him in the Cabinet; his powers and his influence and his name were improving daily; he was acquiring daily greater knowledge of affairs. At home I may say truthfully that he was happy with his wife, who would have laid down her life cheerfully to make him happy, and with his tender children. As for anything outside his home, such as some young men permit themselves, he would have no such thought, and could not have as a man who considered his duty to wife and family or as a Christian. Yet he killed himself—oh, my dear, he killed himself!—and I am left. Why did he do it?

"There was one thing which always weighed heavily upon his mind—the condition of his father. He frequently talked of it. Why, he asked, should a misfortune such as that which had befallen him—the tragic death of a friend and the sudden death of his wife—so completely destroy a strong man, young, healthy, capable of rising above the greatest possible disasters? Why should this misfortune change him permanently, so that he should neglect everything that he had formerly loved, and should become a miserable, silent solitary, brooding over the past, living the useless life of a hermit? Of course, he felt also the neglect in which he and his brother and sister had been left, and the lack of sympathy with which his father had always regarded them. For, remember, his father is not insane; he is able to transact business perfectly. It is only that he refuses to speak or to converse, and lives alone.

"Now, dear Lucy, I am not going to make any suggestion. I want only to tell you exactly what happened. You sent him a book of extracts and cuttings, with supplementary notes. These cuttings were the contemporary account of the murder of Mr. Langley Holme, the inquest, the trial of a man who was acquitted, and the strange effect which the whole produced upon Mr. Campaigne, then quite a young man.

"He received the book, and took it into his study. This was in the morning. At midnight I looked in. He turned his face. My dear, it was haggard. I asked him what was the matter that he looked so ill. He replied, rambling, that the fathers had eaten sour grapes. I begged him to leave off, and to come upstairs. He said something in reply, but I did not catch it, and so I left him.

"He never came upstairs. At five in the morning I woke up, and finding that he was not in bed, I hurried down the stairs full of sad presentiments. Alas! he was dead. Do not ask me how—he was dead!

"Dear Lucy, you are now the only one left of the three children. I have burnt the book. At all events, my children shall not see it or hear of this terrible story. I implore you to burn your copy."

Mrs. Galley wrote after this: "I have read the book again quite through. I cannot understand at all why my brother killed himself. As for the murderer, of course it was the man named John Dunning. Who else could it have been?"

Leonard looked up. It was three o'clock in the morning. His face was troubled with doubts and misgiving.

"Why did they burn the book?" he said. "As for the murder, there must have been someone hidden in the wood. That is clear. No other explanation is possible. But why did my grandfather cut his throat? There is nothing in the book that could lead him to such an act."

CHAPTER XII

ON THE SITE

LEONARD shut the book and threw it aside. He sat thinking over it for a little. Then he thought it was time to go to bed. There was not much of the night left; in fact, it was already broad daylight. But if it had been a night of mid-winter for darkness he could not have been visited by a more terrifying nightmare.

In his sleep the Family History continued. It now took the form of a Mystery—a Mystery in a Shape. It sat upon his afflicted chest and groaned. He was unable to guess or understand what kind of Mystery it was, or, in his sleep, to connect it with anything on the earth or in the world outside this earth. He woke up and shook it off; he went to sleep again, and it returned, unrelenting. It was vague and vast and terrible; a Thing with which the sufferer wrestled in vain, which he could not shake off and could not comprehend.

There are many kinds of nightmares; that of the unintelligible mystery, which will not go away and cannot be driven away, is one of the worst.

When he rose, late in the morning, unrefreshed and tired, he did connect the nightmare with something intelligible. It arose from the book and its story; which, like Chaucer's, was left half told. That, in itself, would have mattered little. A strange thing happened: it began with this morning: there fell upon him quite suddenly an irresistible sense that here was a duty laid upon him: a duty not to be neglected: a thing that had to be done to the exclusion of everything else. He had to follow up this story, and to recover, after seventy years and more, the true history of the crime which cast a shadow so long and so terrible upon all those years and the children of those years. He looked at the papers on his table: they were the half-finished article he had undertaken: his mind bidden to think upon the subject rebelled: it refused to work: it would not be turned in that direction: it went off to Campaigne Park and to seventy years before.

Without words Leonard was mysteriously commanded to follow up the story to its proper conclusion. Without any words he was plainly and unmistakably commanded to follow it up. By whom? He did not ask. He obeyed.

After seventy years the discovery of the guilty man would seem difficult. We find historians grappling with the cases of accused persons, and forming conclusions absolutely opposite, even when the evidence seems quite full and circumstantial in every point. Take the case of Anne Boleyn, for instance; or that of Mary Queen of Scots: two of the most illustrious and most unfortunate princesses. What agreement is there among historians concerning these ladies? Yet there are monumental masses of documents—contemporary, voluminous, official, private, epistolary, confidential, partisan—that exist to help them.

In this case there were no other documents except those in the Book of Cuttings. All that a private investigation could do was to read the evidence that had already been submitted to two Courts, and to arrive, if possible, at some conclusion.

This Leonard proceeded to do. He laid aside altogether the work on which he had been engaged, he placed the book before him, and he read the whole contents again, word for word, albeit with the same strange shrinking.

Then he made notes. The first referred to the man Dunning.

I. *John Dunning.*—The prisoner was rightly acquitted; he was most certainly innocent. The boy showed that he had not been in the wood more than two or three minutes. The deceased was a man six inches taller than Dunning, and strong in proportion. The latter could only have delivered the fatal blow if he had come upon his victim from behind, and while he was sitting. But the medical evidence proves that the blow must have been delivered from the front; and it was also proved that the grass was too wet from recent showers for the deceased to have been sitting down on it.

II. *The Time of Death.*—If the medical evidence is worth anything, the man when found had been lying dead for about two hours, as was proved by the rigor mortis. This absolutely convinces one of Dunning's innocence, and it introduces the certainty of another hand. Whose?

There he paused and began to consider.

There must have been another person in the wood; this person must have rushed upon his victim suddenly and unexpectedly. To rush out of the wood armed with a heavy club torn from a tree was the act of a gorilla. If there had been an escaped gorilla anywhere about, the crime could have been fixed upon him. But gorillas in the year 1826 were not yet discovered.

Perhaps the assailant ran upon him from behind, noiselessly; perhaps Langley Holme heard him at the last moment, and turned so that the blow intended for the back of the head fell upon the fore part.

This was all very well in theory. But why? Who wanted to kill this young gentleman, and why? There was no robbery. The body lay for two hours and more in this unfrequented place; there was plenty of time for the murderer to take everything; the murderer had taken nothing.

Then, why? How to explain it? Here was a young country gentleman, highly popular; if he had enemies, they would not be outside his own part of the country. Most country gentlemen, in those days, had many enemies. These enemies, who were rustics for the most part, satisfied their revenge and their hatred by poaching on the preserves. They also set fire to the hayricks. Langley Holme was staying a welcome guest with his friend and brother-in-law; he was walking along on a summer morning in a wood not a mile away from the House and Park, and there he was discovered lying dead—murdered!

It may be objected that this attempt to solve the insoluble after seventy years was a waste of time; that dead and gone crimes may as well be left alone. Other people's crimes may no doubt be left alone. But this was his own crime, so to speak—a crime inflicted in and upon his own family. Besides, he was dragged by ropes to the consideration of the thing; his mind was wholly charged with it; he could think of nothing else.

Presently he shaped a theory, which at first seemed to fit in with everything. It was really a very good theory, which promised, when he framed it, to account for all the facts brought out in the inquest and at the trial.

The theory supposed an escaped lunatic—a homicidal maniac, of course; that would account for everything. A maniac—a murderous maniac. He must have been lying concealed in the wood; he must have rushed out armed with his club, like that gorilla. This theory seemed to meet every point in the case. He shut up the book; he had found out the truth; he could now go about his own work again, forgetting the mysterious murder which drove his great-grandfather off his balance.

He sighed with satisfaction. He placed the book in a drawer out of the way; he need not worry any more about the thing. So with another sigh of relief he reached out for his books and returned once more to the study of his "subject."

Presently he became aware that his eyes were resting on the page without reading it; that his mind was back again to the Book of Extracts, and that in his brain there was forming, without any volition of his own, one or two difficult questions about that maniac. As, for instance, if there had been such a creature wandering in the fields someone would have seen him; he would probably have murdered more than one person while he was in the mood for murder. There was a little boy, for instance, scaring birds; he would have killed that little boy. Then, the fact of a roving maniac would have been known. He must have escaped from somewhere: his madness must have been known. There would have been some sort of hue and cry after him: either at the inquest or at the trial there would have been some mention of this dangerous person going about at large; some suggestion that he might have been the guilty person. Dangerous maniacs do not escape without any notice taken, or any warning that they are loose.

No. It would not do. Another and a more workable theory must be invented.

He got another. Poachers! Everybody knows the deadly hostility, far worse seventy years ago than at present, that existed between a country gentleman and a poacher. The latter was accustomed, in those days, to get caught in a mantrap; to put his foot into a gin; to be fired upon by gamekeepers; to be treated like a weasel or a stoat. In return the poacher manifested a lamentably revengeful spirit, which sometimes went as far as murder. In this case, no doubt, the crime was committed by a poacher.

The theory satisfied him at first, just as much as its predecessor. Presently, however, he reflected that there is not much for a poacher to do in early June, and that poachers do not prowl about the woods and coverts in broad daylight and at noon; and that poachers do not, as a rule, murder gentlemen belonging to other parts of the country. Besides, poachers on one estate would not bear malice against the squire of another estate fifteen miles distant. Leonard pushed his papers away in despair.

Any other kind of work was impossible; he could think of nothing else. At this point, however, some kind of relief came to him. For he felt that he must make himself personally acquainted with the place itself. He wanted to see the wood of which so much mention was made—the place where the blow was struck, the place where the murderer lay hidden. He wanted the evidence of the wood itself, which was probably the same now as it had been seventy years before, unless it had been felled or built over. In that part of the country they do not destroy woods, and they do not build upon their site; it is a conservative country. As the fields were a hundred years ago, so they are now.

Visitors to the house most conveniently approach it from the Metropolitan Extension Line, which goes to Rickmansworth, Amersham, and Verney. Leonard resolved upon going there that very morning. He took a note-book and started, setting down the points on which he wished to inquire.

He arrived at the station a little before noon; a walk of ten minutes brought him to the house. On the terrace at the back the old man, tall, broad-shouldered, erect, walked as usual up and down, with his hard, resolute air. Leonard did not speak to him; he passed into the garden, and looking at his watch walked along the grass-grown walks, and at the end, turning to the right, entered the park.

It was but a small park: there was only one walk in the direction which the two would have followed; this was now, like the garden walks, overgrown with grass. At the end there was a lodge; but it had stood empty for nearly seventy years; the gates were rusting on their hinges, the windows were broken and the tiles had fallen off the roof.

Beyond the park was an open road—the highroad; beyond the road a narrow path led across a broad field into a small wood; on the right hand was a low rising ground. This, then, was the wood where the thing was done; this was the hillside on which the boy was scaring the birds when he saw the two go in and the one come out.

Leonard crossed the field and entered the wood. He looked at his watch again. It had taken him twenty minutes to walk from the house to the road; he made a note of that fact. He walked through the wood; it was a pretty wood, more like a plantation than a wood—a wood with a few large trees, many saplings, two or three trees lying on the ground and waiting to be cut up. The spring foliage was out, dancing in the sunlight; the varying light and shade were pleasing and restful, the air was soft, the birds were singing. A peaceful, lovely place.

This, then, was the spot where Langley Holme was suddenly done to death. By whom?

Now, as Leonard stood looking into the tangled mass of undergrowth, a curious thing happened. It was the same thing which had happened to the housekeeper, and was mentioned in her notes. By some freak of light and shade, there was fashioned in a part of the wood where the shade was darkest the simulacrum or spectre of a man—only the shoulders and upper part of a man, but still a man.

Leonard was no more superstitious than his neighbours; but at this ghostly presentment he was startled, and for a moment his heart beat quickly with that strange kind of terror, unlike any other, which is called supernatural.

There are men who boast that they know it not, and have never felt it. These are men who would take their work into a deserted house, and would carry it on serenely, alone, through the watches of the livelong night. For my own part, I envy them not. Give me the indications of the unseen world; the whisper of the unseen spirit; the cold breath of the unseen guest; even though they are received with terror and superstitious shrinkings.

It was with such terror that Leonard saw this apparition. A moment after and it was gone; then he perceived that it was nothing but the shadows lying among the undergrowth, so that they assumed a solid form. Yet, as to the housekeeper, to whom that same apparition had appeared, it seemed to him the actual phantom of the murdered man.

He retraced his steps. It took no more than five minutes, he found, to walk through the wood from one end to the other. It was so small, and the undergrowth of so light a character, with no heavy foliage, that any person standing in any part of it would be easily visible; it would be impossible for any man to conceal himself. He made a note, also, of these facts.

He then remembered the boy on the hillside scaring the birds. There was no boy at the moment, but Leonard walked up the low hill in order to learn what the boy had been able to see.

The hill, although low, was a good deal higher than the trees in the wood; it commanded a view of the land beyond the wood — another field with young corn upon it. Leonard observed that one could not see through the wood, but that he could see over it, and beyond it, and on either side of it.

If, for instance, anyone approached the wood from any direction, or ran away from it, it would be quite possible for a boy standing on the hillside to see that person.

Then, in his imagination, he heard the boy's evidence. "I see the Squire and a gentleman with him. They came as far as the wood together. Presently the Squire went away by himself. Then John Dunning came along, and presently he came out, running over to the farm. Then they brought a shutter and carried out something on it covered up. That's all I see."

The words were so clear and plain that when they ceased he looked round, and was astonished to find there was no boy. He sat down on a gate and looked at his notes.

1. The walk from the house to the wood took twenty minutes.

2. The time taken in walking through the wood was five minutes.

3. The wood was nowhere thick enough to conceal a man.

4. The wood could not be seen through from the hillside.

5. But it was overlooked on all sides from the hill.

He considered these things, being now more than ever seized and possessed with the weight and burden of the mystery. Consider. It was no ordinary crime, such as one might read about, when in the annals of a family one member of a long time ago was brutally and wickedly cut off. It was a crime whose effects were felt by every member of his family in the strange seclusion of the head. Whatever advantages might be possessed by any member of this ancient and honourable house were lost; for the head of it, and the owner of all the property, took no notice of anyone; knew nothing of his existence, even; and lived entirely to himself and by himself.

It was, again, the first of all the numerous misfortunes which had fallen upon the family. Lastly, it was a mystery which seemed continually on the point of being cleared up by some theory which would explain and account for everything.

He looked round. The place seemed too peaceful for any deed of violence, the sunshine was warm, the singing of birds filled his ear. The contrast with his own thoughts bewitched him. He would have preferred a thunderous atmosphere charged with electricity.

He argued with himself that the thing took place seventy years ago; that it might be very well left to be cleared up when the secrets of all hearts will be known; that after all these years he could not hope to clear it up; that he was only wasting his time; and so forth. He charged the mystery, so to speak, to leave him. No demon of possession, no incubus, ever refused more resolutely to be driven out. It remained with him, more burdensome, more intolerable, than ever.

He left the hillside and walked back to the road. There, instead of walking through the park again, he turned to the left and entered the village. One must eat; he ordered a chop at the village inn, and while it was getting ready he went to the church. The monuments of his own family were scattered about the church, and on the wall he read again the tablet to the memory of the unfortunate man.

Outside, in the churchyard, was the same old man who had accosted him when he brought Constance here. He was sitting on a tombstone, basking and blinking in the sun. He stood up slowly, and pulled off his hat.

"Hope you're well, sir," he said.

"Oh!" Leonard remembered. "You were the boy who was scaring birds on the day—seventy years ago—when Mr. Holme was murdered."

"Surely, sir—surely. I haven't forgotten. I remember it all—just as yesterday. Better than yesterday. I'm old, master, and I remember what happened when I was a boy better than what happened yesterday. To many old people the same hath happened."

"Very likely; I have heard so. Now sit down and tell me all about it. I've just come down from London to look at the place, and I remembered your evidence."

"I will tell you everything, sir. Will you ask me, or shall I tell my own story?"

"You may tell your own story first, and I will ask you questions afterwards."

So the old man repeated, in a parrot-like way:

"It was on a fine morning in June, getting on to dinner-time. I'd been scaring since five, and I was hungry. I was all alone on the hill, in the field where there's a little wood, and the path runs through the wood. Then I saw two gentlemen—one was the Squire, the other I'd seen at church with the Squire Sunday before, but I didn't know his name. He was tall, but nothing like so tall as the Squire. They were talking high and loud and fast. I remember hearing them, but I couldn't hear the words. They went as far as the wood together. Directly after, the Squire turned back; he looked up and down as if he was expecting somebody, then he turned and walked home fast. The other gentleman didn't go out with the Squire, nor yet at the other end of the wood.

"A long time after, John Dunning came along. He had on his smock-frock; he hadn't been in the wood two minutes before he came running out of it, and he made for the farm. I saw that his smock-frock was red; and the farmin' men brought a shutter and carried out of the wood something covered up. That is all I remember."

"Yes, that is all. That is what you said at the inquest and the trial, is it not?"

"That was it, sir."

"Yes. Was the wood then such as it is now?"

"Just the same."

"Not a close dark wood, but light and open—just as at present?"

"A light and open coppice with plenty of bushes."

"Could you, then, see through the wood?"

"No; I could see over it and beyond it, but not through the road, where I was standing."

"On that day what time was it when you arrived?"

"My time was half-past five. Mother gave me my breakfast and sent me out. I suppose it must ha' been about that time."

"Very well. You went straight to the hillside and began your work, I suppose?"

"No; I went through the wood first."

"What for?"

"To see the birds' nests there."

"Oh! You were in the wood? Did you find anybody there, or any signs of anybody being concealed there?"

"Lord love you! how could a body hide in that little place?"

"There might have been poachers, for instance."

"Not in June. If there was anyone at all, I should have seen him."

"Well, then you went up the hill and began your scaring. Did you see anyone pass into the wood before the Squire and Mr. Holme arrived?"

"No; if there had been anyone, I must have seen him—for certain sure I must. There was no one all the morning—no one that way at all. There very seldom was anyone."

"Where does the path lead?"

"It leads across the fields to the village of Highbeech and the church."

"It is not a frequented way, then?"

"No. Most days there will be only a single person on that way."

"Humph!" Leonard was disconcerted with the old man's positiveness. Nobody in the wood on his arrival, no one passed into it all the morning. Where was the poacher? Where was the murderous maniac? "You were only a little boy at the time," he said. "Don't you think your memory may be at fault? It was seventy years ago, you know."

The old man shook his head.

"Why, for months and months and for years and years I was asked over and over again what happened and what I saw. Sometimes it was the Vicar and his friends who talked about the matter and sent for me. Sometimes it was the men at the Crown and Jug who talked about the murder and sent for me. Sometimes it was the gossips. Don't you think my memory fails, master, because it can't fail. Why," he chuckled, "the very last thing I shall see before I go up to the Throne will be the sight of them two gentlemen going along to the wood."

"Very well, come back to that point. When they arrived at the wood, the Squire turned back."

"Yes: first went in with the other gentleman."

"Oh! It doesn't matter. But he went a little way into the wood, did he?"

"I don't know if it was a little way. It was a bit of a time—I don't know how long, five minutes, perhaps—two minutes, perhaps—I don't know—before he came out."

"Oh! Was this in your evidence?"

"I answered what I was asked. Nobody ever asked me how long the Squire was in the wood."

"Well, they entered the wood, and they were talking in an animated manner. That is not in your evidence, either."

"Because I wasn't asked. As for animated, they were talking high and loud as if they were quarrelling."

"They could not be quarrelling."

"I didn't hear what they said."

"Well: it doesn't matter. The Squire turned back just at the entrance."

Again the sexton shook his head.

"I know what I said," he replied; "and I know what I saw."

"Is there anybody in the village," Leonard asked, "besides yourself, who remembers the—the event?"

"It was seventy years ago," he said. "I'm the oldest man in the village, except the Squire. He remembers it very well, for all his mad ways. He's bound to remember it. There's nobody else."

"Then they suspected one man."

"John Dunning it was. Why, I was only seven years of age, but I knew well enough that it couldn't be John. First, he wasn't big enough—and then, he wasn't man enough—and then, he wasn't devil enough. But they tried him, and he got off and came back to the village. However, he had to go, because, you see, the people don't like the company of a man who's been tried for murder, even though he's been let off; and they wouldn't work with John, so the Squire gave him money, and he went away, out to Australia—him and all his family—and never been heard of since."

"Was no one else ever suspected?"

"There might be some who had suspicions, but they kept their suspicions to themselves."

"Did you yourself have suspicions?"

"It's a long time ago, sir. The Squire and me are the only two people that remember the thing. What's the use, after all these years, of having suspicions? I don't say I have, and I don't say I haven't. If I have, they will be buried with me in my grave."

Leonard returned to London. He now understood exactly the condition of the ground, and he had examined the old man whose evidence was so important. Nothing additional was to be got out of him; but the verbal statement of a contemporary after seventy years concerning the event in which Leonard was so much interested was remarkable.

He returned to his own rooms. Hither presently came Constance.

"My friend and cousin," she said, in her frank manner, as if there had never been any disturbing question between them, "you are looking worried. What is the matter?"

"Am I looking worried?"

"The more important point is—are you feeling worried? Leonard, it has nothing to do with that little conversation we had the other day?"

"No," he replied. "Nothing." It was not a complimentary reply, but, then, Constance was not a girl to expect or to care for compliments.

"Well—is it the discovery of the poor relations?"

"You will think me a very ridiculous person. I don't worry in the least about the poor relations. But I am worried about that crime—that murder of seventy years ago."

"Oh! But why?"

"It concerns you as well as me."

"Do you mean that I ought to worry about it? I cannot, really. It is too long ago. I feel, really, no interest in it at all—except for a little pity about my grandmother, whose childhood was saddened by the dreadful thing. And that, too, was such a long time ago. But why should it worry you?"

"I can hardly tell you why. But it does. Constance, it is the most wonderful thing. You do not suspect me of nerves or idle fancies?"

"Not at all. You are quite a strong person as regards nerves."

"Then you will perhaps explain what has happened. Last night I came home about eleven. I remembered that my newly discovered Great-Aunt had sent me as a present—a cheerful present—a book containing a full account, with cuttings from the papers of the time and notes by a woman who was housekeeper at Campaigne Park, of the crime——"

"Well?"

"I took it out of its brown-paper covering. Again, Constance, am I a man of superstitions?"

"Certainly not!"

"Well——" He considered the point for a few moments, as one perhaps better concealed. Then he resolved upon communicating it. "When I opened it I was seized with a most curious repulsion—a kind of loathing—which it was difficult to shake off. This morning on looking at the book again I had the same feeling."

"Yes, it is strange. But you got over it."

"In spite of it I persisted and resolutely went through the whole book. I am repelled and I am attracted by the subject. I sat up half the night reading it—I have never been so held by any book before."

"Strange!" Constance repeated. "And for a thing so long ago!"

"I threw it aside at last and went to bed—and to dream. And the end—or the beginning—of it is that I am compelled—I use the word advisedly—compelled, Constance, to investigate the whole affair."

"Oh! but you are not in earnest? Investigate? But it happened seventy years ago! What can be learned after seventy years?"

"I don't know. I must investigate and find out what I can."

Constance looked at him with astonishment. He sat at his desk—but with his chair turned towards her. His face was lined and somewhat haggard: he looked like one who is driven: but he looked resolved.

"Leonard, this is idle fancy."

"I cannot help it; I must investigate the case. There is no help for me, Constance—I must. This was the first of the family misfortunes. They have been so heavy and so many that—well, it is weakness to connect them with something unknown."

"I am sorry—I am very sorry—that you have learned the truth—even though it makes me your cousin."

"I am very sorry, too. But Fate has found me—as it found my grandfather and my father and that old, old man. Perhaps my own career is also to be cut short."

"Nonsense, Leonard! You will investigate the case: you will find out nothing: you will throw it aside: you will forget it."

"No; it is not to be forgotten or thrown aside."

"Well, make your inquiry as soon as you can and get it over. Oh, I should have thought you the last person in the world to be moved by fancies of compulsion or any other fancies."

"I should have thought so, too, except for this experience. When I got up, Constance, I resolutely shut the book, and I made up my mind to forget the whole business."

"And you could not, I suppose?"

"I could not. I found it impossible to fix my attention, so I pulled out the book again and went all over it from the beginning once more. Constance, it is the most remarkable story I ever read. You shall read it yourself."

"If I do, not even my duty to our ancestor will make me take it so seriously as you are doing."

"To-day I have been down to the place. I have visited the wood where the thing happened: I found again that old man of the churchyard, who paid you an undeserved compliment." Constance blushed, but not much. "I made him tell me all he remembered: it was not much, but it sounded like the unexpected confirmation of some old document."

"And have you come to any conclusion yet? Have you formed any theory?"

"None that will hold water. I don't know what is going to happen over that business, but I must go on—I must go on."

She laid a hand upon his arm.

"If you must go on, let me go with you. It is my murder as well as yours. Lend me the book."

She carried it off to her own rooms, and that night another incubus sat upon another sleeping person and murdered rest.

CHAPTER XIII

A COMPROMISE

"Come to get another speech, Fred?" Christopher looked up cheerily from the work before him. The sweet spring season, when the big dinners are going on, is his time of harvest, and after June he can send his sheaves of golden grain to the Bank. It promised to be a busy and a prosperous season. "Come for another speech, old man?" he repeated. "I'm doing a humorous one on Literature, but I can make room for you."

"Hang your speeches!" Fred sat down on the table. "You might offer a man a drink." He spoke as one oppressed with a sense of injustice.

"Seem out of sorts, Fred. What's gone wrong? Colonial Enterprise? The great concern which interests all Lombard Street hitched up somehow?" He asked with the exasperating grin of the doubter. But he opened a cupboard and produced a bottle, a glass, and two or three sodas. "Well, old man, there's your drink."

Fred grunted, helped himself liberally, though it was as yet only eleven in the forenoon.

"The great Colonial concern is where it was," he explained vaguely.

"So I supposed. And about Lombard Street?"

"Well, I thought better of the City. I thought there was still some enterprise left in this rotten, stagnant, decaying, and declining old country."

Christopher laughed.

"They won't look at it, eh?"

"On the contrary, they won't do anything till they have looked at it."

"Humph! Awkward, isn't it? I say, Fred, what did you come back for at all? Why not stay in Australia?"

"I came back for many reasons. Partly to look after you, Brother Chris."

"Oh! After me? Why after me?"

"Well, you see, you are the only one left who knew of my existence. Leonard remembered nothing about me. My grandfather's lawyers had never heard of me. And one day there came into my head—it was like a voice speaking to me—it said, 'Fred, you are a Fool. You've been twenty years in this country. You've got an old lunatic of a grandfather who must have piles and piles of money. Perhaps he's dead. And no one but Christopher left to remember you. Get off home as quick as you can. Christopher,' said this remarkable voice, 'is quite capable of putting his hands on the lot and forgetting you.' That is what the voice said, my brother."

"Sometimes it's rats: sometimes it's cats: sometimes it's circles: sometimes it's a voice. Fred, you must have been pretty far gone."

"Perhaps. But I listened to that voice, and, what is more, I obeyed it, and came home. The old man isn't gone yet. So far that's safe. And the lawyers know of my existence. So that's all right. You won't get the chance of forgetting me, after all."

"Very good, very good. There will be very soon, I should say, the division of a most almighty pile, Fred. You are quite welcome to your share."

"Much obliged, I'm sure. Do you know how much it is?"

"I am afraid to calculate. Besides, what will has he made?"

"Will, my boy! He's got £6,000 a year, and he spends nothing and he gives nothing. All that money, with something he had from his mother, has been rolling up and rolling up. How much is it? A million? Two millions? And here am I hard up for want of a few pounds, and you, a Fraud and an Impostor, working like a nigger, and all that money waiting to be spent as it should be spent. It's maddening, Chris—it's maddening."

"So it is, so it is. But nothing can be done. Well, you were on the highroad to D.T., and, instead of seeing rats, you heard a voice calumniating your brother, and you came home; and you put your vast concern in your pocket—the waistcoat pocket held it all, no doubt."

"What the devil does it matter which pocket held it?"

Christopher leaned back and joined the tips of his fingers.

"I wasn't going to spoil your game, Fred, though that devil of a voice did speak such utterances. But I knew all along. I smelt a fake, so to speak. You a man of business? You the head of a great Colonial Enterprise? No, no; it was too thin, my brother—too thin. Not but what you looked the part—I will say that."

"Upon my word, I thought it was going to come off. I got hold of a company promoter. He said he's steered craft more crazy than mine into Port. Talked of a valuation: talked of assigning 50,000 shares to me as owner of the Colonial business——"

"Well, but, Fred, come to the facts; sooner or later the facts would have to be faced, you know. What was the Colonial business?"

"It was a going concern fast enough when I left it. Whether it's going now I don't know. A lovely shanty by the roadside, stocked with a large assortment of sardines, Day and Martin, tea, flour, and sugar. What more do you want? The thing I traded on was not the shanty, but the possible 'development.'"

"The development of the shanty. Excellent!"

"The development, I say, out of this humble roadside beginning. I made great use of the humble beginning: I thought they would accept the first steps of the development. I proposed a vast company with stores all over Australia for the sale of everything. Barlow Brothers were to serve the Australian Continent. We were to have our sugar estates in the Mauritius: our coffee estates in Ceylon: our tea estates in Assam: our flour-mills everywhere: our vineyards in France and Germany——"

"I see—I see. Quite enough, Fred; the scheme does you great honour. So you went into the City with it."

"I did. I've wasted buckets full of champagne over it, and whisky enough to float a first-class yacht. And what's the result?"

"I see. And you've come to an end."

"That is so. The very end. Look!" He pulled out his watch-chain. There was no watch at the end of it. "The watch has gone in," he said. "The chain will go next. And there's the hotel bill."

"Rather a heavy bill, I should imagine."

"I've done myself well, Christopher."

"And how are you going to pay that bill? And what are you going to do afterwards?"

"I thought of those accumulations. I went down to see the old man. He's quite well and hearty—wouldn't speak to me. Pretends to be deaf and dumb. But the housekeeper says he understands everything. So he knows of my existence. The woman gave me the address of his solicitors, and I've been to see them. I wanted an advance, you know, just a little advance on the accumulations."

"Ah!"

"But they won't acknowledge that they have any power. 'My dear Sir,' I said, 'I don't ask whether you have any power or not—I don't care whether you advance me a thousand on my reversionary interest, or whether you lend it yourself.' No, sir, the fellow wouldn't budge. Said I must prove the possession of reversionary interest: said he wasn't a money-lender: said I had better go to a bank and show security. Here I am one of the heirs to a noble fortune. I don't know how much, but it must be something enormous. Why, his estate is worth £6,000 a year, and I know that there was money besides which he had from his mother. Enormous! Enormous! And here I am wanting a poor thousand."

"It seems hard, doesn't it? But, then, are you sure that you are one of the heirs?"

"The old man is off his head. Everything will be divided. He can't live long."

"No. But he may live five or six years more."

"Well, Christopher, the long and the short of it is that you will have to find that money. You may charge interest: you may take my bond: you will do what you like: but I must have that money."

"The long and the short of it, Fred, is this: I am not going to give, or to lend, or to advance, any money to you at all. Put that in your pipe."

"Oh!" Fred helped himself to another whisky-and-water. "You won't, eh? Then, what do you think of my blowing this flourishing concern of yours, eh?"

Christopher changed colour.

"What do you think, Christopher, of my going to call on Pembridge Crescent, and letting out in the most natural and casual way in the world, that I've just come from the rooms in Chancery Lane where you carry on your business?"

"Fred, you—you—you are a most infernal scoundrel!"

"What business? asks my sister-in-law. What business? asks my niece. What business? asks my nephew. Why, says I, don't you know? Hasn't he told you? Quite a flourishing income—almost as flourishing as Barlow Brothers. It's in the Fraudulent Speech Supply Line. That's a pretty sort of shell to drop in the middle of your family circle, isn't it?"

"Fred, you were always the most cold-blooded villain that ever walked."

"That's what I shall do, my dear brother. More than that, I shall go and see Leonard. That aristocratic young gentleman, who thinks so much about his family, will be greatly pleased, will he not?"

We need not follow the conversation, which became at this point extremely animated. Memories long since supposed to be forgotten and buried and put away were revived, with comments satirical, indignant, or contemptuous. Language of the strongest was employed. The office boy put down his novelette, and wondered what Jack Harkaway would do under such circumstances. Indeed, the past lives of the two brothers lent themselves singularly to the recollection of romantic adventures and episodes of a startling character. Presently—we are not Cain and Abel—the conversation became milder. Some kind of compromise began to be considered.

"Well, I don't mind," said Fred at length. "I don't care so long as I can get the money. But I must have the money—or some money—and that before long."

"You can put your case before Leonard, if you like. He won't give you much, because he hasn't got much to give. I think he has a few hundreds a year from his mother. He might advance on his reversions, but he isn't that sort of man at all."

"I'll try. But, look you, Christopher, if he refuses I'll take it out of you. How would you like all the world to know how you live? And, by the Lord, sir, if I have to tell all the world, I will."

"I was a great fool, Fred, to let you into the secret. I might have known, from old experience, what you would do with it to suit your own purpose. Always the dear old uncalculating, unselfish, truthful brother—always!"

Fred took another drink and another cigar. Then he invoked a blessing upon his brother with all the cordiality proper for such a blessing and retired.

CHAPTER XIV

CONSULTATION

THE rôle of coincidence in the history of the Individual is much more important than any writer of fiction has ever dared to represent. Not the coincidence which is dear to the old-fashioned dramatist, when at the very nick and opposite point of time the long-lost Earl returns; the coincidence of real life does not occur in this way. A man's mind is much occupied, and even absorbed, by one subject: he goes about thinking upon that subject and upon little else. Then all kinds of things happen to him which illustrate this subject. That is what coincidence means.

For instance, I was once endeavouring to reconstruct for a novel a certain scene among the overgrown byways and the secluded and forgotten lanes of history. I had nothing at first to help me: worse still, I could find nothing, not even in the British Museum. The most profound knowledge of the books and pamphlets in that collection, in the person of the greatest scholar, could not help me. I was reluctantly making up my mind to abandon the project (which would have inflicted irreparable damage on my novel) when a sheaf of second-hand catalogues came to me. It was by the last evening post. I turned over two or three, without much curiosity, until among the items I lit upon one which caught my eye. It was only the title of a pamphlet, but it promised to contain the exact information which I wanted. The promise was kept. I was too late to buy the pamphlet, but I had the title, and it was found for me in the British Museum, and it became my "crib." Now that, if you please, was a coincidence; and this kind of coincidence happens continually to every man who thinks about anything.

It is said of a most distinguished numismatist that he cannot cross a ploughed field without picking up a rose noble. That is because his thoughts are always turned to rose nobles and other delightful coins. If one is studying the eighteenth century, there is not a museum, a picture-gallery, a second-hand catalogue, which does not provide the student with new information. Every man absorbed in a subject becomes like a magnet which attracts to itself all kinds of proofs, illustrations, and light.

These things are mentioned only to show that the apparently miraculous manner in which external events conspired together to keep up the interest in this case was really neither remarkable nor exceptional. For the interest itself, the grip with which the story of the newspaper cuttings caught and held both these readers, was a true miracle. In every group of situations there is the central event. In this case, the mystery of the wood was the central event.

"It is my murder, Leonard," Constance repeated, "as much as yours. It was my great-grandfather who was murdered, if it was your great-grandmother who was also killed by that crime. Let me sit with you while you work it out."

"You too, Constance?" Leonard saw in her eyes something that reminded him of his own overpowering interest in the thing. "You too?"

"Take back the book, Leonard."

"You have read it?"

"I read it over and over again—I have been reading it all the livelong night."

"And you—you also—feel—with me—the same——" He did not finish the sentence.

"I feel—like you—constrained to go on—why—I cannot tell you. It is not pity, for one cannot feel pity for a man of whom one knows nothing except that he was young and handsome and unfortunate, and that he was an ancestor. It is not desire for revenge—how can one take revenge for a crime when everybody concerned is dead and gone?"

"Except the man who suffered most."

"Except that old, old man. Well, I cannot understand it. But the fact is so. Like you, I am drawn by ropes to the subject."

"As for me I can think of nothing else. I am wholly possessed by the story and by the mystery. We will work at it together—if any work is possible."

They sat down together and they read the book aloud, both making notes. They read parts of it over again. They compared notes. They went to the club together and dined together: they went home and they spent the evening together: they separated with the assurance that everything had been done which could be done, and that they must reluctantly abandon any further investigation.

In the morning they met again.

"I was thinking last night," said Constance, "about the Inquest. There are two or three points— —"

"I was thinking about the Trial," said Leonard. "There are a few doubts in my mind— —"

"Let us have out the book again."

Once more it was produced. Once more it lay on the table: once more they sat on opposite sides and read and considered and took counsel together—with no result: once more they locked up the book, and agreed that further investigation was impossible.

"To-morrow," said Leonard, "I shall go on with my work again. This is like the following of Jack-a-Lantern."

"To-morrow," said Constance, with a sigh. "Strange that we should have been led to consider the subject at all. Let the dead bury their dead. It is an old story, and nothing more remains to be found out. Why have we been so foolish?"

Despite this agreement, they continued at their hopeless task. They sat together day after day; during this time they talked and thought of nothing else. Again and again they agreed there was nothing more to be found. Again and again they made a show of putting the book away and locking it up. Again and again they took it out again and read it till they knew it all by heart. Together they went once more to Campaigne Park; they visited the fatal wood, they wandered about the deserted rooms of the house, haunted by the dreadful memory. How could they expect to find anything now after all these years?

"We have," said Leonard, repeating the words a hundred times, "all the evidence that can now be discovered—the evidence of the wood and the place, the evidence of one survivor, the evidence of the trial. If the truth cannot be discovered, why should we go on? Moreover, after all these years nothing more can be discovered."

"Nothing more, except the hand that did it."

Why should they go on? Because they could not choose but go on. They were compelled to go on. If they spoke of other things, their thoughts and their talk wandered back to this same subject. As may always happen when two persons are engaged on the subject and absorbed in it, their faces assumed the same expression—that of one who searches and finds not. With such a face the alchemist was accustomed every day to enter his laboratory, hoping against hope, beaten back every evening, returning in the morning. But with a difference—for the alchemist knew what he wanted to find out, and these two were in search of they knew not what.

They went together, in the vain hope of finding or hearing something more, to call upon the lady of the Commercial Road. She was most gratified to be recognised as a cousin of this young lady; she desired nothing better than to talk of the family and its misfortunes. But she threw no more light upon the story, knowing, in fact, less than they themselves knew. They left her; they agreed once more that it was absurd to continue a quest so hopeless; they agreed once more to lock up the book. Next day they took it out and laid their heads together again.

"How long is this going to last?" Constance asked.

"I don't know," Leonard replied wearily. "Are we possessed? Are we bewitched?"

"Are we two persons who do not believe in possession or in witchcraft, yet are really possessed—I don't know by whom, or why, or anything at all about it—but if there is not possession, then the old stories mean nothing."

"We might make a wax image, and call it by the name of the witch, and stick pins in it——"

"If we knew the name of the witch. Why, it seems as if we could speak and think of nothing else. If one were superstitious ——"

"If," echoed the other doubtfully, "one were superstitious ——"

"It might seem like part of the hereditary misfortunes; yet why should I share in your sorrows?" Here she blushed because she remembered how, before the misfortunes were even heard of, she had been invited to share in the good fortune. But Leonard observed nothing. The quest left no room for any thoughts of love.

"No," he replied gravely, "you must not share in our troubles. Constance, I, too, ask myself every day how long this will last. Why cannot I throw off the sense of being driven on against my own will in a search which must be hopeless?"

"Yes, I, too, am driven, but it is to follow you. What does it mean? Is it imagination of a morbid kind?" She paused. Leonard made no reply. "After all," she continued, "there is nothing to do but to accept the situation, and to go on and see what happens."

Leonard groaned. "Suppose," he said, with a wintry smile, "that we are doomed to go on day after day till the end of things, just as that old man has walked up and down his terrace day after day for seventy years. What a fearful tramp! What a monotony! What a life!"

"A dreary prospect. Yet, to go over the same story day after day, every day, seems little better than that walk up and down the terrace, does it?"

"Leave it, Constance. Give it up and go back to your own work."

He took up the fatal book and threw it to the other end of the room.

"Frankly, I would leave it if I could. The thing weighs upon me. I understand what possession means. I am possessed. I must follow you."

"Constance, we are growing ridiculous. We are two persons of culture, and we talk of possession and of an unseen force that drags us."

"But since we are dragged ——"

"Yes, since we are dragged"—he crossed over the room, picked up the book, and brought it back—"and we are dragged—let us obey."

It was then three weeks since this inquiry had begun. It was now the sole object of their lives. They hunted in the British Museum among old papers, they went to the Hall and turned out desks and drawers and cupboards of letters, documents, papers, and accounts. They found enough to reconstruct the daily life of the old man before the tragedy, and the history of his predecessors. They were the simple annals of peaceful country life, with no events but those that one expects—births of children, buying of lands, festivities.

You know that when Sisyphus had rolled his ball—or was it a wheel?—to the top of the hill, the thing incontinently rolled all the way down again. Then, with a sigh, the prisoner walked after it, as slowly as was consistent with a show of obedience, and began again. So Leonard, with a sigh, began again, when one theory after the other broke down.

At this point the coincidences commenced. They were talking together one morning.

"If," said Leonard, "we could only hear the man Dunning on the subject! He would be more interesting, even, than the ancient boy who scared the birds."

"He must be dead long ago. Yet, if he could be found ——"

At this moment—no coincidence, I have explained, can be considered remarkable—Leonard's servant opened the door and brought him a bulky letter. It had an Australian postage stamp upon it. He looked carelessly at the address, and tossed it on the table to wait his convenience. As it lay on its back Constance read, printed across the securing fold, the words "John Dunning's Sons."

"John Dunning's Sons," she said. "This is strange." She took up the letter and pointed out the name. "Just as we were talking of John Dunning. Open the letter, Leonard, and read it. Oh, this is wonderful! Open it at once."

Leonard tore open the envelope. Within there was a letter and an enclosure. He read both rapidly.

"Good Heaven!" he cried. "It is actually the voice of the man himself, Constance; it is the voice we were asking for. It is his voice speaking from the grave."

He read aloud both the letter and the enclosure. The following was the letter:

"Dear Sir,

"I found the enclosed paper only yesterday, though it was written ten years ago, and my grandfather, by whom it was written, died very shortly after it was written. I will not trouble you with the causes which led to our overlooking it for so many years, but hasten to send it on to you in accordance with the writer's wishes.

"The circumstances to which he refers happened seventy years ago. No doubt everyone who can remember the events has long since departed. I do not suppose that you even know the fact—to my grandfather of vital importance—that his acquittal was secured by the kind offices of your ancestor, who was then the owner of Campaigne Park, and I do not suppose that you have ever heard of the great kindness, the sympathy, the desire for justice, which prompted those good offices, nor of the further generosity which sent my grandfather out to Australia. He began life as an agricultural labourer in England; he would have remained in that humble position all his days but for the calamity which turned out so great a blessing—his trial for murder: he came out here: he died one of the richest men in the colony, for everything that he touched turned to gold.

"The paper which I enclose is a proof that gratitude is not wholly dead in the world. I gather, from the published notes on the Members of Parliament and their origin, that you are now the head of the House. Seeing that you were distinguished in the University of Oxford, and are a member of several clubs, as well as in the House, I do not suppose that there is anything we can do to carry out the wishes of my grandfather as regards yourself personally. It may happen, however, that members of your family might come out to this country, and might not be so fortunate as yourself. In that case, will you please to inform those members that our worldly wealth is great, that the origin of all our property was the generosity of your ancestor, that my grandfather's wishes are commands, and that there is nothing which we can do for any member of your family, if the opportunity should occur, which we will not do cheerfully and readily.

"I remain, dear sir,
"Very faithfully yours,
"CHARLES DUNNING."

"I should very much like to make the acquaintance of Mr. Charles Dunning," said Constance. "Now for what the grandfather says."

Leonard opened the other paper and read:

"Being now in my eighty-sixth year, and therefore soon to be called away, I desire to place in writing, in order that it may be sent after my death to the present head of the Campaigne family, first my thanks and heartfelt gratitude for what was done for me by the late Squire in and after my trial for murder. I have enjoined upon my children and my grandchildren that they are to part with their last farthing, if the occasion arises, for the benefit of any descendants of that good man. I suppose that he is dead and beyond the reach of my prayers. I can only hope that he speedily recovered from the loss of his dear lady, and that he enjoyed a long and happy life.

"It is a dreadful thing to be accused of murder. All my life I have remembered the charge and the trial. After the case was over, the people of the village were cruel hard. The charge was thrown in my teeth every day: no one would work with me, and no one would sit with me. So I had to come away. If there is anyone living who remembers the case and me, I would ask him to read and to consider two points that I found out after the trial."

"This is indeed the Voice of the Dead," said Constance, speaking low.

"The first point is that I had witnesses, but I was too much stunned to think of them, who could prove that I was at work all the morning until just before noon in another place.

"The second point may be more important. The path through the wood leads to a stile opening on the lane to the village of Highbeech. There is a cottage in the lane opposite the stile. On the morning of the murder the woman of the cottage was washing outside the door. She told me after the trial that not a soul had gone into the wood from her end of it all the morning; she could not see the other end, but she saw me coming down the hill on my way to the wood, and I had not been in the wood half a minute before she saw me running back again and up the hill to the farm-yard on the top. I hope that if there is any doubt left in the mind of anyone as to my innocence, this new evidence will make it clear."

The paper was signed "John Dunning."

"There is no doubt left," said Constance. "Still, what bearing has the evidence of the cottage woman on the case? What do you think? Has the Voice contributed anything?"

"We will consider presently. Meantime, all he wanted was to clear himself. I think that was effectually done at the trial. Still, he would naturally catch at anything like corroboration. It proves that no one went into the wood from the other end. As for anything else, why, it would seem, with the boy's evidence, to mean that nobody went into the wood at all that morning except those two gentlemen."

"Then we come back to the old theory: the lurking in the wood of poacher, madman, or private enemy."

"We asked for a Voice from the Grave, and it came," said Leonard. "And now it seems to have told us nothing."

He placed the paper in the book, leaving the letter on the table.

They looked at each other blankly. Then Leonard rose and walked about the room. Finally he took up a position before the fireplace, and began to speak slowly, as if feeling his way.

"I suppose that it is natural that I should connect this crime with that great question about the inheritance of punishment or consequences."

"It is quite natural," said Constance. "And yet — —"

"My mother and my grandmother, as I now understand, believed that the misfortunes which they so carefully concealed from me were the inheritance of the forefathers' sins. And since these misfortunes began with this crime, it was natural that they should attribute the cause to the ancestor who died before the crime. Now, all I can learn about that ancestor is, that he was a country gentleman and Justice of the Peace, a Member of Parliament, and that he left behind him no record or memory of anything uncommon. Now, to produce this enormous list of misfortunes, one must be a Gilles de Retz at least."

"I am not acquainted with that example."

"He was a great master in every kind of villainy. About these misfortunes, however. My great-grandfather, as you know — — My grandfather died by his own hand: his brother was drowned at sea: his sister has been unfortunate throughout her life: his son, my father, died young: my uncle Frederick went abroad under a dread of disgrace, which we may forget now he has come home again. The list of misfortunes is long enough. But we cannot learn any cause — which may, even to the superstitious, account for it — under anything of inheritance."

"Why should we try to account for the misfortunes? They are not caused by you."

"I try because they are part of the whole business. I cannot escape or forget the chain of misfortune."

"If you only could, Leonard! And it is so long ago, and no misfortune has fallen upon you. Oh, what did I say once — in this very room?"

"The misfortune that has fallen upon me is the knowledge of all these misfortunes — these ruined lives. The old selfish contentment is gone. I lived for myself. That is henceforth impossible. Well" — he shook himself as a dog after a swim — "I am now what you wanted me to be — like other people." He relapsed into silence. "I cannot choose," he said presently, "but connect these misfortunes with that first and greatest. The point of doubt is whether to speak of consequence or punishment."

"Must it be one or the other?"

"The child must suffer for the father's sin. That is most certain. If the father throws away his property, the son becomes a pauper. If the father loses his social position, the children sink down with him. If the father contracts disease, the children may inherit. All this is obvious and cannot be disputed."

"But that is not punishment for generations of innocent children."

"It is consequence, not punishment. We must not confuse the two. Take the case of crime. Body and mind and soul are all connected together, so that the face proclaims the mind and the mind presents the soul. The criminal is a diseased man. Body and mind and soul are all connected together. He lives in an evil atmosphere. Thought, action, impulse, are all evil. He is wrapped in a miasma, like a low-lying meadow on an autumn morning. The children may inherit the disease of crime just as they may inherit consumption or gout. That is to say, they are born with a tendency to crime, as they may be born with a tendency to consumption or gout. It is not punishment, I repeat. It is consequence. In such children there is an open door to evil of some kind or other."

"Since all men have weaknesses or faults, there must be always such an open door to all children."

"I suppose so. But the son of a man reputed blameless, whose weaknesses or faults are presumably light or venial, is less drawn towards the open door than the son of the habitual criminal. The son of the criminal naturally makes for the open door, which is the easy way. It is the consequence. As for our own troubles, perhaps, if we knew, they, too, may be the consequence—not the punishment. But we do not know—we cannot find the crime, or the criminal."

CHAPTER XV

"BARLOW BROTHERS"

"The theory of consequence"—Leonard was arranging his thoughts on paper for better clearness—"while it answers most of the difficulties connected with hereditary trouble, breaks down, it must be confessed, in some cases. Given, for instance, a case in which a boy is carefully educated, has no bad examples before him, shows no signs of vice, and is ignorant of the family misfortunes. If that boy becomes a spendthrift and a prodigal, or worse, when there has never before been such a thing in the family, how can we connect the case with the faults or vices of a grandfather altogether unlike his own, and unknown to him? I should be inclined rather to ascribe the case to some influences of the past, not to be discovered, due to some maternal ancestry. A man, for instance, may be so completely unlike any other member of the family that we must search for the cause of his early life in the line of his mother or his grandmother."

He was just then thinking of his uncle—the returned Colonial, in whom, except for his commanding stature and his still handsome face, there was nothing to remind the world of the paternal side. Whenever he thought of this cheerful person, with whom life seemed a pleasant play, certain doubts crossed his mind, and ran like cold water down his back. He had come home rich—that was something. He might have come home as poor as when he started. Rich or poor, he would have been the same—as buoyant, as loud, as unpresentable.

In fact, at this very moment, when these reflections were forming a part of Leonard's great essay on the after-effects of evil—an essay which created only last month so great a stir that people talked of little else for a whole evening—the rich Australian was on his way to confess the fact that things were not exactly as he had chosen to present them.

He did confess the truth, or as much of the truth as he could afford to express, but in an easy and irresponsible manner, as if nothing mattered much. He was a philosopher, to whom nothing did matter. He came in, he shook hands and laughed buoyantly; he chose a cigar from Leonard's box, he rang the bell for whisky and a few bottles of soda; when the whisky and the soda had arrived and were within reach, he took a chair, and laughed again.

"My boy," he said, "I'm in a tight place again."

"In what way?"

"Why, for want of money. That's the only possible tight place at my age. At yours there are many. It is only a temporary tightness, of course." He opened the soda-water and drank off the full tumbler at a gulp. "Temporary. Till the supplies arrive."

"The supplies?" Leonard put the question in a nasty, cold, suspicious manner, which would have changed smiles into blankness in a more sensitive person. But uncle Fred was by no means sensitive or thin-skinned. He was also so much accustomed to temporary tightness that the incongruity of tightness with his pretensions of prosperity had not occurred to him.

"Supplies?" he replied. "Supplies from Australia, of course."

"I thought that you were a partner in a large and prosperous concern."

"Quite true—quite true. Barlow Brothers is both large and prosperous."

"In that case it is easy for you to draw upon your bankers or the agents for your bank or some friends in the City. You go into the City every day, I believe. Your position must be well known. In other words, I mistrust this temporary tightness."

"Mistrust? And from you? Really, Leonard——"

"I put things together. I find in you none of the habits of a responsible merchant. I know that everywhere character is essential for commercial success——"

"Character? What should I be without character?"

"You come home as the successful merchant: you drink: you talk as if you were a debauched youngster about town: your anecdotes are scandalous: your tastes are low. Those are the outward signs."

"I am on a holiday. Out there—it's very different. As for drink, of course in a thirsty climate like that of New South Wales—and this place—one must drink a little. For my own part, I am surprised at my own moderation."

"Very well. I will not go on with the subject, only—to repeat—if you are in a tight place, those who know your solvency will be very willing to relieve you. I hope you are not here to borrow of me, because——"

The man laughed again. "Not I. Nobody is likely to borrow of you, Leonard. That is quite certain—not even the stoniest broke. Make your mind quite easy. As for my friends in the City, I know very well what to do about them. No; I am here because I want to throw myself upon the family."

"The family consists of your brother, who may be able to help you——"

"I've asked him. He won't—Christopher was always a selfish beast. Good fellow to knock about with and all that—ready for anything—but selfish—damned selfish."

"And your aunt Lucy——"

"I don't know her. Who is she?"

"She is not able to assist you. And of myself."

"You forget the Head of the Family—my old grandfather. I am going to him."

"You will get nothing out of him—not even a word of recognition."

"I know. I have been down there to look at him. I have been to see his solicitors."

"You will get nothing from them without their client's authority."

"Well, you know the family affairs, of course. I suppose that a word from you authorising or advising the transfer of a few thousands—or hundreds—out of that enormous pile——"

"I have no right to authorise or advise. I know nothing about my great-grandfather's affairs."

"Tell me, dear boy, what about those accumulations? We mentioned them the other day."

"I know nothing about them."

"Of course, of course. I'm not going to put questions. The bulk of everything will be yours, naturally. I have no objection. I am not going to interfere with you. Only, don't you think you could go to the people, the agents or solicitors, and put it to them, that, as a son of the House, I should like an advance of—say a thousand pounds?"

"I am quite certain beforehand they will do nothing for you."

"You're a better man of the world than I thought, my boy. I respect you for it. Nobody is to have a finger in the pie but yourself. And you look so damned solemn over it, too."

"I tell you that I know nothing."

"Just so—just so. Well, you know nothing. I've made a rough calculation—but never mind. Let the accumulations be. Very good, then, I shall not interfere. Meantime, I want some money. Get me from those lawyers a thousand."

"I cannot get you anything. As for myself, I have not got a thousand pounds in the world. You forget that all I have is my mother's small fortune of a few hundreds a year. It is not in my power to lend you anything."

He laughed again in his enjoyment of the situation. "Delicious!" he said. "And I said that I wasn't going to borrow anything. This it is to be a British swell. Well, I don't mind. I will draw upon you at six months. Come. Long before that time I shall be in funds again."

"No. You shall not even draw upon me at six months," Leonard replied, with some vague knowledge of what was implied. "You told me you were rich."

"Every man is rich who is a partner in a going concern."

"Then, again, why are you in this tight place?"

"My partner, you see, has been playing the fool. Barlow Brothers, General Stores, Colonial Produce, will be smashed if I can't raise a few hundreds."

"Your going concern, as you call it, is going to grief. And what will you do?"

"You shall just see what I wanted. Barlows' is a General Store in a rising town. There are great capabilities in Barlow Brothers. I came over here to convert Barlow Brothers into a Limited Liability Company, capital £150,000. Branches everywhere. Our own sugar estates, our own tea and coffee plantations. That was my idea!"

"It was a bold idea, at any rate."

"It was. As for Barlows' General Store, I confess, between ourselves, and considering that you don't belong to the City, I don't mind owning up to you that it is little better than a shanty, where I sold sardines and tea-leaves and bacon. But the capabilities, my dear boy—the capabilities!"

"And you brought this project to London! Well, there have been greater robberies."

Uncle Fred took another glass of whisky-and-soda. He laughed no more. He even sighed.

"I thought London was an enterprising city. It appears not. No promoter will so much as look at the Company. I was willing to let my interest in it go for £40,000. If you'll believe me, Leonard, they won't even look at it. A few hundreds would save it, a few thousands would make it a Colossal Success. For want of it we must go to the wall."

"You were hoping to sell a bankrupt business as a flourishing business."

"That is so. But it hasn't come off."

"Well, what shall you do?"

"I shall have to begin again at the bottom. That's all."

"Oh!" Leonard looked at him doubtfully, for he seemed in no way cast down. "You will go back to Australia, then." There was some consolation in the thought.

"I shall go back. I don't know my way about in London. I will go back and begin again, just as before, at the bottom rung. I shall have to do odd jobs, I dare say. I may possibly have to become a shepherd, or a night-watchman, or a sandwich-man. What does it matter? I shall only be down among the boys who can't get any lower. There's a fine feeling of brotherhood down there, which you swells would never understand."

"Have you no money left at all?"

"None. Not more than I carry about with me. A few pounds."

"Then the fine show of prosperity was all a sham?"

"All a sham. And it wouldn't work. Nobody in the City will look at my Company."

"Would it not be better to try for some definite kind of work? You can surely do something. You might write for the papers, with all your experience."

"Write for the papers? I would rather go on tramp, which is much more amusing. Do something? What am I to do? Man, there isn't on the face of the earth a more helpless person than a bankrupt trader at forty-five. He knows too much to be employed in his own trade. He's got to go down below and to stay there. Never mind. I can turn my hand to anything. If I stayed at home I should have to be a sandwich-man. How would you like that? Even my old grandfather would come back to the present life, if it were only to burst with rage, if he met his grandson walking down Regent Street between a pair of boards. You wouldn't like it yourself, would you? Come out to Sydney next year, and very likely you'll see that, or something like it."

"Then you go out to certain misery."

"Misery? Certain misery?" The Colonist laughed cheerfully. "My nephew, you are a very narrow-minded person, though you are a scholar and a Member of Parliament. You think that it is misery to take off a frock-coat and a tall hat, and to put on a workingman's jacket and bowler. Bless you, my boy! that's not misery. The real misery is being hungry and cold. In Australia no one is ever cold, and very few are ever hungry. In my worst times I've always had plenty to eat, and though I've been many times without a shilling, I've never in all my life been miserable or ashamed."

"But there is the companionship."

"The companions? They are the best fellows in the world. Misery? There isn't any with the fellows down below, especially the young fellows. And, mind you, it is exciting work, the hand-to-mouth life. Now, by the time I get out, the business will be sold up, and my partner, who is a young man, will be off on another lay; they always put out the old man as soon as they can. What shall I do? I shall go hawking and peddling. I shall become Autolycus."

"And afterwards?"

"There is no afterwards, till you come to the hospital, which is a really pleasant place, and the black box. I've done it before, and I'll do it again." He mixed another soda-and-whisky and drank it off. "It's thirsty work along the roads under the sun—a red-hot burning sun, not like your red frying-pan skulking behind a cloud. Wherever you stop you get a drink. Then you bring out your wares. I've got a tongue that runs like an engine newly oiled. And where you put up for the night there are the boys on the road, and there are songs and stories. Respectability go hang!"

He laughed again. He put on his hat and swung out of the room, laughing as at the very finest joke in the world—to come home as a gentleman, and to go back as a tramp.

CHAPTER XVI

AND ANOTHER CAME

ALMOST immediately after the colonial merchant—the wholesale trader in sardines and tea-leaves from a shanty—had departed, there came another. They might almost have passed each other on the stairs.

It was none other than the Counsel learned in the Law, the pride and prop of his family, the successful barrister, Mr. Christopher Campaigne.

"Good heavens!" cried Leonard, "what is the matter with this man?" For his uncle dropped speechless, limp, broken up, into a chair, and there lay, his hands dangling, his face filled with terror and care. "My dear Uncle Christopher," he said, "what has happened?"

"The worst," groaned the lawyer—"the very worst. The impossible has happened. The one thing that I guarded against. The thing which I feared. Oh, Leonard! how shall I tell you?"

Come with me to the chambers where the Professor of Oratory was preparing, as in a laboratory, his great effects of laughter and of tears. It was morning—high noon. He was engaged upon what is perhaps the most fascinating branch of a most delightful profession—a speech of presentation. Before him, in imagination, stood the mug; beside him the recipient; and in front of him a vast hall filled with sympathetic donors. Such a speech is the enunciation and the magnifying of achievements. It must be illustrated by poetical quotations; the better known and the more familiar they are, the more effective they will prove. The speaker should tell one funny story at least; he must also contrive, but not obtrusively—with modesty—to suggest his own personal importance as, if anything, superior to that of the recipient; he must not grovel before greatness.

All these points the professional manufacturer of oratory understood and had at his fingers' ends. He was quite absorbed in his work, insomuch that he paid no kind of attention to footsteps outside, nor even, at first, to an angry voice in the outer office, which, as we have seen, was only protected by the boy, who had nothing else to do, unless the reading of Jack Harkaway's adventures be considered a duty.

"Stand out of my way!" cried the voice, apparently infuriated. "Let me get at him!"

The professional man looked up wonderingly. Apparently a row on the stairs. But his own door burst open, and a young man, quite a little man, with hot cheeks and eyes aflame, rushed in brandishing a stick. The orator sprang to his feet, seizing the office ruler. He leaned over his table, six feet three in height, with this formidable weapon in his hand, and he faced the intruder with calm, cold face.

We must not blame the assailant; doubtless he was of tried and proved courage, but he was only five feet five. Before that calm face of inquiry, on which there was no line of terror or of repentance, his eyes fell. The fire and fury went out of him quite suddenly. Perhaps he had not developed his æsthetic frame by rude exercise. He dropped his stick, and stood irresolute.

"Oh," said his enemy quietly, "you think better about the stick, do you? The horse-whipping is to stand over, is it? Now, sir"—he rapped the table horribly with the ruler, so that the little man trembled all over; the adventure unexpectedly promised pain as well as humiliation—"what do you mean? What do you come here for, making this infernal racket? What——"

Here he stopped short, because to his unspeakable dismay he saw standing in the doorway none other than his own son, Algernon, and Algernon's face was not good to look at, being filled with shame, amazement, and bewilderment—with shame because he understood, all in a moment, that his father's life had been one long lie, and that by this way, and none other, the family income had been earned. Had not his friend on the way told him that the man Crediton was known in certain circles as the provider of good after-dinner speeches for those who could afford to pay for them?—how it was whispered that the rare and occasional evenings on which the speeches were crisp and fiery and witty and moving all through were those for which Crediton had supplied the whole?—and how for his own speech, about which he had been most shamefully treated, he had paid twenty guineas? So that he understood without more words, and looked on open-mouthed, having for the moment no power of speech or utterance.

The father first recovered. He went on as if his son was not present.

"Who are you, sir, I say, who come to my quiet office with this blackguard noise? If you don't tell me on the spot, I will take you by the scruff of your miserable little neck and drop you over the banisters."

"I—I—I wrote to you for a speech."

"What speech? What name? What for?"

His client, whose eyes at first were blinded by excess of wrath, now perceived to his amazement that Mr. Crediton was none other than his friend's father, whom, indeed, he had met at the family mansion in Pembridge Crescent.

"Good Lord!" he cried, "it's—it's Mr. Campaigne!"—he glanced from father to son, and back again—"Mr. Campaigne!"

"And why not, sir—why not? Answer me that."

Again the ruler descended with a sickening resonance.

"Oh, I don't know why not. How should I know?" the intruder stammered. "It's no concern of mine, I'm sure."

"Then come to the point. What speech? What name? What for?"

"The Company of Cartmakers. The speech that you sent me—it arrived by post."

"A very good speech, too. I did send it. Much too good for you or for the fee you paid. I remember it. What is the matter with it? How dare you complain of it!"

"The matter, sir—the matter," he stammered, feeling much inclined to sit down and cry, "is that you sent the same speech to the proposer. Mine was the reply. The same speech—do you hear?—the same speech to the proposer as to me, who had to reply. Now, sir, do you realise—— Oh, I am not afraid of your ruler, I say;" but his looks belied his words. "Do you understand the enormity of your conduct?"

"Impossible! How could I do such a thing—I who have never made a mistake before in all my professional career?" He looked hard at his son, and repeated the words "professional career." "Are you sure of what you say?" He laid down his ruler with a very serious air. "Are you quite sure?"

"Certain. The same speech, word for word. Everything—every single thing—was taken out of my mouth; I hadn't a word to say."

"How did that happen, I wonder? Stay, I have type-written copies of both speeches—the toast and the reply. Yes, yes, I always keep one copy. I am afraid I do understand how I may have blundered." He opened a drawer, and turned over some papers. "Ah, yes, yes. Dear me! I sent out the second copy of your speech to the other man instead of his own. Here is his own duplicate—the two copies—which fully explains it. Dear, dear! Tut, tut, tut! I fear you were unable to rise to the occasion and make up a little speech for yourself?"

"I could not; I was too much astonished, and I may add disgusted, to do—er—justice to myself."

"No doubt—no doubt. My clients never can do justice to their own genius without my help. Now sit down, sir, and let us talk this over for a moment."

He himself sat down. His son meanwhile stood at the open door, still as one petrified.

"Now, sir, I confess that you have reason to complain. It was a most unfortunate accident. The other man must have observed something wrong about the opening words. However, most unfortunate." He opened a safe standing beside him, and took out a small bundle of cheques. "Your cheque arrived yesterday morning. Fortunately, it is not yet paid in. I return it, sir—twenty guineas. That is all I can do for you except to express my regret that this accident should have occurred. I feel for you, young gentleman. I forgive your murderous intentions, and I assure you, if you will come to me again, I will make you the finest after-dinner orator in the town. And now, sir, I have other clients."

He rose. The young man put the cheque in his pocket.

"It will be," he said grandly, "my duty to expose you—everywhere." He turned to his companion. "To expose you both."

"And yourself, dear sir—and yourself at the same time."

The Agent rattled the keys in his pocket, and repeated the words, "Yourself at the same time."

"I don't care—so long as I expose you."

"You will care when you come to think about it. You will have to tell everybody that you came to me to buy a speech which you were about to palm off as your own. There are one or two transactions of the same nature standing over, so to speak. Remember, young gentleman, there are two persons to be exposed: myself, whom the exposure will only advertise, and you yourself, who will be ruined as an orator—or anything else."

But the young man was implacable. He had his cheque back. This made him stiffer and sterner.

"I care nothing. I could never pretend again to be an orator after last night's breakdown. I was dumfoundered. I could say nothing: they laughed at me, the whole Hall full of people—three hundred of them—laughed at me—and all through you—through you. I'll be revenged—I'll make you sorry for last night's business—sick and sorry you shall be. As for you——" He turned upon Algernon.

"Shut up, and get out," said his friend. "Get out, I say, or——"

Algernon made room for him, and the aggrieved client marched out with as much dignity as he could command.

Left together, father and son glared at each other icily. They were both of the same height, tall and thin, and closely resembling each other, with the strong type of the Campaigne face; and both wore pince-nez. The only difference was that the elder of the two was a little thin about the temples.

The consciousness of being in the wrong destroyed the natural superiority of the father. He replied with a weak simulacrum of a laugh.

"Surely the situation explains itself," he said feebly, opening the door for explanation.

"Am I to understand that for money you write—write—write speeches for people who pretend—actually pretend—that they are their own?"

"Undoubtedly. Did not your friend confess to you why he was coming here?"

"Well—of course he did."

"And did you remonstrate with him on account of his dishonesty?"

Mr. Algernon Campaigne shirked the question, and replied by another. "And do you regard this mode of money-making—I cannot call it a profession—this mode—honourable—a thing to be proud of?"

"Why not? Certain persons with no oratorical gifts are called upon to speak after dinner or on other occasions. They write to me for assistance. I send them speeches. I coach them. In fact, I am an oratorical coach. They learn what they have to say, and they say it. It is a perfectly honourable, laudable, and estimable way of making money. Moreover, my son, it makes money."

"Then, why not conduct this—this trade—openly under your own name?"

"Because, in the nature of things, it is a secret business. My clients' names are secret. So also is the nature of our transactions."

"But this place is not Lincoln's Inn. How do you spare the time from your law work?"

"My dear boy, there has been a little deception, pardonable under the circumstances. In point of fact, I never go to Lincoln's Inn. There is no practice. I've got a garret which I never go near. There never has been any practice."

"No practice?" The young man sank helplessly into a chair. "No practice? But we have been so proud all along of your distinguished career."

"There has never been any legal practice at all. I adopted this line in the hope of making a little money at a time when the family was pretty hard up, and it succeeded beyond my expectations."

Algernon sat down and groaned aloud.

"We are done for. That—that little beast is the most spiteful creature in the world, and the most envious. He is mad to be thought clever. He has published some things—I believe he bought them. He goes about; he poses. There isn't a man in London more dangerous. He will tell everybody. How shall we face the storm?"

"People, my son, will still continue to want their after-dinner speeches."

"I am thinking of my sister, myself, and our position. What will my mother say? What will our friends say? Good Lord! we are all ruined and shamed. We can never hold up our heads again. What on earth can we say? How can we get out of it? Who will call upon us?"

The parent was touched.

"My dear boy," he said humbly, "I must think the matter over. There will be trouble, perhaps. Leave me for the present, and—still for the present—hold your tongue."

His son obeyed. Then Mr. Crediton resumed his work, but the interruption was fatal. He was fain to abandon the speech of presentation, and to consider the prospect of exposure. Not that any kind of exposure would destroy his profession, for that had now become a necessity for the convenience of the social life—think what we should suffer if all the speeches were home-made!—but there was the position of his wife and family: the reproaches of his wife and family: the lowering of his wife and family in the social world. It would be fatal for them if he were known as a secret purveyor of eloquence; secrecy can never be considered honourable or ennobling: dress it up as you will, the cloven foot of fraud cannot be disguised.

He went out because he was too much agitated to keep still or to do any work, and he wandered through the streets feeling pretty small. How would the exposure come? This young fellow had been brought to the house; he called at the house; he came to their evenings and posed as poet, story-teller, orator, epigrammatist; he knew a whole lot of people in their set: he could certainly make things very disagreeable. And he was in such a rage of disappointment and humiliation—for he had broken down utterly and shamefully—that he certainly intended to be nasty.

After a tempestuous youth in company with his brother, this man had settled down into the most domestic creature in the world. Twenty-five years of domestic joys had been his portion; they were made possible by his secret profession. His wife adored and believed in him; his children, while they despised his æsthetics, respected his law. In a word, he occupied the enviable position of a successful barrister, a gentleman of good family, and the owner of a good income. This position was naturally more than precious: it was his very life. At home he was, in his own belief, a great lawyer; in his office he was Mr. Crediton the universal orator. They were separate beings; and now they were to be brought together. Crediton would be known to the world as Campaigne, Campaigne as Crediton. He was a forlorn and miserable object indeed.

As he passed along the street he discovered suddenly that he was passing one of the entrances to Bendor Mansions. A thought struck him.

"I must ask someone's advice," he murmured. "I cannot bear the trouble all alone and unsupported. I will tell Leonard everything."

Leonard sprang to his feet, astonished at this extraordinary exhibition of despair.

"My dear uncle Christopher!" he exclaimed, "what does this mean? What has happened?"

The unhappy man, anxious to take counsel, yet shrinking from confession, groaned in reply.

"Has anything happened at home? My aunt? My cousins?"

"Worse—worse. It has happened to me."

"Well.... But what has happened? Man, don't sit groaning there. Lift up your head and tell me what has happened."

"Ruin," he replied—"social ruin and disgrace. That is all. That is all."

"Then, you are the second member of our truly fortunate family who has been ruined this very day. Perhaps," Leonard added coldly, "it might be as well if you could let me know what form your ruin has taken."

"Social ruin and disgrace. That is all. I shall never be able to look anyone in the face any more."

"What have you done, then?"

"I have done only what I have been doing blamelessly, because no one ever suspected it, for five-and-twenty years. Now it has been found out."

"You have been doing something disgraceful for five-and-twenty years, and now you have been found out. Well, why have you come to me? Is it to get my sympathy for disgracing your name?"

"You don't understand, Leonard."

He lost his temper.

"How the devil am I to understand if you won't explain? You say that you are disgraced — —"

"Let me tell you all — everything — from the beginning. It came from knocking about London with my brother Fred. He was a devil: he didn't care what he did. So we ran through our money — it wasn't much — and Fred went away."

"I have heard why. A most shameful business."

"Truly, yes. I always told him so. Since he came home, however, we have agreed not to mention it."

"Go on. You were left with no money."

"I had just been called. I was engaged. I wanted to get married."

"You rapidly acquired an extensive practice — —"

"No — no. That is where the deception stepped in. My dear nephew, I never had any practice at all. If any cases had been sent to me I could not have taken them, because, you see, I never opened a law-book in my whole life."

"You — never — opened — a law-book? Then — how — —"

"I loathed the sight of a law-book. But I was engaged—I wanted to be married—I wanted to live, too, without falling back on your mother."

"Pray go on."

"I knew a man who wanted to get a reputation for an after-dinner speaker. He heard me make one or two burlesque speeches, and he came to me. After a little conversation, we talked business. I wrote him a speech. It succeeded. I wrote him another. That succeeded. He leaped into fame—leaped, so to speak, over my back—oratorical leap-frog—by those two speeches. Then my price ran up. And then I conceived the idea of opening out a new profession. For five-and-twenty years I have pretended to go to chambers in Lincoln's Inn, and I have gone to an office in Chancery Lane, where, under another name, I have carried on the business of providing speeches for all occasions."

"Good Heavens!" cried Leonard. "And this is the man of whom we were proud!" His face had been darkening from the beginning, and it was now very hard and dark. "I understand, I suppose. The beginning of the story I had heard already. You got through your fortune in company with your brother—in riotous living."

"Quite so—quite so."

"Was there not something about a cheque?"

"Fred's affair—not mine."

"Your brother says it was your affair. Don't think I want to inquire into the horrid story. I have found quite enough shame and degradation among my family without wanting to know more."

"If Fred says that, it is simply disgraceful. Why, everybody knew—but, as you say, why rake up old scandals?—at the time when it happened. But why, as you say——"

"Why, indeed? Except to make quite sure that there is no longer a shred of family pride possible for us. I now learn, on your own confession, that you entered upon a general course of imposition, and deception, by which you have managed to live ever since, and to maintain your family with credit because you have escaped detection."

"Excuse me. I don't call it deception. Nobody is deceived, except pleasantly. Is it wrong to present a fellow-creature in an agreeable and quite unexpected character before the world? Can you blame me for raising the standard of after-dinner oratory? Can you blame me for creating reputations by the dozen?"

"I make no doubt that you persuaded yourself that it was laudable and honourable. Nevertheless——"

"You must consider how it grew. I told you I was myself a good after-dinner speaker. I was hard up. Then this man—old friend, now a Colonial Judge—came to me for help. I wrote him a speech, and he bought it—that is to say, he lent me ten pounds for it—really he bought my secrecy. That's how it began. Money was necessary. There was an unexpected way of making money. So it spread."

"I have no doubt that the practice of imposition was duly paid for."

"You must consider—really. There is nothing envied so much as the reputation of good after-dinner speaking. I supply that reputation. People go where they are likely to hear good speeches. I supply those speeches."

"I do not deny the position. But you are, nevertheless, helping a man, for money, to deceive the world."

"To deceive the world? Not at all. To delight the world. Why, I am a public benefactor. I open the purses at charity dinners, I send the people home in good temper. Do you think the people care two pins who is speaking if they can be amused?"

"Then, why this secrecy?"

"Why not?" He walked about the room, swinging his arms, and turning from time to time on Leonard as he made his points and pronounced his apology. "Why not? I ask. You talk as if some fraud was carried on. Nobody is defrauded; I earn my fees as much as any barrister. Look you, Leonard: my position is unique, and—and—yes, honourable, if you look at it rightly."

"Honourable! Oh!"

"Yes; I am the Universal After-Dinner Speaker. I supply the speeches for every occasion. I keep up the reputation of the City for eloquence.

Why, we were rapidly sinking; we were already acknowledged to be far below the American level. Then I came. I raised the standard. Our after-dinner speeches—mine—are becoming part of our national greatness. Why? Because I, sir—I, Christopher Campaigne—took them in hand."

"Yet, in secrecy."

"I carry on this business alone—I myself—hitherto without recognition. The time may come when the national distinctions will be offered to the—in fact, the After-Dinner Demosthenes."

"You look so far forward?"

"I confess that the work is light, easy—to me, at least—and pleasant. It is also well paid. People are willing to give a great deal for such a reputation as I can make for them. Nobody ever wants to see me. Nobody knows who I am. Nobody wants to know. That is natural, come to think of it. The whole business is done by correspondence. I work for none but persons of wealth and position. Confidence is respected on both sides. Sometimes the whole of a dinner, so to speak, passes through my hands. I have even known occasions on which I have sat unrecognised at a dinner-table, and listened to my speeches being delivered well or ill through the whole evening. Imagine, if you can, the glow and glory of such an evening."

"I can imagine a ruddy hue—of shame. After five-and-twenty years of deception, however, there is not much shame left. What has happened now? You have been found out, I suppose?"

"Yes; I have been found out. There was a little mistake. I sent a man the wrong speech—the response instead of the proposer's speech. To the proposer I sent the same speech in duplicate. I cannot imagine how the mistake was possible, but it happened. And you may imagine the feelings of the poor young man who heard his own brilliant speech which was in his pocket actually delivered, a few words only changed, by the man whom he was about to answer. When his turn came he rose; he was overcome; he blurted out three or four words, and sat down."

"Oh! And then?"

"In the morning he came to beard me in my own den. He had never seen me before, but he knew my address. He came with a big stick, being a little man. Ho, ho! and he marched in flourishing his stick. You should have seen him when I stood over him with the office ruler." He laughed again, but at the sight of Leonard's dark face he checked his sense of humour. "Well, the misfortune was that I know the fellow at home, and he comes to our place, and knows me, and, worse than that, my own son, Algernon, was with him to see fair — —"

"Oh, Algernon was with him. Then, Algernon knows?"

"Yes, he knows. I packed off the fellow, and had it out with Algernon. It was a tough business. I'm sorry for Algernon. Perhaps, he won't put on quite so much side, though. Yes," he repeated thoughtfully, "I had it out with that young man. He knows now what the real profession is."

"Well, what next?"

"I don't know what next."

"Shall you continue your trade of deception and falsehood?"

"Shall I go into the workhouse?"

"Upon my word, it would be better."

His uncle rose and took up his hat.

"Well, Leonard, if you have nothing but reproaches, I may as well go. I did think that you would consider my position — my very difficult position. I have at least supported my family, and I have confided the whole to you. If you have nothing to say except to harp upon deception — as if that mattered — I may as well go."

"Stop! let's consider the thing. Is there no other way of livelihood?"

"None. The only question is whether I am to conduct the business henceforth under my own name or not."

"I don't know that I can advise or help in any way. Why did you come to me?"

"I came for advice — if you have any to give. I came because this misfortune has fallen upon me, and you are reputed to be wise beyond your years."

"The fact of your occupation is misfortune enough."

"Well? You have nothing more to say? Then I must go."

He looked so miserable that Leonard forgot his indignation, and inclined his heart to pity.

"You are afraid of exposure," he said, "on account of your wife and children."

"On their account alone. For my own part, I have done no wrong, and I fear no exposure."

They were brave words, but he was as the donkey in the lion's skin. He spoke valiantly, but his knees trembled.

"I should think," Leonard replied, "that this young man, for his own sake, would be careful not to spread abroad his experience, because he would expose himself as well as you. He proposed deliberately to impose upon the audience, as his own, an oration prepared by another man and bought by himself. That is a position, if it were known and published, even less dignified than your own. I think that Algernon should put this side of the case to him strongly and plainly."

"He may leave himself out and whisper rumours abroad."

"Algernon should warn him against such things. If, however, the man persists in his unholy ambition to obtain a false reputation, he will probably have to come to you again, since there is no other practitioner."

Mr. Crediton jumped in his chair.

"That's the point. You've hit it. That's the real point. I'm glad I came here. He's not only got his ambition still, but he's got his failure to get over. He must come to me. There is no other practitioner. He must come. I never thought of that." He rubbed his hands joyously.

"He may not be clever enough to see this point. Therefore Algernon had better put it to him. If Algernon fails, you must make a clean breast to your wife and daughter, and send it round openly among your personal friends that you are willing to supply speeches confidentially. That seems the only way out of it."

"The only way—the only way, Leonard. There will be no clean breast at all, and that venomous beast will have to come to me again. I am so glad that I came here. You have got more sense than all the rest of us put together."

CHAPTER XVII

YET ANOTHER!

WHEN he was gone Leonard threw himself into the nearest chair, and looked around him. He gazed with bewildered face, not upon the study full of books, the papers which showed the man of learning, the reports which spoke of the man of affairs, the engravings on the wall which spoke of the man of culture. These are accidental: anyone may show them. The artist sprung from the gutter, the self-made scholar, the mere mushroom, might possess and exhibit all these things. He saw strewn around him the wreck and ruin of all that he had hitherto considered the essential, namely, the family honour.

There are none so full of family pride as those who show it least. To Leonard it had always been the greatest happiness merely to feel that the records of his family went back to times beyond the memory of man. It was not a thing to be talked about, but a prop, a stay, a shield, anything that helps to make a man at peace with himself. No one knew when the Campaignes first obtained their estate; in every century he found his ancestors—not distinguished—indeed, they had never produced a man of the first rank—but playing a part, and that not an unworthy one. It was the record of an honourable line. There were no traitors or turncoats in it: the men were without reproach, the women without a spot or stain among them all.

I suppose that nobody, either at school or college, ever knew or suspected the profound pride which lay at the heart of this quiet and self-possessed scholar. It was the kind of pride which is free from arrogance. He was a gentleman; all his people had been gentlemen. By gentlemen he meant people of good birth and breeding, and of blameless life. The word, we well know, is now used so as to include the greater part of male man. To most people it means nothing and matters nothing. Even with people who use limitations the door is always open to those who choose to lead the gentle life, and are privileged to follow the work which belongs to the gentle life.

He was a gentleman—he and all his people. He had no feeling of superiority, not the least—no more than a man may entertain a feeling of superiority on account of his stature. Nor had he the least feeling of contempt for those who have no such advantages. A man who has a grandfather may affect to despise one who has no grandfather, but not a man who has a long line terminating like the ancestry of a Saxon king in dim shapes which are probably Woden, Thor, and Freyya.

The grand essentials of family pride are ancestry and honour. The former cannot very well be taken away, but without the latter it is not worth much. One might as well take pride in belonging to a long line in which gallant highwaymen, footpads, costers, hooligans, and Marylebone boys have succeeded each other for generations with the accompaniments and distinctions of Tyburn Tree and the cart-tail.

Therefore, I say, Leonard sat among the ruins of the essentials regardless of the accidentals. The man who had just left him had stripped off all that was left of his former pride; he could feel no further support or solace in the contemplation of his forefathers. Think what he had learned and endured in less than a month. It was line upon line, precept upon precept. It was like unto the patriarch to whom, while one messenger of evil was speaking, there came also another, saying, "Thus and thus has it been done. Where is now thy pride?"

First, he learned that he had cousins living in one of the least desirable quarters of London; the man-cousin could not by any possible stretch be considered as possessing any of the attributes of a gentleman; the girl occupied a station and followed a calling which was respectable, but belonging to those generally adopted by the Poor Relation. He was thus provided with poor relations. Constance had said that he wanted poor relations in order to be like other people. And then they came as if in answer to her words.

He had learned also that his grandfather almost at the outset of a promising career had committed suicide for no reason that could be discovered; that his father had died young, also at the outset of a promising career, was a misfortune, but not a blot.

Two persons were left of his father's generation. He had welcomed one as the prodigal, who had gone forth to the husks and returned bearing sheaves of golden grain. At least there was the pretence of the golden grain. The other he had regarded all his life with respect as one in successful practice in a most honourable profession. Where were they now? One was a bankrupt grocer or general store-keeper, the owner of a shanty in an Australian township, a miserable little general shop selling sardines and tea and oil and blacking, which he wanted to turn into a company as a great business; one who made no pretence at truth or honesty; the companion of tramps; devoid of honour or even the respect or care for honour. He had been driven out by his family as a spendthrift, a profligate, and a forger. He had come home unchanged and unrepentant and ready to swindle and to cheat if he could do so without the customary penalties.

As for the other man, the pretended barrister, he stood revealed as one who was living under false pretences. He had an equal right to stand in pillory beside his brother. Once a prodigal and a spendthrift like him: now living a daily lie which he had carried on for five-and-twenty years. Good heavens! Christopher Campaigne, Barrister-at-Law of Lincoln's Inn, the successful Lawyer, on whom his family reposed a confidence so profound and a pride so unbounded — who does not take pride in a successful lawyer? — was nothing more than a common pretender and an impostor. He wrote speeches and sold them to humbugs who wished to be thought clever speakers. Honourable occupation! Delightful work! A proud and distinguished career!

So there was nobody left except himself to maintain the family honour.

Certain words which you have already heard came back again. It seemed to him as if Constance was saying them all over again: "You are independent as to fortune; you are of a good house; you have no scandals in your family records; you have got no poor or degraded relations ... you are outside humanity.... If you had some family scandals, some poor relations who would make you feel ashamed, something that made you like other people, vulnerable — —" Now he had them all.

The door was opened. His servant brought him a card: "Mr. Samuel Galley-Campaigne."

"Another!" Leonard groaned and sprang to his feet. "Another!" The sight or the thought of this man, the caricature of his own family, tall and thin, like himself, but with every feature vulgarized, and the meanness of petty gains, petty cares, petty scheming and self-seeking stamped upon his face, irritated Leonard unspeakably. And he was a cousin! He stiffened involuntarily. His attitude, his expression, became that of the "supercilious beast" formed by Mr. Galley on his previous business.

The cousin came in and bowed slightly, not holding out his hand. There was a look in his face which meant resolution held back by fear, the desire to "try on" something, and the doubt as to whether it would be successful. It is an expression which may be remarked on 'Change and in every market-town on market-day.

It has been wisely, perhaps frequently, remarked that trouble brings out a man's true character far more certainly than prosperity, which may encourage him to assume virtues not really his own. The lines about the uses of adversity must be referred to the bystander rather than the patient, because the former is then enabled to contemplate and observe the true man for the first time. Mr. Galley, for instance, who was smug in prosperity, was openly and undisguisedly vulgar in adversity. At this moment, for instance, he was struggling with adversity; it made him red in the face, it made him speak thick, it made him perspire inconveniently, and it made his attitude ungraceful.

He came up the stairs; he knocked at the door with an expression of fixed resolution. One might have expected him to bang his fist on the table and to cry out: "There! that's what I want, and that's what I mean to have." He did not quite do that, but he intended to do it when he called, and he would have done, I have no doubt, but for the cold, quiet air with which his cousin received him.

"Mr. Campaigne," he began, "or cousin, if you like——"

"Mr. Campaigne, perhaps," said Leonard the supercilious.

"Well, Mr. Campaigne, then, I've come to have a few words of explanation—explanation, sir!" he repeated, with some fierceness.

"By all means. Pray take a chair."

He took a chair, and was then seized by the doubt of which we have spoken. Perhaps the cause was the commanding position of his cousin, standing over him six foot three in height, and with a face like that of a Judge not personally interested in the case before him.

"The point is this: I've got a bill against your family, and I want to know whether I am to present it to you or to my great-grandfather?"

"A bill? Of what nature?"

"A bill for maintenance. We have maintained my grandmother for fifty years. She has been kept partly by my grandfather, partly by my family, and partly by myself, and it's time that your family should do their duty."

"That is a very remarkable claim."

"Putting it at £50 a year, which is cheap for the lavish way she's been kept, that makes £2,500. At compound interest it mounts up to £18,000 and odd. I shall be contented to square the claim for £18,000."

"You propose to send in a bill—a bill for keeping your own grandmother?"

"That is just what I am going to do."

"You must surely be aware that such a claim would not be entertained for a moment. No Court of Law would so much as look at it."

"I am aware of the fact. But this is not a claim of an ordinary kind; it is a claim that rests on equity—on equity, not on Law."

"What is the equitable side of the claim?"

"Well, it's this way: My grandfather, who failed for an enormous amount—which showed the position he occupied in the City—married my grandmother in the reasonable expectation that she would bring him a fortune. It is true that the old man was then not more than fifty or so, but he did not count so much on a will as on a settlement."

"I understand that the marriage was undertaken without consultation with my great-grandfather, or, under the circumstances, with his solicitors."

"That was, no doubt, the case; but when one marries into so wealthy a family, and when the head of it is not in a position to be consulted, the least that can be expected is a settlement—a settlement of some kind. My grandfather said that he expected nothing less than twenty thousand—twenty thousand. He dated his subsequent misfortunes to the failure of this expectation, because he got nothing. Perhaps, Mr. Campaigne, as you were not born then, you can hardly believe that he got nothing."

"I am in ignorance of the whole business."

"Quite so—quite so. I think, therefore, that I am quite justified in asking your people to pay me just the bare sum—out-of-pocket expenses—which we have expended upon my grandmother."

"Oh!"

The tone was not encouraging, but the other man was not versed in these external signs, and went on, unabashed:

"You saw yourself the other day the style in which we live, I believe, Mr. Campaigne; you will acknowledge that it was a noble Tea."

Leonard bowed solemnly.

"An account rendered, under any circumstances, for the maintenance of a grandmother, a mother, and a wife I should myself tear up and throw into the fire. But it is no concern of mine. You can send your claim to my great-grandfather——"

"My great-grandfather as much as yours."

"To his solicitors, whose name and address you probably know; if not, I will furnish you with them. If that is all you have to say——"

He moved towards the door.

"No, no. I mean this. We had a right to expect a fortune, and there has been none."

"You said that before. Again, Mr. Galley, I cannot discuss this matter with you. Take your claim to the right quarter."

"I'm not obliged to keep the old woman," he replied sulkily.

"I decline to discuss your views of duty."

"I want to wake up the old man to a sense of justice. I will, too. If he's mad we will find out. If he isn't, I will make him pay—even if I have to expose him."

Leonard stepped to the door and threw it open. Mr. Galley rose. His face betrayed many emotions. In fact, the conversation had not proceeded quite on the lines he hoped.

"Don't be in a hurry," he said. "Give me a little time."

Leonard closed the door and returned to the hearth-rug.

"Take time, Mr. Galley."

"I don't want," he said, "to behave ungentlemanly, but I'm in desperate trouble. If you think it's no good sending in a claim, I withdraw it. The fact is, Mr. Campaigne, I want money. I want money desperately."

Leonard made no reply. This was discouraging.

"I've been speculating—in house property—backing a builder; and the man is going. That is what has happened to me. If I can't raise a thousand pounds in the course of a day or two I must go too."

"You will not raise anything by sending in a bill for the maintenance of your grandmother. Put that out of your head, Mr. Galley."

He groaned.

"Then, will you lend me a thousand pounds, Mr. Campaigne? You were very friendly when you came to see us the other day. The security is first-class—the shells of three unfinished houses—and I will give you eight per cent. for the accommodation. Good security and good interest. There you are. Come, Mr. Campaigne: you are not a business man, and I don't think you can make, as a rule, more than three per cent. at the outside."

"I have no money either to lend or to advance."

"I have been to the bank, but they won't look at the business. It's a mean, creeping, miserable bank. I shall change it."

"Well, Mr. Galley, I am sorry to hear that you are in trouble, but I cannot help you."

"If I do go bankrupt," he said savagely, "the old woman will go into the workhouse. That's one consolation. And she's your great-aunt."

"You forget your sister, Mr. Galley. From what I know of Board Schools, I should say that she is quite able to maintain her grandmother. If not, there may be other assistance."

"There's another thing, then," he persisted. "When I spoke to you first, I mentioned the word 'accumulations.' "

"No one mentions any other word just now, I think," Leonard replied, with a touch of temper.

"They must be enormous. I've been working it out. Enormous! And that old man can't live much longer. He can't. He's ninety-five."

"Mr. Galley, I put it to you as a lawyer, or, at least, as a solicitor: Do you think that your great-grandfather has lived all these years without making a will?"

"He can't make a will. He is a madman."

"Ask his solicitors for an opinion on that subject. The old man will not speak, but he receives communications and gives instructions."

"I shall dispute the will if I'm not named in it. I shall expect a full share. I shall show that he's a madman."

"As you please. Meanwhile, it is doubtful whether the testator ever heard your name."

"He knows his daughter's name. And what's hers is mine."

"I must open the door again, Mr. Galley, if you talk nonsense. I hear, by the way, that you have made that lady sign certain papers. As a solicitor, you must know that such documents would be regarded by the Court with extreme suspicion."

"If I have to go bankrupt I shall let the whole world know that you wouldn't lift a finger to save your own cousin."

"As you please."

"And if there's a will that turns out me, I'll drag the whole thing into Court and expose you. I will expose you, by — —"

Leonard opened the door again.

"This time, Mr. Galley, you will go."

He obeyed. He dropped his hat on his head, he marched out, and he bawled on the stairs as he went down:

"I'll expose you—I'll expose you—I'll expose you!"

These terrifying and minatory words rang up and down the stairs of that respectable mansion like the voice of an Accusing Angel, so that everybody who heard them jumped and turned pale, and murmured:

"Oh, good Lord! What's come out now?"

CHAPTER XVIII

THE LIGHT THAT BROKE

IT was Sunday morning. Leonard sat before the fire doing nothing. He had done nothing for three weeks. He had no desire to do anything: his work lay neglected on the table, books and papers piled together. He was brooding over the general wreck of all he had held precious: over the family history; the family disgraces and disasters; and the mystery which it was hopeless to look into but impossible to forget.

The bells were ringing all around: the air was full of the melody, or the jingle of the bells of many Churches.

Then Constance knocked at his door. "May I come in?" she asked, and came in without waiting for an answer. "I was proposing to go to the Abbey," she said. "But things have got on my nerves. I felt that I could not sit still for the service. I must come and talk to you."

"I suppose that we know the very worst now," said Leonard. "Why do you worry yourself about my troubles, Constance?"

"Because we are cousins—because we are friends. Isn't that enough?"

She might have added, as another reason, that the events of the last three weeks had drawn them more closely together—so closely that it wanted but a word—if once their minds were free from the obsession of the mystery—to bind them so that they should never again drift asunder.

Leonard replied, with a wintry smile: "Without you to talk things over, Constance, I believe I should go mad."

"And I feel so guilty—so guilty—when I think of what I said so lightly about scandals and poor relations with all this hanging over your head."

"Nothing more, I should think"—he looked about the room, as if to make sure that no telegrams or letters were floating in the air—"can happen now—except to me. Everybody else is laid low. One cousin has brought me a bill for the maintenance of his grandmother for fifty years—says he will take eighteen thousand pounds down. One ought really to be proud of such a cousin."

"The solicitor of the Commercial Road, I suppose. But, really, what does it matter?"

"Nothing. Only at the moment there is a piling up; and every straw helps to break the camel's back. The man says he is going to be a bankrupt. My uncle Frederick—that large-souled, genial, thirsty, wealthy, prosperous representative of colonial enterprise—now turns out to be an impostor and a fraud——"

"Oh, Leonard!"

"An impostor and a fraud," he repeated. "He has a small general store in an Australian township, and he has come over to represent this as a big business and to make a Company out of it. The other uncle—the learned and successful lawyer——"

"Don't tell me, Leonard."

"Another time, then: we ought certainly to have heard the worst. Let us go to the village and bury the Family Honour before the altar in the Church, and put up a brass in memory of what our ancestors created."

"No. You will guard it still, Leonard. It could not be in better hands. You must not—you cannot, bury your own soul."

Leonard relapsed into silence. Constance stood over him sad and disheartened. Presently she spoke.

"How long?" she asked.

"How long?" he replied. "Who can say? It came of its own accord—it was uninvited. Perhaps it will go as it came."

"You would rather be left alone?" she asked. "Let me stay and talk a little. My friend, we must have done with it. After all, what does it matter to us how a crime was committed seventy years ago?"

"It concerns your own ancestor, Constance."

"Yes. He, poor man, was killed. Leonard, when I say 'poor man' the words exactly measure the amount of sorrow that I feel for him. An ancestor of four generations past is no more than a shadow. His fate awakens a little interest, but no sadness."

"I should say the same thing, I suppose. But my ancestor was not killed. He was condemned to a living death. Constance, it is no use; whether I will or no, the case haunts me day and night." He sprang to his feet, and threw up his arms as one who would throw off chains. "How long since I first heard of it through that unfortunate old lady of the Commercial Road? Three weeks? It seems like fifty years. As for any purpose that I had before, or any ambition—it is gone—quite gone and vanished."

"As for me, I am haunted in the same manner."

"I am like a man who is hypnotised—I am no longer a free agent. I am ordered to do this, and I do it. As for this accursed Book of Extracts"—he laid his hand upon the abomination—"I am forced to go through it over and over again. Every time I sit down I am prompted by a kind of assurance that something will be discovered. Every time I rise up, it is with disgust that nothing has occurred to me."

"Are we to go on all our lives looking for what we can never find?"

"We know the whole contents by heart. Yet every day there is the feeling that something will start into light. It is madness, Constance. I am going mad—like my grandfather, who killed himself. That will end the family tale of woes, so far as I am concerned."

"Send the book back to its owner."

He shook his head. "I know it all. That will be no use."

"Burn the dreadful thing."

"No use. I should be made to write it all out again."

"I dropped an envelope in your letter-box last night. Have you opened it?"

"I don't think I have read a single letter for the last three weeks."

"Then it must be among the pile. What a heap of letters! Oh, Leonard, you are indeed occupied with this business. I found last night three letters from Langley Holme to his wife. They were written from Campaigne Park; but on what occasion I do not know. I thought at first that I might have found something that would throw a little light upon the business. But of course, when one considers, how could he throw light upon his own tragic end?"

He took the packet carelessly. "Do the letters tell us anything?"

"Nothing important, I believe. They show that he was staying at the Park."

"We know that already. It is strange how we are continually mocked by the things we learn. It was the same with the letter from Australia."

"That was an interesting letter—so are these—even if they tell us nothing that we do not know already."

He opened the envelope, and took out the packet of letters. There were three: they were written on square letter paper: the folds had been worn away, and the letters were now dropping to pieces. The ink was faded as becomes ink of the nineteenth century. Leonard laid them on the table to read because they were in so ragged a condition. "The date," he said, "is difficult to make out, but the last letter looks like '6'—that would make it 1826. You say that there is nothing important in them."

"Nothing, so far as I could make out. But read them. You may find something."

The first letter was quite unimportant, containing only a few instructions and words of affection. The next two letters, however, spoke of the writer's brother-in-law:

"My little dispute with Algernon is still unsettled. He makes a personal matter of it, which is disagreeable. He really is the most obstinate and tenacious of mortals. I don't like to seem to be thinking or saying anything unkind about him. Indeed, he is a splendid fellow all round, only the most obstinate. But I shall not budge one inch. Last night in the library he entirely lost command of himself, and became like a madman for a few minutes. I had heard from others about the ungovernable side of his temper, but had never seen it before. He really becomes dangerous at such times. He raged and glared like a bull before a red rag. Since Philippa is happy, she has certainly never seen it."

In the third letter he spoke of the same dispute.

"We had another row last night. Row or no row, I am not going to budge one inch. We are going to discuss the matter again—quietly, he promises. I will write to you again and tell you what is settled. My dear child, I am ashamed to see this giant of a man so completely lose control of himself. However, I suppose he will give way when he sees that he must."

"There seems to have been a slight dispute," said Leonard. "His brother-in-law lost his temper and stormed a bit. But they made it up again. Well, Constance, that is all—a little quarrel made up again undoubtedly."

He replaced the letters in the envelope and returned them to Constance.

"Keep them," he said. "They are valuable to you as letters from your ancestor. Like the letter from Mr. John Dunning, which we received with amazement as a voice from the grave, they help us to realise the business—if one wanted any help. But we realised it before—quite vividly enough—and that," he sighed, "is all. We are no whit advanced. There were no more papers?"

"I searched the desk over and over again, but I could find nothing more. Now, Leonard." She took a chair and placed it beside his own at the table. "Leave the fire and take your chair, and we will begin and finish. This time must be the very last. It is high time that we should make an end of this. As for me, I came here this morning just to say that whatever happens I am determined that we must make an end. The thing is becoming dangerous to your peace of mind."

"We cannot make an end."

"Yes—yes—we are now persons bewitched. Let us swear that after this morning we will put away the book and the papers and cease from any further trouble about it."

"If we can," he replied gloomily.

"Leonard, for the first time in your life you are superstitious."

"We may swear what we like. We shall come back to the case again to-morrow."

"We will not. Let us resolve. Nay, Leonard, you must not continue. To you it is becoming dangerous."

Leonard sighed. "It is weary work. Well, then, for the last time." He laid the packet of papers upon the table. He opened the dreadful book—the Book of Fate. "It is always the same thing. Whenever I open the book there is the same sense of sickness and loathing. Are the pages poisoned?"

"They are, my friend."

He began the old round. That is to say, he read the case as they had drawn it up, while Constance compared it with the evidence.

" 'These are the facts of the inquest, of the trial, of the effects of the crime, the evidence of place, and the evidence of time:

" 'The two leave the house, they walk together through the Park; they cross the road, they get over the stile, they enter the wood. Then the Squire turns back——' "

"After some short time," Constance corrected. "According to the recollection of the ancient man who was the bird-scarer, he went into the wood."

" 'Then the Squire walked homewards rapidly. If the housekeeper gave the time correctly, and it took him the same time to get home as to reach the wood—I have timed the distance—he may have been ten minutes—a quarter of an hour in the wood.

" 'Two hours or so later, the boy saw a working man, whom he knew well by sight and name, enter the wood. He was dressed in a smock-frock, and carried certain tools or instruments over his shoulder. He remained in the wood a few minutes only, and then came running out, his white smock spotted with red, as the boy could see plainly from the hillside. He ran to the farmyard beyond the field, and returned with other men and a shutter. They entered the wood, and presently came out carrying "something" covered up. The boy was asked both at the inquest and the trial whether anyone else had entered the wood or had come out of it. He was certain that no one had done so, or could have done so without his knowledge.

" 'The men carried the body to the house. They were met on the terrace by the housekeeper, who seemed to have shrieked and run into the house, where she told the women-servants, who all together set up a shrieking through the house. Someone, after the mistress was thus terrified, blurted out the dreadful truth. In an hour the Squire had lost his wife as well as his brother-in-law.

" 'At the inquest, the Squire gave the principal evidence. He said that he walked with his brother-in-law as far as the wood, when he turned back.' "

"Not 'as far as the wood.' He said that on entering the wood he remembered an appointment, and turned back. Remembering the evidence of the boy and your timing of the distance, we must give him some little time in the wood."

"Very well—the longer the better, because it would show that there was nobody lurking there.

" 'Then John Dunning deposed to finding the body. It lay on its back; the fore-part of the head was shattered in a terrible manner; the unfortunate gentleman was quite dead. Beside the body lay a heavy branch broken off. It would seem to have been caught up and used as a cudgel. Blood was on the thicker end.

" 'A medical man gave evidence as to the fact of death. He reached the house at about one, and after attending the unfortunate lady, who was dying or dead, he turned his attention to the body of the victim, who had then been dead sometime, probably two hours or thereabouts. The valet deposed, further that the pockets were searched, and that nothing had been taken from them.

" 'The coroner summed up. The only person who had gone into the wood after the deceased gentleman was the man John Dunning. Who but John Dunning could have committed this foul murder? The verdict of the jury was delivered at once—"Wilful murder against John Dunning."

" 'We have next the trial of John Dunning. Mr. Campaigne was so fully persuaded in his own mind of the man's innocence that he provided him, at his own expense, with counsel. The counsel employed was clever. He heard the evidence, the same as that given at the inquest, but instead of letting it pass, he pulled it to pieces in cross-examination.

" 'Thus, on examining Mr. Campaigne, he elicited the very important fact that Mr. Holme was six feet high and strong in proportion, while the prisoner was no more than five feet six, and not remarkably strong; that it was impossible to suppose that the murdered man would stand still to receive a blow delivered in full face by so little a man. That was a very strong point to make.

" 'Then he examined the doctor as to the place in which the blow was received. It appeared that it was on the top of the head, behind the forehead, yet delivered face to face. He made the doctor acknowledge that in order to receive such a blow from a short man like the prisoner the murdered man must have been sitting or kneeling. Now, the wood was wet with recent rain, and there was nothing to sit upon. Therefore it required, said the doctor, a man taller than Mr. Holme himself to deliver such a blow.' "

Leonard stopped for a brief comment:

"It shows how one may pass over things. I passed over this point altogether at first, and, indeed, until the other day, perhaps, because the newspaper cutting is turned over at this place. The murderer, therefore, was taller than Langley Holme, who was himself six feet high. The point should have afforded a clue. At all events, it effectively cleared the prisoner."

" 'It appears that the crime created the greatest interest in the neighbourhood. There were kept up for a long time after the acquittal of John Dunning, discussions and arguments, for and against, as to his guilt or innocence. No one else was arrested and no one tried, and the police left off looking after the case. Indeed, there was nothing more than what I have set down in these notes.

" 'The friends of Mr. Campaigne, however, speedily discovered that he was entirely changed in consequence of the double shock of the deaths of brother and sister, brother-in-law and wife, in one day. He ceased to take interest in anything; he refused to see his friends; he would not even notice his children; he gradually retreated entirely into himself; he left his business affairs to an agent; he dismissed his servants. He sent his children to the care of a distant cousin to get them out of the way; he never left the house at all except to walk on the terrace; he kept neither horses nor dogs; he never spoke to anyone; he had never been known to speak for all these years except once, and then two or three words to me."

"The following," he went on, "is also a part of the case:

" 'We have been a very unfortunate family. Of Mr. Campaigne's three children, the eldest committed suicide for no reason discoverable, the next was drowned at sea, the third married a bankrupt tradesman, and dropped very low down in the world. Of the next generation, the eldest, my father, died at an early age and at a time when his prospects were as bright as those of any young member of the House; his second brother has just confessed that he has led a life of pretence and deception; and his younger brother, who was sent abroad for his profligacy, told me yesterday that he is about to become bankrupt, while another member of the family is threatened with ruin, and, to judge from his terror, with worse than ruin.' "

"There are still two or three facts that you have omitted," said Constance. "We had better have them all."

"What are they?"

"You have not mentioned that the boy went into the wood early in the morning and found no one; that the woman in the cottage — this was the voice of the grave that we asked for and obtained — said that nobody at all had been through the wood that day until the gentlemen appeared."

"We will consider everything. But remember, Constance, we are sworn not to go through this ceremony again whatever the force that draws us."

"We have forgotten; there is the half-finished letter that we found upon the table. Read that again, Leonard."

It was in one envelope among the papers. Leonard took it out.

"There is nothing in it that we do not know. Langley was staying in the house."

"Never mind; read it."

He read it:

" 'Algernon and Langley have gone into the study to talk business. It is this affair of the Mill that is still unsettled. I am a little anxious about Algernon; he has been strangely distrait for the last two or three days. Perhaps he is anxious about me. There need be no anxiety; I am quite well and strong. This morning he got up very early, and I heard him walking about in the study below. This is not his way at all. However, should a wife repine because her Lord is anxious about her? Algernon is very determined about that Mill, but I fear that Langley will not give way. You know how firm he can be behind that pleasant smile of his.'

"Nothing much in that letter, Constance, is there?"

"I don't know. It is the voice of the dead. So are these letters of Langley's to his wife. They speak of a subject of disagreement: neither would give way. Mr. Campaigne was at times overcome with anger uncontrolled. Leonard, it is wonderful how much we have learned since we first began this inquiry—I mean, this new evidence of the quarrel and Mr. Campaigne's ungovernable temper and his strange outburst in the evening. Oh! it is new evidence"—her face changed: she looked like one who sees a light suddenly shine in the darkness—a bright and unexpected light. "It is new evidence," she repeated with wondering, dazzled eyes. "It explains, everything"—she stopped and turned white.

"Oh!"

She shrank back as if she felt a sudden pain at her heart: she put up her hands as if to push back some terrible creature. She sprang to her feet. She trembled and shook: she clasped her forehead—the gesture was natural to the face of terror and amazement and sudden understanding.

Leonard caught her in his arms, but she did not fall. She laid her hand upon his shoulder, and she bowed her head.

"Oh, God, help us!" she murmured.

"What is it? Constance, what is it?"

"Leonard, no one—no one—no one was in the wood but only those two—and they quarrelled, and the Squire was taller than his brother—

and we have found the truth. Leonard, my poor friend—my cousin—we have found the truth."

She drew herself away from him, and sank back into her chair, hiding her face in her hands.

Leonard dropped the papers.

"Constance!" he cried. For in a moment the truth flashed across his brain—the truth that explained everything—the despair of the wretched man, the resolve to save an innocent man, a remorse that left him not by day or night, so that he could do nothing, think of nothing, for all the long, long years that followed; a remorse which forbade him to hold converse with his fellow-man, which robbed him of every pleasure and every solace, even the solace of his little children. "Constance!" he cried again, holding out his hands as if for help.

She lifted her head but not her eyes; she took both his hands in hers.

"My friend," she whispered, "have courage."

So for a brief space they remained, he standing before her, she sitting, but holding both his hands, with weeping eyes.

"I said," he murmured, "that nothing more would happen. There wanted only the last—the fatal blow."

"We were constrained to go on until the truth came to us. It has come to us. After all these years—from the memory of the old man who scared the birds: from the innocent man who was tried—he spoke from the grave: from the murdered man himself. Leonard, this thing should be marvellous in our eyes, for this is not man's handiwork."

He drew away his hands.

"No. It is Vengeance for the spilling of blood." She made no reply, but she rose, dashed the tears from her eyes, placed the papers in the book, closed it, tied it up again neatly with tape, and laid the parcel in the lowest drawer of the table.

"Let it lie there," she said. "To-morrow, if this Possession is past, as I think it will be, we will burn it, papers and all."

He looked on, saying nothing. What could he say?

"What are we to do with our knowledge?" he asked after a few minutes.

"Nothing. It is between you and me. Nothing. Let us nevermore speak of the thing. It is between you and me."

The unaccustomed tears blinded her eyes. Her eyes were filled with a real womanly pity. The student of books was gone, the woman of Nature stood in her place; and, woman-like, she wept over the shame and horror of the man.

"Leave me, Constance," he said. "There is blood between us. My hands and those of all my house are red with blood—the blood of your own people."

She obeyed. She turned away; she came back again.

"Leonard," she said, "the past is past. Courage! We have learned the truth before that unhappy man dies. It is a sign. The day of Forgiveness draws nigh."

Then she left him softly.

CHAPTER XIX

THE SIGNS OF CHANGE

LEONARD was left alone. He threw himself into a chair and tried to think. He could not. The power of concentration had left him. The tension of the last three weeks, followed by the wholly unexpected nature of the discovery, was too much for a brain even so young and strong as his. The horror of the discovery was not even felt: he tried to realise it: he knew that it ought to be there: but it was not: all he felt was an overwhelming sense of relief. He fell asleep in the chair before the fire. It was then about noon on Sunday. From time to time his man looked in, made up the fire, for the spring day was still chilly, but would not awaken his master. It was past seven in the evening when he woke up. Twilight was lying about the room. He remembered that Constance had laid the papers in a drawer. He opened the drawer. He took out the papers and the book. He held them in his hand. For the first time since his possession of those documents he felt no loathing of the book and its accursed pages: nor did he feel the least desire to open it or to read any more about the abominable case. He returned the packet to the drawer. Then he perceived that he was again down-laden with the oppression of sleep. He went into his bedroom and threw himself dressed as he was upon the bed, when he instantly fell sound asleep.

He was neither hungry nor thirsty: he wanted no food: he wanted nothing but sleep: he slept the clock round, and more. It was ten on Monday morning when he woke up refreshed by his long and dreamless sleep, and in a normal condition of hunger.

More than this, although the discovery—the tragic discovery—was fresh in his mind, he found himself once more free to think of anything he pleased.

He dressed, expecting the customary summons to the Book and the Case. None came. He took breakfast and opened the paper. For three weeks he had been unable to read the paper at all. Now, to his surprise, he approached it with all his customary interest. Nothing was suggested to his mind as to the book. He went into the study, he again opened the drawer; he was not afraid, though no compulsion obliged him, to take out the book: since he was not constrained, as before, to open it, he put it back again. He remarked that the loathing with which he had regarded it only the day before was gone. In fact, he heeded the book no longer: it was like the dead body of a demon which could do no more harm.

He turned to the papers on his writing-table; there were the unfinished sheets of his article lying piled up with notes and papers in neglect. He took them up with a new-born delight and the anticipation of the pleasure of finishing the thing; he wondered how he had been able to suspend his work for so long. There was a pile letters, the unopened, unanswered letters of the last three weeks; he hurriedly tore them open: some of them, at least, must be answered without delay.

All this time he was not forgetful of the Discovery. That was now made: it was complete. Strange! It did not look so horrible after four-and-twenty hours. It seemed as if the discovery was the long-looked for answer to the mystery which explained everything.

He sat down, his mind clear once more, and tried to make out the steps by which the truth had been recovered. To give his thoughts words, "We started with two assumptions, both of which were false; and both made it impossible to find the truth. The first of these was the assumption that the two were fast and firm friends, whereas they were for the moment at variance on some serious affair—so much at variance that on one occasion at least before the last, one of them had become like a madman in his rage. The second was the assumption that the Squire had turned and gone home at the entrance of the wood. Both at the inquest and the trial that had been taken for granted. Now, the boy had simply said that they went into the wood together, and that one had come out alone.

"In consequence of these two assumptions, we were bound to find some one in the wood who must have done the deed. The boy declared that no one was in the wood at half-past five in the morning, and that he saw no one but these two go in till John Dunning went in at noon. The cottage woman said that no one at all had used that path that day. The coppice was so light that the two who went in must have seen anybody who was lurking there. If we remove the two assumptions—if we suppose that they entered the wood quarrelling—if we remember that the evening before one of them had become like a madman for rage—if we give them ten minutes or a quarter of an hour together—if we remember the superior height of one, which alone enabled the blow to fall on the top of the other's head—if we add to all this the subsequent behavior of the survivor, there can no longer be the least room for doubt. The murderer was Algernon Campaigne, Justice of the Peace, Master of Campaigne Park."

All this he reasoned out coldly and clearly. That he could once more reason on any subject at all gave him so much relief that the blow and shame of the discovery were greatly lessened. He remembered, besides, that the event happened seventy years before; that there could be no further inquiry; that the secret belonged to himself and to Constance; and that there was no need to speak of it to any other members of his family.

By this time, what was left of the family honour? He laughed bitterly as he reflected on the blots upon that once fair white scutcheon. Suicide—bankruptcy—the mud and mire of dire poverty—forgery—shame and pretence, and at last the culminating crime beyond which one can hardly go—the last crime which was also the first—the slaying of a man by his brother—MURDER!

A knock at the door roused him. Was it more trouble? He sat up instinctively to meet it. But he was quite calm. He did not expect trouble. When it comes, one generally feels it beforehand. Now he felt no kind of anticipation. It was, in fact, only a note from Constance:

"I write to tell you that the misfortunes of your House are over. There will be no more. I am certain of what I say. Do not ask me how I learned this, because you would not believe. We have been led—and this you will not believe—by the hand of the man who was killed, and none other—to the Discovery which ends it all.

"CONSTANCE."

"The Discovery," he thought, "which is worse than all the rest put together. No more misfortunes? No more consequences, then. What does she mean? Consequences must go on."

You remember how, one day, there came to a certain Patriarch one who told of trouble, and almost before he had finished speaking there came also another with more trouble, and yet a third with more. You remember also how to this man there came, one after the other, messengers who brought confession of fraud and disgrace.

This afternoon the opposite happened. There came three; but there were not messengers of trouble, but of peace, and even joy.

The first was his cousin Mary Anne.

"I've come," she said, "with a message from my brother. Sam is very sorry that he carried on here as he says he did. I don't know how he carried on, but Sam is very nasty sometimes, when his temper and his troubles get the better of him."

"Pray do not let him be troubled. I have quite forgotten what he said."

"It seems that he brought his precious bill against granny, and showed it to you. He says that he's put it in the fire, and that he didn't mean it, except in the hope that you'd lend him a little money."

"I see. Well, my cousin, is that all?"

"Oh, he begs your pardon humbly. And he says that the builder has got the Bank to back him after all: and he'll be contented to wait now for his share of the accumulations."

"I am sorry that he still entertains hopes in that direction."

"Oh! he thinks about nothing else. He has got the whole amount worked out: he knows how much there will be. If it is left to you or to anybody else he will dispute the will. He'll carry it up to the Lords, he says."

"Very good. We may wait until the will is produced. Meantime, Mary Anne, there is a little point which he seems to forget. It his grandmother and not himself who could have a right to dispute the will. Can he be so poor in law as not to know that?"

"He makes granny sign papers. I don't know how many she has signed. He is always thinking about some other danger to be met, and then he draws up a paper and makes her sign it with me as witness. Granny never asks what the paper means."

"Signing documents is dangerous. You must not allow it, my cousin. If there is anything coming to your branch of the family from Campaigne Park, you are as much concerned as Sam."

She laughed. "You don't know Sam. He means to have it all. He says that he's arranged to have it all."

"Let us talk about something else. Is your grandmother content to go on living as she does now?"

"No. But she has always been so unhappy that a few years more of Sam's bad temper and selfishness don't seem to matter. I came here this morning partly to tell you that I've arranged it at last. I had it out with Sam yesterday. I told him that he could go on living with mother, and I would take granny—she's so vexed, you can't think—that Sam should have gone and made out a bill for her keep and presented to you—that I was able to persuade her. Granny will live with me—I can afford it—and mother will go on with Sam. And I do hope, Mr. Campaigne, that you will come and see her sometimes. She says, have you read the book?"

"Yes. I will go to see her sometimes. Tell her so. And as for the book, I have read it all through."

"And did it do you good to read the book? To me it always makes that old gentleman so grand and good—finding lawyers for the poor innocent man and all."

"Tell her the book has produced all the effect she desired and more."

While she was still speaking, Uncle Fred burst in. Mary Anne retired, making way for the visitor, who, she perceived, from the family likeness, was a large and very magnificent specimen of the Campaigne family.

He burst in. He came in like an earthquake, making the furniture crack, and the glasses rattle, and the picture-frames shake. He showed the most jovial, happy, benevolent air possible. No one could look happier, more benevolent, and more contented with himself.

"Congratulate me, my dear boy!" he cried, offering the most friendly hand in the world. There was a fine and large forgiveness in that extended hand. The last conversation was forgotten and dismissed from memory. "Barlow Brothers is saved!"

"Oh! how have you saved it?"

"I will tell you how. It has been a most wonderful stroke of luck for Australian enterprise. Nothing short of a national disaster has been averted."

"Indeed! I gathered from your last communication that the business was—well, not worth saving."

"Not worth saving? My dear Leonard! it is colossal—colossal!"

Leonard is still mystified, whenever he thinks of it, by this abrupt change of front. What did he mean?

"I am immediately going back to Australia to put things on a right footing."

"Oh! You have made a Company in the City after all!"

"No," he replied with decision. "The City has had its chance and has refused its opportunity. I leave the City to lament its own shortsighted refusal. I am sorry for the City. I now return to Australia. The firm of Barlow Brothers may rise conspicuous and colossal, or it may continue to be a purveyor of sardines and blacking, or it may go smash."

At this point his eye fell upon a letter. It was one of the documents in the Case; in fact, it was the letter from Australia which came with John Dunning's memorandum. By accident it had not been put away with the rest. He read the superscription on the seal: "John Dunning's Sons."

"John Dunning's Sons?" he asked. "John Dunning's Sons?"

"It's an old story. Your grandfather helped John Dunning in early life." Leonard took out the letter. "His family write to express the gratitude—a post-mortem gratitude—of the late John Dunning to the family generally. Would you like to read it?"

Uncle Fred read it. His jovial face became grave—even austere in thoughtfulness. He folded the letter and put it in his pocket.

"By your leave," he said. "My dear boy, the Dunnings are the richest people in the colony. I am a made man. Their gratitude simply warms my heart. It inspires once more the old youthful belief in human nature. With this letter—with this introduction—Barlow Brothers vanish. Damn the sardine boxes! Fred Campaigne returns to Australia, and Fortune smiles. My boy, farewell. With this letter in my pocket, I start to-morrow."

"Stop, stop!" cried Leonard. "How about the colossal business? How about the saving of that important shanty where you dispensed sardines?"

Uncle Fred looked at his watch.

"But you say that you have saved it—how?"

"I have just time"—again he looked at his watch—"to keep—ah! a most important appointment. I shall go out to Australia next week. On the way out I will amuse myself by writing you an account of the Barlow Brothers—in several chapters—The Conception, The First Box of Sardines, The Shanty, the Realisation, the Millionaire. Novels would not be more thrilling."

"But you abandon this Colossal undertaking?"

"I give it up. Why? Because an easier way lies open. I should be more than human if I did not take the easier way."

"You are going out to Mr. Dunning with that letter in your pocket?"

"I am, going, sir, to throw myself into the arms of gratitude. Human Nature! Human Nature! How lovely a thing is Human Nature when it is grateful!"

Leonard grunted.

"I am not sure," he said, "that I did right in giving you that letter."

"You can have it back again. I know the contents. And now, my dear nephew, there is but one small duty to perform—I allude to the Hotel Bill. My brother has found the passage-money—Christopher was always a selfish beast, but his language at parting with that money was inexcusable. He refuses the Hotel Bill."

"And so you come to me. Why should I pay your Hotel Bill?"

"There is no reason that I know of except the fact that I have referred the Hotel Clerk to you as a Member of Parliament and a gentleman."

"You come home boasting of your wealth, being next door to penniless."

"You forget—the Accumulations——"

"And you end with the confession that you were lying."

"You mean putting the best foot forward—presenting myself in the enviable light of the successful uncle—the modern Nabob."

"And you levy money on your people?"

"I borrow on my reversionary interests—in the Accumulations."

"I will pay your bill on the understanding that you take yourself off. How much is it?"

Uncle Fred named the amount. It was a staggerer.

"Good Heavens! Man, you must have bathed in champagne."

"There has been champagne," Fred replied with dignity. "I had to support my position. City men lunched with me and dined with me. We discussed the Fourth Act in the Comedy of Barlow Brothers—the Realisation. As for the Bill, I borrow the amount."

Leonard sat down and wrote a cheque. Uncle Fred took it, read it, folded it, and sighed with a tear of regret that he had not named double the amount.

"Thanks," he said. "The act was ungraciously performed. But the main thing is to get the cheque. That I have always felt, even when I got it out of old Sixty per Cent. Well, I go back to a land which has been hitherto inhospitable. Farewell, my nephew. I shall bask: I shall batten, whatever that means: I shall fatten: I shall swell out with fatness in the sunshine—the Sydney sunshine is very fattening—of gratitude, and the generosity of a Sydney millionaire."

He buttoned his coat, and went away with loud and resounding footsteps, as he had come, the furniture cracking, the picture-frames rattling. So far, Leonard has not received the promised explanation of the Mystery of Barlow Brothers; nor has that check been returned.

There remained one more credit to the Family. It was Christopher, the eminent and learned counsel.

He, too, called half an hour after the departure of his brother.

"I came," he said, "first of all to warn you against giving or lending any more money to that fraud—my brother Fred."

"You are too late, then. I have paid his hotel bill. You have paid his passage out——"

"No, I paid his hotel bill; you paid his passage out."

"Oh, well! so long as he goes——"

"I paid his hotel bill because he threatened to go into the City and expose my real name."

"Go into the City? What could he do in the City? Whom does he know in the City? Your brother is just a mass of lies and impostures. What does it matter if he is really going?"

"He must go. Nobody except you and me will lend or give him any money. He goes as he came—the wealthy Australian. He has promised my people to make them rich by his will: he hinted at an incurable disorder: and he bade farewell for ever—with my cheque in his pocket!"

"Let him go. You had something else to say?"

"Yes. It was about my own affairs. They know all, Leonard."

"They know all? Who told them?"

"I've had a terrible time with the wife and daughter. But they know all. That vindictive little Beast called at the house, went upstairs, and told them everything. Then he went away grinning. There was a terrible scene."

"So I should suppose."

"Yes. It's all right, though, at last. I persuaded them, with a good deal of trouble, that the profession was rather more holy than the Church. I set forth the facts—the honour and glory—the secret diffusion and cultivation of a better taste—higher standards—a Mission—nobler æsthetics—and the income—especially the income."

"That would be a serious factor in the case."

"Yes. And I pointed out the educational side—the advance of oratory. So they came round, little by little. And I clinched the thing by offering to go back to the Bar; in which case, I told them, we should have to live at Shepherd's Bush, in a £40 a year semi-detached, while Algernon went into the City as a clerk at fifteen shillings a week, which is more than his true value."

"Well, since it did well I congratulate you. The profession will be continued, of course?"

"Of course. But I confess I was surprised at the common-sense of Algernon. He will immediately enter at the Bar: he will join me; there will henceforth be two successful lawyers in the family instead of one."

"And what about the threatened exposure?"

"Algernon has gone to see the BEAST. He is to promise him that if a word or a hint is dropped, everybody shall know where he—the BEAST—buys his stories, and his poems, and his epigrams, as well as his after-dinner speeches. Algernon has fished it all out. Why, sir, the man is a Fraud—a common Fraud! He buys everything!"

So with this tribute to truth and honesty the weaver of speeches for other people went away. Only the day before Leonard would have received this communication with disgust as another humiliation. The way of deception—the life of pretence—was kept open. It would have been a tearing down of more family pride. Now it was nothing. The pretence of it, the ready way in which his cousin Algernon had dropped into it, belonged to someone else—not to himself. The family honour—such as he had always regarded it and believed in it—was gone—smashed and broken up into fragments. The House of the Campaignes, like every other family, had its decaying branches; its dead branches; its off-shoots and humble branches; its branches of dishonour.

There is no such thing existing as a family where men have been always Bayards and its women always beyond reproach. Upon him had fallen the blow of finding out the things concealed: the blot on the scutcheon, the ugly stories of the past: the poor relations and the unworthy relations. The discovery humiliated him at the outset: it became rapidly a thing apart from himself and outside himself. Uncle Fred might be an impostor and fraud. Very good. It mattered nothing to him. Uncle Christopher was a pretender and a humbug—what did it matter? The East-End solicitor was a person with no pretence at honour and honesty—what did it matter? They belonged to him by blood relationship; yet he was still—himself.

Only one thing remained. And now even the horror of that was more tolerable than the humiliation of the first revelations. It was the terrible story of the crime and the seventy years of expiation in which there had been no expiation, because nothing can ever atone for a crime or make it as if it had not been.

Men pray for forgiveness—"neither reward us after our iniquities."

There should be another and a less selfish prayer that all shall be in the world as if the iniquity had never been committed: that the consequences of the iniquity shall be stayed, miraculously stayed—because, but for a miracle, they must take their course according to the great law of Nature, that nothing can happen save under conditions imposed by the record of the past. The dream of the sinner is that he shall be forgiven and shall go straight to the land of white clothing and hearts at peace for ever, while down below the children and the grandchildren are in the misery of the consequences—the inevitable consequences of his follies and his crimes. So every soul stands or falls by itself, yet in its standing or in its falling it supports or it drags down the children and the grandchildren.

These thoughts, and other thoughts like unto these, crowded into the brain of the young man when he sat alone—the *dossier* of the crime locked up in the drawer—the disgraces of his cousins pushed aside—and the crime which caused so much little more than a memory and an abiding pity. Everything had come to Leonard which Constance, not knowing what the words might mean, desired for him. How great the change it made in him, as yet he hardly suspected.

CHAPTER XX

HE SPEAKS AT LAST

WAS it really the last day of Visitation? Punishment or Consequence, would there be no more?

Punishment or Consequence, it matters little which. One thing more happened on this eventful day. It came in a telegram from the ancestral housekeeper.

"Please come down as soon as you can. There is a change."

A change! When a man is ninety-five what change do his friends expect? Leonard carried the telegram to Constance.

"I think," he said, "it must be the end."

"It is assuredly the end. You will go at once—to-day. Let me go with you, Leonard."

"You? But it would only distress you."

"It will not distress me if I can take him, before he dies, a simple message."

"You sent me a message. How did you know that it was a message?"

"I knew it was a message, because I saw it with my mind's eye written clear and bright, and because I heard it plain and unmistakable. It came to me in the night. I thought it was a dream. Now I think it was a message."

"You said that all the misfortunes were over. Like your message, it was a dream. Yet now we get this telegram."

"Why—do you call this a misfortune? What better can we desire for that poor old man but the end?"

They started at once; they caught a train which landed them at the nearest station a little before seven. It was an evening in early spring. The sun was sinking, the cloudless sky was full of peace and light, the air was as soft as it was fragrant; there was no rustle of branches, even the birds were hushed.

"It is the end," said Constance softly, "and it is peace."

They had not spoken since they started together for the station. When one knows the mind of his companion, what need for words?

Presently they turned from the road into the park. It was opposite the stile over which, seventy years ago, one man had passed on his way to death, and another, less fortunate, on his way to destruction.

"Let us sit down in this place," said Leonard. "Before we go on I have something to say—I should like to say it before we are face to face with that most unhappy of men."

Constance obeyed and sat down upon the stile.

"When we came here before," he began, with a serious voice and grave eyes, "I was fresh from the shame and the discovery of the family misfortunes. And we talked of the sins of the fathers, and the eating of sour grapes, and the consolation of the Prophet——"

"I remember every word."

"Very well. I think you will understand me, Constance, when I say that I am rejoiced that I made the discovery of this fatal family history with all that it entailed—the train of evils and shames—yes, even though it has led to these weeks of a kind of obsession or possession, during which I have been unable to think of anything else."

"What do you think now? Are the sins of the fathers visited upon the children, or was the Prophet right?"

"I see, with you, that it is impossible to avoid the consequences of the father's life and actions. The words 'Third or Fourth Generation' must not be taken literally. They mean that from father to son there is a continual chain of events linked together and inseparable, and always moulding and causing the events which follow, and this though we know not the past and cannot see the connecting links that form the chain. In a higher stage humanity will refrain from some things and will be attracted by other things entirely through the consideration of their effect upon those who follow after. It will be a punishment self-imposed by those who fall that they must, in pity and in mercy, have no children to inherit their shame."

"You put my own thoughts into words. But about the children I am not so sure; their very shames may be made a ladder such as Augustine made his sins."

"There is nothing so true as the inheritance of consequences, except that one does not inherit the guilt. Even with the guilt there is sometimes the tendency to certain lines of action. 'Nothing so hereditary as the drink craving,' says the physician. So I suppose there may be a hereditary tendency in other directions. Some men—I have known some—cannot sit down to steady work; they must lie about in the sun; they must loaf; they have a *vitium*, an incurable disease, as incurable as a humpback, of indolence, mind and body. Some seem unable to remain honest—we all know examples of such men; some cannot possibly tell the truth. What I mean"—Leonard went on, clearing his own mind by putting his wandering thoughts into argumentative array—"is that the liability to temptation—the tendency—is inherited, but the necessity which forces a man to act is not inherited; that is due to himself. What says the Prophet again? 'As I live, saith the Lord God'—saith the Lord God. It is magnificent; it is terrible in its depth of earnestness. He declares an inspiration; through him the Lord strengthens His own word—veritably strengthens His own word—by an oath, 'As I live, saith the Lord God.' Can you imagine anything stronger, more audacious, but for the eternal Verity that follows?"

The speaker's voice trembled; his cheek, touched by the setting sun, glowed; the light of the western sky filled his eyes. Constance, woman-like, trembled at the sight of the man who stood revealed to her—the new man—transformed by the experience of shames and sorrows.

"As the soul of the father, so also the soul of the son is Mine; but if a man doeth that which is lawful and right, he shall surely live, saith the Lord God."

" 'Saith the Lord God!' " Leonard repeated. "What must have been the faith of a man who could so attribute his words? How to sound the depths of his faith and his insight?"

"He verily believed that he heard the voice of the Lord."

"We live for and by each other," Leonard returned. "We think that we stand by ourselves, and we are lifted up by the work of our forefathers; we talk as if we lived alone, and we are but links in the chain; we are formed and we form; we are forged and we forge. I have been like unto one who stands in a crowd and is moved here and there, but believes all the time that he is alone on a hill-top." He was silent for awhile. Presently he went on. "All that has followed the crime," he said, "has been in the nature of consequence. The man who committed the act retired from the world; he deserted the world; he gave up his duties; he resigned his children to others. One of them went to sea; he was drowned; others were drowned with him—that was but a consequence. His daughter, neglected and ill educated, ran away with a vulgar adventurer whom she took for a gallant gentleman—that was a consequence. His son found out the dreadful truth and committed suicide; his boys had no father; two of them fell into evil ways—that was a consequence. My own father died young, but not so young as to leave me a mere infant—that was a misfortune, but not a consequence. In other words, Constance, the sins of that old man have been visited upon the children, but the soul of the son has been as the soul of the father. That is the sum and substance of the whole. The consequences are still with us. That poor lady in the Commercial Road is still in the purgatory of poverty which she brought upon herself. Her son is, and will continue, what he is. Her daughter rises above her surroundings. 'She shall surely live, saith the Lord God.' My two uncles will go on to the end in their own way, and so, I suppose, shall I myself."

He stopped; the light went out of his eyes. He was once more outwardly his former self.

"That is all, Leonard?"

"That is all. I want you to understand that at the end—if this is the end—I desire to feel towards that old man no thought or feeling of reproach, only of pity for the fatal act of a moment and the long punishment of seventy years—and you, whose ancestor he smote——"

"Only with forgiveness in the name of that ancestor and of pity akin to yours and equal to yours. Come, Leonard: perhaps the end has come already."

The Fourth Generation

They entered the Park by the broken gate and the ruined Lodge.

"I have been looking for some such call," said Constance. "This morning I sent you that message. I knew it was a true message, because there fell upon me, quite suddenly, a deep calm. All my anxieties vanished. We have been so torn"—she spoke as if the House was hers as well—"by troubles and forebodings, with such woes and rumours of woes, that when they vanished suddenly and unexpectedly I knew that the time was over."

"You are a witch, Constance."

"Many women are when they are interested. Oh, Leonard! what a happiness that there is always an end of everything—of sorrow, nay, of joy! There must come—at last—the end, even of Punishment or of Consequence." She looked up and round. "The evening is so peaceful—look at the glories of the west—it is so peaceful that one cannot believe in storm and hail and frost. It seems to mean, for us, relief—and for him—forgiveness."

Everything was, indeed, still—there was no sound even of their own footsteps as they walked across the springy turf of the park, and the house when they came within view of it was bathed in the colours of the west, every window flaming with the joy of life instead of the despair of death. Yet within was a dying man.

"Death is coming," said Constance, "with pardon upon his wings."

The news that there was a "change"—word meaning much—at the Hall had reached the village. The pride of the people, because no other village in England entertained a recluse who lived by himself in a great house and allowed everything to fall into decay, was to be taken from them. No more would strangers flock over on Sunday mornings from the nearest town and the villages round, to look over the wall at the tall stalwart figure pacing his terrace in all weathers with the regularity of a pendulum. In the village house of call the men assembled early to hear and tell and whisper what they had heard.

Then the old story was revived—the story which had almost gone out of men's memories—how the poor gentleman, then young, still under thirty, with a fine high temper of his own—it was odd how the fine high temper had got itself remembered—lost in a single day his wife and his brother-in-law, and never held up his head again, nor went out of the house, nor took notice of man, woman, or child, nor took a gun in his hand, nor called his dogs, nor rode to hounds, nor went to church.

These reminiscences had been told a thousand times in the dingy little room of the village public-house. They reeked, like the room, of beer and tobacco and wet garments. For seventy years they had been told in the same words. They had been, so far, that most interesting form of imaginative work—the story without an end. Now the end had arrived, and there would be no more to tell.

The story was finished. Then the door opened, and the ci-devant scarer of birds appeared. He limped inside, he closed the door carefully; he looked around the room. He supported himself bravely with his two sticks, and he began to speak.

"We're all friends here? All friends? There's nobody here as will carry things to that young man? No."

"Take half a pint, Thomas."

"By your leave. Presently. I shall lend a hand to-morrow or next day to digging a grave. We must all come to it. Why not, therefore?"

He looked important, and evidently had something more to say, if he could find a way to say it.

"We're all thinking of the same thing," he began. "It's the old Squire who will soon be lyin' dead, how he never went out of the place for seventy long years—as long as I can remember. Why? Because there was a man murdered and a woman died. Who was the man murdered? The Squire's brother-in-law. Who murdered him? John Dunning, they said. John Dunning, he was tried and he got off and he went away. Who murdered that man? John Dunning didn't. Why? Because John Dunning didn't go to the wood for two hours afterwards. Who murdered that man, I say?"

At this point he accepted the hospitality of the proffered glass of beer.

"I know who done it. I always have known. Nobody knows but me. I've known for all these years; and I've never told. For why? He would ha' killed me, too. For certain sure he would ha' killed me. Who was it, then? I'll tell you. It was the man that lies a-dyin' over there. It was the Squire himself—that's who it was. No one else was in the wood all the morning but the Squire and the other gentleman. I say, the Squire done it; the Squire and nobody else. The Squire done it. The Squire done it."

The men looked at each other in amazement. Then the blacksmith rose, and he said solemnly:

"Thomas, you're close on eighty years of age. You've gone silly in your old age. You and your Squire! I remember what my father said, 'The Squire, he left Mr. Holme at the wood and turned back.' That was the evidence at the Inquest and the Trial. You and your Squire! Go home, Thomas, and go to bed and get your memory back again."

Thomas looked round the room again. The faces of all were hard and unsympathetic. He turned and hobbled out. The days that followed were few and evil, for he could speak about nothing else, and no one heeded his garrulous utterances. Assuredly, if there had been a lunatic asylum in the village he would have been enclosed there. A fatal example of the mischief of withholding evidence! Now, had this boy made it clear at the inquest that the two gentlemen were together in the wood for ten minutes or a quarter of an hour, one knows not what might have followed.

Thomas did not go home. He turned his steps in the direction of the Hall, and he hobbled along with a purpose in his face. His revelation had been received with scorn and derision. Perhaps in another place it would be received with more respect.

The housekeeper met Leonard and Constance at the open door. It had stood open all day, as if for the admission of the guest whose wings were hovering very near.

"He's in the library," said the woman, with the corner of her apron brushing away the tears with which women-servants always meet the approach of Azrael. "I wanted him to go upstairs and to bed, but he takes no notice. He's been in the library nearly all day."

"Did he go out this morning after breakfast?"

"He took his breakfast as usual, and he went out afterwards as usual, walking as upright as a post, and looking as strong and as hard as ever. After a bit he stopped and shook all over. Then he turned round and went indoors. He went into the library, and he sat down before the fire."

"Did he speak?"

"Never a word. I offered him a glass of wine, but he only shook his head. At one o'clock I took him his dinner, but he could eat nothing. Presently he drank a glass of wine. At four o'clock I took him his tea, but he wouldn't touch it. Only he drank another glass of wine. That's all he's had since the morning. And now he is sitting doubled up, with his face working terrible."

They opened the door of the library softly and went in. He was not sitting 'doubled up': he was lying back in his ragged old leather chair, extended—his long legs stretched out, his hands on the arms of the chair, his broad shoulders and his great head lying back—splendid even in decay, like autumn opulent. His eyes were open, staring straight upwards to the ceiling. His face was, as the housekeeper put it 'working.' It spoke of some internal struggle. What was it that he was fighting in his weary brain?

"Leonard," the girl whispered, "it is not despair in his face. It is not defiance. Look! It is doubt. There is something he cannot understand. He hears whispers. Oh, I think I hear them, too! I know what they are and whose they are." She drew down her veil to hide her tears.

The sun had now gone down. The shadows of the twilight lay about the corners of the big room, the rows of books looked ghostly; the western light began to fall, and the colours began to fade. A fire burned in the grate, as it always burned all the year round; the flames began to throw flickering lights and shadows about the room; they lit up the face of the old man, and his figure seemed to stand out clear and apart, as if there were nothing in the room but himself; nay, as if there were no room, no furniture, no house, nothing but that one sole figure in the presence—the unspeakable presence—of the Judge.

His face was changing; the housekeeper spoke the truth. The defiance and the stubbornness were going out of it. What was come to take their place? As yet, nothing but doubt and pain and trouble. As for the whispers, there was no proof that there were any whispers, save from

The Fourth Generation

the assurance of the girl who heard them with the ear of faith. Leonard stepped forward and bent over him.

"Sir," he said solemnly, "you know me. I am your great-grandson—the grandson of your eldest son, who killed himself because he discovered a secret—your secret. And he could no longer endure it and live. I am his grandson."

The words were plain, even brutal. Leonard intended that there should be no mistake about them. But, plain as they were, they produced no effect. There was not even a gleam in the old man's eye to show that he heard.

"You are ninety-five," Leonard went on. "It is time to speak. I have brought with me one who will recall a day—if you have ever forgotten it—of tragic memories, the day when you lost at once your wife and your brother-in-law. You have never forgotten that day, have you?"

The old man made no reply. But he closed his eyes, perhaps as a sign that he refused to listen.

"Sir, I have a message for you. It is from the man whom you saved from the gallows—the innocent man whom you saved at a trial for murder. He sent a message from his death-bed—words of gratitude and of prayer. The good deed that you did has grown, and borne fruit a hundredfold—your good deed. Let the grateful words of that man be some comfort to you."

Again the old man made no sign.

At this point an unexpected interruption took place, for the door was opened, and a man, a villager, came clumping in noisily. Seventy years agone he was the boy who had done the bird-scaring.

"They told me"—he addressed Leonard, but he looked at the figure in the chair—"that you were here, and they said that he was going at last. So I came. I minded what you said. Did never a one suspect? That's what you said. I don't care for him now." He nodded valiantly at the figure of his old master. "He won't hurt no one—no more."

He clumped across the room, being rheumatic, and planted himself before the chair, bringing his stick down with a bump on the floor.

"Did never a man suspect?" He looked round and held up his finger.

He suspected. And he knew.

"Old man"—he addressed himself directly to the silent figure—"who done that job? You done it. Nobody else done it. Nobody else couldn't ha' done it. Who done it? You done it. There was nobody else in the wood but you before John Dunning came along."

Leonard took him by the arm, and led him unresisting out of the library. But he went on repeating his story, as if he could not say it often enough to satisfy his conscience.

"I always meant to tell him some day before I died. Now I have told him. I've told all the people too—all of them. Why should I go on putting of it away and hiding of it? He ought to ha' swung long ago, he ought. And he shall too. He shall yet, though he be ninety years and more. Who done it? Who done it? Who done it? He done it. He done it. He done it, I say."

They heard his voice as Leonard led him to the door; they heard his voice when Leonard shut the door upon him, repeating his refrain in a senile sing-song.

"What matter?" said Leonard. "Let him sing his burden all over the village. The time has gone by when such as he can hurt."

But the old man still made as if he had heard nothing. He remained perfectly impassible. Not even the Sphinx could be more obstinately fixed on betraying no emotion. Presently he stirred—perhaps because he was moved; he pulled himself up with difficulty; he sat supported by the arms of the chair, his body bending under the weight of the massive head and broad shoulders, too heavy at last even for that gigantic frame; his head was bent slightly forward; his eyes, deep set, were now fixed upon the red coals of the fire, which burned all the year round to warm him; his face was drawn by hard lines, which stood out like ropes in the firelight. His abundant white hair lay upon his shoulders, and his long white beard fell round him to the waist.

And thus he had been for seventy years, while his early manhood passed slowly into the prime of life, while the first decay touched his locks with tiny streaks of grey, while early age fell upon him, while his face grew furrowed, while his eyes sank and his cheek-bones stood out, while his teeth fell out and his long face was shortened and his ancient comeliness vanished. So he had remained while his neglected children grew up, while Consequences fell unheeded and unknown upon his house, ignorant of what went on in the outer world, though a new world grew up around him with new thoughts, new ideals, new standards, and a new civilisation. The Great Revolution which we call the Nineteenth Century went on around him, and he knew nothing; he lived, as he was born, in the eighteenth century, which was prolonged to the days of King George the Fourth. If he thought at all in his long life, his thoughts were as the thoughts of the time in which he was born.

Did he think at all? Of what could he think when day followed day, and one was like another, and there was no change; when spring succeeded winter unheeded; and cold and heat were alike to one who felt neither; and there was no book or newspaper or voice of friend to bring food for the mind or to break the monotony of the days?

The anchorite of the Church could pray; his only occupations were prayer and his mighty wrestling with the Devil. Since this anchorite of the Country House could not pray, there was left with him, day and night, the latter resource. Surely, after seventy long years, this occupation must have proved wearisome.

Leonard went on: "Speak."

The old man made no sign.

"Speak, then. Speak, and tell us what we already know."

There was still no reply.

"You have suffered so long. You have made atonement so terrible: it is time to speak—to speak and end it."

His face visibly hardened.

"Oh! it is no use," Leonard cried in despair. "It is like walking into a brick wall. Sir, you hear me—you understand what is said! You cannot tell us one single thing that we do not know already."

He made a gesture of despair, and stepped back.

Then Constance herself stepped forward. She threw herself at his feet; like a Greek suppliant she clasped his knees, and she spoke slowly and softly:

"You must hear me. I have a right to be heard. Look at me. I am the great-grand-daughter of Langley Holme."

She raised her veil.

The old man screamed aloud. He caught the arms of the chair and sat upright. He stared at her face. He trembled and shook all over, insomuch that at the shaking of his large frame the floor also trembled and shook, and the plates on the table and the fender rattled.

"Langley!" he cried, seeing nothing but her face—"Langley! You have come back. At last—at last!"

He could not understand that this was a living woman, not a dead man. He saw only her face, and it was the face of Langley himself.

"Yes," she said, boldly. "Langley come back. He says that you have suffered long enough. He says that he has forgiven you long ago. His sister has forgiven you. All is forgiven, Langley says. Speak—speak—in the very presence of God, Who knows. It was your hand that murdered Langley. Speak! You struck him with the club in the forehead so that he fell dead. When he was brought home dead, your punishment began with the death of your wife, and has gone on ever since. Speak!"

The old man shook his head mechanically. He tried to speak. It was as if his lips refused to utter the words. He sank back in the chair, still gazing upon the face and trembling. At last he spoke.

"Langley knows—Langley knows," he said.

"Speak!" Constance commanded.

"Langley knows——"

"Speak!"

"I did it!" said the old man.

Constance knelt down before him and prayed aloud.

"I did it!" he repeated.

Constance took his hand and kissed it.

"I am Langley's child," she said. "In his name you are forgiven. Oh, the long punishment is over! Oh, we have all forgiven you! Oh, you have suffered so long—so long! At last—at last—forgive yourself!"

Then a strange thing happened. It happens often with the very old that in the hour of death there falls upon the face a return of youth. The old man's face became young; the years fell from him; but for his white hair you would have thought him young again. The hard lines vanished with the crow's-feet and the creases and the furrows; the soft colour of youth reappeared upon his cheek. Oh, the goodly man—the splendid face and figure of a man! He stood up, without apparent difficulty; he held Constance by the hand, but he stood up without support, towering in his six feet six, erect and strong.

"Forgiven?" he asked. "What is there to be forgiven? Forgive myself? Why? What have I done that needs forgiveness? Let us walk into the wood, Langley—let us walk into the wood. My dear, I do not understand. Langley's child is but a baby in arms."

His hand dropped. He would have fallen to the ground but that Leonard caught him and laid him gently on the chair.

"It is the end," said Constance. "He has confessed."

It was the end. The Recluse was dead.

CHAPTER XXI

THE WILL

ONE of the London morning papers devoted a leading article to the subject of the modern Recluse. The following is a passage from that excellent leader:

"The Hermit, or the Recluse, has long disappeared from the roadside, from the bridge-end, from the river bank. His Hermitage sometimes remains, as at Warkworth, but the ancient occupant is gone. He was succeeded by the Eccentric, who flourished mightily in the last century, and took many strange forms; some lived alone, each in a single room; some became misers and crept out at night, to pick up offal for food; some lived in hollow trees; some never washed, and allowed nothing in the house to be washed. There were no absurdities too ridiculous to be practised by the Eccentric of the last century.

"For reasons which the writer of social manners may discover, the Eccentric has mostly followed the Recluse; there are none left. Therefore, the life of the late Algernon Campaigne, of Campaigne Park, Bucks, an Eccentric of the eighteenth-century type, will afford a pleasing exception to the dull and monotonous chronicles of modern private life.

"This worthy, a country gentleman of good family and large estate, was married in quite early manhood, having succeeded to the property at twenty-one or so. His health was excellent; he was a model of humanity to look at, being much over six feet high and large of frame in proportion. He had gone through the usual course of public school and the University, not without distinction; he had been called to the Bar; he was a magistrate; and he was understood to have ambitions of a Parliamentary career. In a word, no young man ever started with fairer prospects or with a better chance of success in whatever line he proposed to take up.

"Unfortunately, a single tragic event blasted these prospects and ruined his life. His brother-in-law, a gentleman of his own rank and station, and his most intimate friend, while on a visit at Campaigne Park, was brutally murdered—by whom it was never discovered. The shock of this event brought the young wife of Mr. Campaigne to premature labour, and killed her as well on the same day.

"This misfortune so weighed upon the unhappy man that he fell into a despondent condition, from which he never rallied. He entered into a voluntary retirement from the world. He lived alone in his great house, with no one but an old woman for a housekeeper, for the whole remainder of his life—seventy years. During the whole of that time he has preserved absolute silence; he has not uttered a word. He has neglected his affairs; when his signature was absolutely necessary, his agent left the document on his table, and next day found it signed. He would have nothing done to the house; the fine furniture and the noble paintings are reported to be ruined with damp and cold; his garden and glass-houses are overgrown and destroyed. He spent his mornings, in all weathers, walking up and down the brick terrace overlooking his ruined lawns; he dined at one o'clock on a beefsteak and a bottle of port; he slept before the fire all the afternoon; he went to bed at nine. He never opened a book or a newspaper or a letter. He was careless what became of his children, and he refused to see his friends. A more melancholy, useless existence can hardly be imagined. And this life he followed without the least change for seventy years. When he died, the day before yesterday, it was on his ninety-fifth birthday."

More followed, but these were the facts as presented to the readers, with a moral to follow.

They buried the old man with his forefathers "in sure and certain hope." The words may pass, perhaps, for he had been punished, if punishment can atone for crime. Constance brought him a message of forgiveness, but could he forgive himself? All manner of sins can be forgiven. The murdered man, the dishonoured woman, the wronged orphan, the sweated workwoman, the ruined shareholder, the innocent man done to death or prison by perjury—all may lift up their hands in pity and cry aloud with tears their forgiveness, but will the guilty man forgive himself? Until he can the glorious streets of the New Jerusalem will be dark, the sound of the harp and the voices of praise will be but a confused noise, and the new life itself will be nothing better than an intolerable prolonging of the old burden.

"Dust to dust, ashes to ashes."

Then they went away, and when they were all gone the old bird-scarer came hobbling to the grave, and looked into it, and murmured, but not aloud, for fear the man in the grave might arise and kill him too:

"You done it! You done it! You done it!"

The funeral party walked back to the house, where for the first time for seventy years there was a table spread. All were there—the ancient lady, daughter of the dead man, stately with her black silk and laces, with the bearing of a Duchess, leaning on the arm of her grand-nephew; the two grandsons, Fred and Christopher; the wife and children of the latter; Mr. Samuel Galley and Mary Anne his sister; and Constance, great-grandniece of the deceased. With them came the agent, a solicitor from the neighbouring town.

After luncheon the agent produced the Will.

"This Will," he said, "was drawn up by my great-grandfather in the year 1826, exactly one month after the tragic event which so weighed upon his client's mind."

"Was he in his right mind?" asked Sam, turning very red. "I ask the question without prejudice."

"Sir, he was always in his right mind. He would not speak, but on occasion he would write. He was never, down to the very end, in any sense out of his mind. I have letters and instructions from him year after year for seventy years—my firm has acted for this family for a hundred years—which will establish his complete sanity should that be questioned."

"Well, the Will," said Sam. "Let's get to the Will."

"I will read the Will."

For the will of a rich man, it was comparatively short; there was in it, however, a clause which caused Leonard to glance curiously and inquiringly at Constance.

"I don't understand," said Sam. "There's something left to me——"

"No, sir—to your grandmother. To you, nothing."

"It's the same thing. What is hers is mine."

"No," said the lady concerned, stiffly. "You will find, my grandson, that you are mistaken."

"Well," said Sam, disconcerted, "anyhow, you've got a share. What I want to know is the meaning of that clause about somebody's heirs. What have they got to do with it?"

"Perhaps," said Leonard, "you might kindly explain the Will."

"Certainly. The testator had at the time of making his will a certain amount of personal property to bequeath. The property consisted partly of invested moneys, chiefly his mother's fortune. As he was an only child, the whole of this personal property came to him. Partly it consisted of a town-house in Berkeley Square, also part of his mother's property not entailed, and his pictures, his library, and his furniture, carriages, horses, etc. The latter part he has bequeathed to the heir of the Campaigne estate—to you, Mr. Leonard. The former part, consisting of the invested moneys, he bequeathes to his three children in equal portions. As the second child was drowned and left no heirs, this money will be divided equally between the elder son and the daughter—you, Mrs. Galley; and as the elder son is dead, his heirs will receive the money shared between them."

"With all the Accumulations!" cried Sam. "Ah!" with a long, long breath of relief.

"No, not the Accumulations; they are especially provided for. The testator expressly states that only the amount actually standing in his name at that date shall be divided, as I have set forth. 'And,' he continues, 'seeing that I may live some years yet, very much against my wish, and that I shall not spend on myself or on my house or in any way, being now and henceforth dead to the world and waiting in silence for my removal whenever it may come, there will be interest on this money, which I desire shall be invested year after year by my solicitors. And on my death I desire that the difference between the money then and the money now, whatever it may be, shall be given in equal shares to the heirs of Langley Holme, my late brother-in-law, who was foully murdered near my house, for a reason which he alone knows,' "

"This is very wonderful," said Frederick. "All the accumulations— seventy years of compound interest! an immense fortune—to be given to strangers or very distant cousins? Are we going to allow this will to stand without a protest? You are the chief, Leonard. What do you say?"

"The question is whether the testator was sane at the time of making his will," said Leonard.

"He was sane, then, I believe," said the solicitor, "and he was certainly sane at the end. I have here a note written by him three years ago. All our communication was by writing. I ventured to ask him whether he desired to make any change in his testamentary disposition. Here is his reply."

He took a note out of his pocket-book. It was quite short.

"Nothing has happened to cause any alteration in my will. The reasons which made me set apart all moneys saved and accumulated for the heirs of Langley Holme still exist. I do not know who the heirs are.—A. C."

"Is that the letter of a person of unsound mind?"

"I for one shall dispute the will," said Sam, standing up and thrusting his hands in his pockets.

"Pardon me, sir, you have no *locus standi.*"

"I don't care. It is an iniquitous will."

"As you please, sir—as you please."

"Will you tell us the amount of the money which will come to us?" said Fred.

"There was a sum of £90,000 invested in the Three per Cents. The half of that sum, or £45,000, will be divided among you three gentlemen as the grandson and the sons of Mr. Campaigne's eldest son. The other half will be given to you, Mrs. Galley."

"Humph!" said Sam. "But when I get the will set aside— —"

"As for the accumulations, they amount at the present moment to a very large sum indeed, an immense sum—more than a million of money. The late Langley Holme left one daughter, whose only descendant is the young lady here present, Miss Constance Ambry."

Constance rose.

"We will talk about this business at another time," she said.

Leonard followed her out of the damp and grave-like house into the ruined garden. And they sat down together in silence.

"Fifteen thousand pounds!" said Fred. "It is no more at present rates of interest than £400 a year. But it's a pleasant little nest-egg to take out to Australia—with the Dunnings to place if— —"

"Fifteen thousand pounds," said Christopher to his son. "It's a nice little addition. But, my boy, the Bureau is worth ten times as much."

They walked away. They rambled about the house of Ruin and Decay. Presently they walked to the station: the dream of huge wealth was shattered. But still, there was a *solatium*.

Mrs. Galley turned to the lawyer.

"Sir," she said, "when will that money be my very own?"

"Immediately. It has only to be transferred. If you wish for an advance— —"

"I wish for protection against my grandson."

"Quite right." It was Mary Anne, who had not hitherto said a word.

"He claims everything as his own."

"Madame," said the lawyer, "we have acted, father and son, for four generations for your family. Let me assure you that if you allow us your confidence, you shall be amply protected."

Sam looked from one to the other. Then he put on his hat and walked away gloomily.

"My dear," said Mrs. Galley, laying her hand on her grand-daughter's shoulder, "I am again a gentlewoman. We will live, you and I, in a country house, with a garden and flowers and servants and a pony carriage. No, my dear, I will never go back to the Commercial Road. He is welcome to everything there. Let us stay here in the village and among the people where I was born—you and I together. Oh, my dear—my dear! It is happiness too great. The hand of the Lord is lifted: His wrath is stayed."

Leonard and Constance returned to town together.

In the carriage the girl sat beside Leonard in silence, her hands folded, her eyes dropped.

"You are a great heiress, Constance," he said. "I learn that the accumulations now amount to an immense sum. What will you do with all this money?"

"I do not know. I shall pretend to myself that I haven't got any. Perhaps in time someone may help me to use it. I have enough already. I do not want to buy anything that costs large sums. I do not want to dress more expensively. I have as good society as I can desire, and I cannot, I believe, eat any more than I have always done."

"Yet, how happy would some people be at such a windfall!"

"The difficulty of doing something with it will be very terrible. Let us never talk about it. Besides, that cousin of yours is going to set the will aside, if he can."

She relapsed into silence. It was not of her newly-acquired fortune that she was thinking.

They drove from the station to the "Mansions." They mounted the stairs to the first-floor.

"Let me come in with you, Leonard," she said. "I want to say something. It had better be said to-day and at once, else it will become impossible."

He observed that she was embarrassed in her manner, that she spoke with some constraint, and that she was blushing. A presentiment seized him. Presentiment is as certain as coincidence. He, too, changed colour. But he waited. They remained standing face to face.

"Tell me first," she said, "is the Possession of your mind wholly gone? Are you quite free from the dreadful thing?"

"Happily, yes. I am quite free. My mind is completely clear again. There is plenty to think about—one is not likely to forget the last few weeks—but I can think as I please. My will is my own once more."

"I also am quite free. The first thing that I want to say is this: What are we to do with our knowledge?"

"You are the person to decide. If you wish, it shall be proclaimed abroad."

"I cannot possibly wish that."

"Or, if you wish, a history of the case shall be written out and shown to every member of the family, and placed with the other documents of our people, so that those who follow shall be able to read and understand the history."

"No. I want the story absolutely closed, so that it can never again be reopened. In a few years the memory of the event itself will have vanished from the village; your cousins of the Commercial Road will certainly not keep the story alive; besides, they know nothing. There remains only the Book of Extracts. Let us first burn the Book of Extracts."

Leonard produced the volume. Constance tore out the leaves one by one, rolled them up, laid them neatly in the grate, put the cover on the top, and set light to the whole. In one minute the dreadful story was destroyed; there was no more any evidence, except in the piles of old newspapers which are slowly mouldering in the vaults of the British Museum.

"Never again!" she said. "Never again will we speak of it. Nobody shall know what we discovered. It is our secret—yours and mine. Whose secret should it be but yours and mine?"

"If it were a burden to you, I would it were all mine."

"It is no burden henceforth. Why should that be a burden which has been forgiven? It is our secret, too, that the suffering was laid upon us, so that we might be led to the discovery of the truth."

"Were we led? You would make me believe, Constance—even me—in supernatural guidance. But it seems natural, somehow, that you should believe that we were, as you say, led."

"You, who believe nothing but what you see, you will not understand. Oh! it is so plain to me—so very plain. You have been forced—compelled against your will—to investigate the case. Who compelled you? I know not; but since the same force made me follow you, I think it was that murdered man himself. Confess that you were forced; you said so yourself."

"It is true that I have been absorbed in the case."

"Who sent your cousin from the East End? Who fired your imagination with half-told tales of trouble? Who sent you the book? How do you explain the absorbing interest of a case so old, so long forgotten?"

"Is it not natural?"

"No, it is not natural that a man of your willpower should become the slave of a research so hopeless—as it seemed. Who was it, after we had mastered every detail and tried every theory and examined every scrap of evidence, and after you had examined the ground and talked to the surviving witness—I say, after the way had been prepared—who was it sent the two voices from the grave—the one which made it quite certain that those two were the only persons in the wood, and the other which showed that they were quarrelling, and that one was ungoverned in his wrath? Can you explain that, Leonard?"

"You believe that we were led by unseen hands, step by step, towards the discovery, for the purpose of those who led."

"There were two purposes: one for the consolation of that old man, and the other for yourself."

"How for myself?"

"Look back only a month. Are you the same or are you changed? I told you then that you were outside all other men, because you had everything—wealth sufficient, pride of ancestry, intellectual success, and no contact with the lower world, the vulgar and the common, or the criminal or the disreputable world. You remember? Yes—are you changed?

"If to possess all these undesirable things can change one, I am changed."

"If to lose the things which separate you from the world, and to receive the things which bring you nearer to the world, do change a man, then you are changed. You will change more and more; because more and more you will feel that you belong to the world of men and women—not of caste and books. When all is gone, there still remains yourself—alone before the world."

He made no reply.

"Where is now your pride of birth? It is gone. Where is your contempt for things common and unclean? You have had the vision of St. Peter. If there are things common and unclean, they belong to you as well as to the meaner sort—for to that kind you also belong."

"Something of this I have understood."

"And there was the other purpose. While with blow after blow it is destroyed, you were led on and on with this mystery; voices from the dead were brought to you, till at last the whole mystery was made plain and stood out confessed—and with it I was moved and compelled to follow you, till at the end I was taken to see the dying man, and to deliver to him the forgiveness of the man he slew. Oh, Leonard, believe me; if it is true that the soul survives the death of the body, if it is possible for the soul still to see what goes on among the living, then have you and I been directed and led."

Again he made no reply. But he was moved beyond the power of speech.

"Forgiveness came long since. Oh! I am sure of that—long since. That which followed—was it Consequence or Punishment?—lasted for seventy years. Oh, what a life! Oh, what a long, long agony! Always to dwell on one moment; day after day, night after night, with never a change and no end; to whirl the heavy branch upon the head of the brother, to see him fall back dead, to know that he was a murderer. Leonard! Leonard! think of it!"

"I do think of it, Constance. But you must not go on thinking of it."

"No, no—this is the last time. Forgiveness, yes—he would forgive. God's sweet souls cannot but forgive. But Justice must prevail, with the condemnation of self-reproach, till Forgiveness overcomes—until, in some mysterious way, the sinner can forgive himself."

She sat down and buried her face in her hands.

"You say that we have been led—perhaps. I neither deny nor accept. But whatever has been done for that old man whom we buried this morning, whatever has been done for the endowment of myself with cousins and people—well, of the more common sort—one thing more it has accomplished. Between you and me, Constance, there flows a stream of blood."

She lifted her head; she rose from the chair; she stepped closer to him; she stood before him face to face, her hands clasped, her face pale, the tears yet lying on her cheek, her eyes soft and full of a strange tender light.

"You asked me three or four weeks ago," she said, "to marry you. I refused. I told you that I did not know the meaning of Love or the necessity for Love. I now understand that it means, above all, the perfect sympathy and the necessity for sympathy. I now understand, besides, that you did not then know, any more than I myself, the necessity of sympathy. You were a lonely man, content to be lonely, and sufficient for yourself. You were a proud man—proud through and through, belonging to a caste separated from the people by a long line of ancestry and a record full of honour. You had no occasion to earn your daily bread; you were already distinguished; there was no man of your age in the whole country more fortunate than you, or more self-centred. I was able to esteem you—but you could not move my heart. Are you following me, Leonard?"

"I am trying to follow you."

"Many things have happened to you since then. You have joined the vast company of those who suffer from the sins of their own people; you have known shame and humiliation——"

"And between us flows that stream."

Even for a strong and resolute woman, who is not afraid of misunderstanding and does not obey conventions, there are some things very hard to say.

"There is one thing, and only one thing, Leonard, that can dry that stream."

His face changed. He understood what she meant.

"Is there anything? Think, Constance. Langley Holme was your ancestor. He was done to death by mine."

"Yes. There is one way. Oh, Leonard, in this time of trouble and anxiety I have watched you day by day. I have found the man beneath the scholar. If I had accepted your offer three weeks ago, it would have been out of respect for the scholar. But a woman can only love a man — not a scholar, believe me, nor a student, nor a poet, nor an artist, nor anything except a man."

"Constance! It is impossible! You are his daughter."

"It is fortunate that I am, as you say, the daughter of the man who was killed. He suffered less than the other. The suffering was but a pang, but the other's — oh, it was a lifelong agony! If I marry the son of the man who did the wrong, it is because the message I carried to the dying man was a sign that all was forgiven, even to " 'the third and fourth generation.' "

"Tell me, Constance, is this pity, or — —"

"Oh, Leonard, I know not what flowers there are which grow out of pity and sympathy, but — —"

She said no more, because there was no need.

THE END.

Copyright © 2023 Esprios Digital Publishing. All Rights Reserved.